Beverly Hills Demon Slayer

NEW YORK TIMES BESTSELLING AUTHOR
ANGIE FOX

MORE BOOKS FROM ANGIE FOX

The Accidental Demon Slayer series
The Accidental Demon Slayer
The Dangerous Book for Demon Slayers
A Tale of Two Demon Slayers
The Last of the Demon Slayers
My Big, Fat Demon Slayer Wedding
Beverly Hills Demon Slayer
Night of the Living Demon Slayer – coming 2015

The Monster MASH trilogy
Immortally Yours
Immortally Embraced
Immortally Ever After

Short Stories
Gentlemen Prefer Voodoo
(from the My Zombie Valentine anthology)
Murder on Mysteria Lane
(from The Real Werewives of Vampire County
anthology)
What Slays in Vegas
(from the So I Married a Demon Slayer anthology)
Date with a Demon Slayer
(from The Mammoth Book of Southern Gothic
Romance) – coming November 20, 2014

To learn more about upcoming releases, sign up for
Angie's quarterly newsletter at www.angiefox.com

To Rachel Flesher and the Angie Fox Street Team
for their crazy fun help in naming this book

ACKNOWLEDGEMENTS

Special thanks to Sherrie Hill and Alexx Miller for early reads.

Chapter One

A low *thud* jarred me awake. Followed by a slow metallic rattle.

"Dimitri?" I rubbed at my new husband's shoulder while trying to sit up. He had me pinned in a love hug, one powerful arm securing me against his chest, a leg stretched over both of mine, keeping me safe.

Thud.

I definitely heard it that time.

My eyes strained against the absolute darkness. I rolled as far as I could to see the digital readout on our bedside clock. It was exactly 3:00 a.m.—the devil's hour.

I shoved at him harder. "Dimitri!"

He ground his hard, wonderfully naked body against mine. "Mmm." He traced a hand over the curve of my bare breast. "Want to go again?" he murmured, his sexy Greek accent thick with sleep.

Okay, that might be why I usually woke him up, but I was beginning to think we had a situation. "I heard a noise."

His lips brushed the top of my head. "Could be Pirate again," he said against my hair, referring to my dog, who was not at all happy to be locked out of our bedroom.

"Maybe."

Then again, I was a demon slayer. And even though life had been peaceful lately, that never lasted long.

I opened up my slayer senses. My powers kept me tuned in to any kind of trouble, whether it was from supernatural nasties, burglars, or lately, the nest of bunnies chewing through the siding under the deck.

Tonight, I picked up more than gnawing little teeth. I couldn't pinpoint the source yet, but I knew it wasn't anything cute and furry.

It sounded again. Another low *thud*. "Oh, hell."

Dimitri didn't even ask. In a single motion he rolled off the bed and onto his feet.

"What are you picking up?" he asked, finding a pair of boxers as my mind reached out like fingers through the mist.

"I'm not exactly sure." But it felt wrong, like an angry dark tangle of emotions and…something else.

"I'll check it out," he said, moving quickly through the dark. Now that I'd woken up, I could make out the familiar shadows of our bedroom. But Dimitri was a shape-shifting griffin and his eyes could pick up things mine couldn't.

He stood like a lone sentry, to the side of a window overlooking the street. Light blue curtains covered the glass. He leaned his head against the wall and checked out the situation through a gap where the fabric didn't quite reach.

Stiffness bit at the center of my back as I straightened. "Anybody out there?"

He watched for one long heartbeat. Then another.

"No." He parted the curtains, letting in the light from the streetlamps.

I used it to try to find my nightshirt.

In the meantime, he reached into our closet and came out with a lacrosse stick.

Of all the… "Are you serious?"

The side of his mouth quirked. "You'd be surprised how well I handle a stick."

I refused to say anything. It would be too easy.

When you got right down to it, his body was his weapon. I wasn't so lucky. A few years ago, when I taught preschool, I considered it a good day when I had enough energy to hit the treadmill at the gym. That was before I learned I was a demon slayer. Maybe someday, I'd actually get used to my powers—and have the hard body, too.

Then again, Dimitri liked me exactly how I was.

"I'm coming with you." I reached next to my nightstand for the utility belt that held the tools of my trade. I still couldn't locate my sleep shirt, so I just grabbed the T-shirt Dimitri had worn to bed, the one I'd ripped off him and tossed onto the floor. Soft and navy blue, it reached down to my mid-thigh. It would have to do.

A shiver ran through me as I cinched my utility belt around my waist. The cracked and faded black leather hovered at a balmy eighty-six degrees, no matter what.

It held five switch stars, which were the weapon of demon slayers like me. They were round and flat, kind of like Chinese throwing stars. Only they were slightly larger, and much, much more deadly. The blades would begin to churn as soon as I touched them.

I flicked on the hall light to reveal a basket of clean laundry we'd both neglected to fold and put away. A quick glance into the small spare bedroom/office showed a neatly made bed and a desk in need of a professional organizer. No change there.

"Is it demonic?" Dimitri asked, his voice low.

"It's violent and in pain." I didn't know any more than that.

The night was completely silent, as if it were waiting too. I vowed to start keeping a flashlight next to the bed as we padded down the short carpeted hallway. Dimitri edged slightly ahead of me as we hit the stairs.

He raised the stick and I caught a movement at the bottom a split second after he did. Dimitri charged after it. I hurried right behind him and hit the light.

Good thing my husband was a look-first-and-bash-later type because my dog, Pirate, stood in the hardwood entryway, his tail wagging like it was three in the afternoon.

He gave a wet doggy snurfle. "What's going on? Are we having breakfast?"

Dimitri scanned the room behind Pirate. "Lizzie heard a noise."

"Ooh, fun!" My dog whipped his stubby tail hard enough to stir up a breeze. "What did it sound like?"

Interesting that he didn't know. Pirate could hear the mailman from two blocks away.

My dog was mostly white, with a dollop of brown on his back that wound up his neck and over one eye. He had your typical Jack Russell terrier energy, and attitude—and ever since I'd come into my powers, the little guy could speak to me...in real sentences.

Of course, that didn't always work out for him. The first time he asked why Dimitri and I were jumping on the bed, the poor doggy was banned from our room.

Dimitri moved past Pirate and through the living room.

"Let's attack!" my dog said, following.

"Where?" I asked. I sure didn't see anyone down here.

"No idea!" he said, not letting it deter him in the least.

We didn't exactly have the largest town house on the block. We had a main living room and then a dining area with a kitchen behind it. It would be hard for someone to hide.

Dimitri headed over to investigate the closet that held our water heater and a few cleaning supplies. Pirate stopped at the refrigerator.

"Help me out here," I said to the dog who had barked at a cricket not too long ago.

Pirate turned in a circle and sat. "Don't look at me. I just heard you getting up. Thought you might be in the mood for a late-night snack. If you listen real close, you can hear my stomach almost growling."

Unbelievable. "You have dog food," I told him.

"Yeah, but that's just for emergencies."

Dimitri walked past Pirate, completely ignoring him. "Where's Flappy?"

"He's sleeping," Pirate said, leading us to the sliding glass door overlooking the deck.

Last year, Pirate had adopted a dragon. Because a pet should have a pet.

I couldn't believe I let him get away with that.

We peered out and spotted the darkened form of a mottled white-and-gray dragon. He sprawled on his back, with his legs splayed open and his arms curled out in front of him like a dead bug. His massive head rested on a stack of my nice, new deck chair cushions and his mouth hung open, drooling on them.

Dimitri cursed under his breath. "I told him to stay off the deck. He's too heavy."

Besides, we'd built him a very nice dragon lair in our parking space.

"He wants to be close to us," Pirate said fondly.

Yes, well, I didn't regret our "no dragons in the house" rule.

Thud.

"There!" I hissed. "Did you hear that?" Pirate's ears quirked. Dimitri cocked his head and concentrated.

After the thud, we heard a metallic clatter, like something being dragged. *That's* what I'd heard upstairs.

It ended almost as soon as it began. But it was enough. "It came from outside." I was sure of it.

Strange the dragon hadn't moved.

A muscle worked in Dimitri's jaw. "I didn't hear anything," he said, cautiously.

Pirate's nails clacked against the hardwood as paced in front of the door. "I didn't either, but I say we go outside and I'll bark anyway."

Why me, then?

Maybe I'd been relying on my powers more than I realized.

Dimitri slid open the glass door. Cool air blew in, along with the sounds of the waves pounding against the shore. We lived on the California coast, just south of Los Angeles. Normally, I loved it. Now? "I can't see much past Flappy."

I reached for the back porch light.

"Wait," Dimitri said quickly. He glanced at me over his shoulder, and in that moment I could tell he was all about the challenge, the hunt. His eyes shone with it as he cocked a grin. "Do you want to scare whatever's out there or do you want to try to catch it?"

Ah, yes: reason number 412 why I fell in love with this man.

I couldn't help but return his smile. "Let's catch it."

He ducked back inside, running a quick, affectionate hand along my side as he located a pair of black dress pants he'd discarded under the kitchen table. I grabbed a pair of undies that had gotten tangled up in one of the chair legs. We had our choice of things to wear, seeing as we'd broken in that table earlier this evening and had neglected to clean up.

I loved my new life. *Mostly*, I reminded myself as the dragon sighed out a loud, throaty *mmmrfle* and rolled over.

The boards of the deck creaked and I had a sudden vision of the whole thing collapsing. While non-magical people couldn't see Flappy, they would notice if our entire deck fell apart underneath him.

"Quickly," Dimitri said, as he buttoned his pants. A leather belt sheath held a dagger.

"Just a sec." I opened one of the upper kitchen cabinets to reveal a shelf full of recycled glass baby-food jars. Each one held a different spell I'd been working on. My biker witch grandma had been teaching me how to brew protective wards, although her recipes left a lot to be desired. Exactly how was one supposed to measure a pinch of white sage? Or a sprinkle of graveyard dirt? And did that mean dirt from an actual grave, or could you just scoop something out of one of the flower beds near the front gates?

Plus, I'd been forced to halve the recipes because I couldn't fit full-size jars onto my utility belt. I grabbed two of my new anti-demonic spells, which looked a lot like jars filled with brackish green and brown sludge, and hoped I was better at spell work than I was at making chicken potpie.

Dimitri gave me a lingering look when he spied his undershirt hanging from our kitchen light. Lucky for me, he didn't bother putting it on. He just grabbed it and stuffed one end of it in his pocket. "Ready?"

We slipped out into the night, with Pirate on our heels. Flappy let out a loud *brrwaaaaa-ker-snuffle*. It sounded like a half snore, half god-knew-what. He rolled over, his tail flicking one of my pink seashell candleholders off the table by the barbecue pit. It landed with a soft *thump* on the sand below.

Lovely.

"Now I can hear it," Pirate said.

"That's not the noise." I stepped over Flappy's thick tail and tried to see down into the darkened area at the bottom of the steps. Beyond it stretched a rock retaining wall. A wooden pathway cut across it and led down to the beach. I couldn't see too far past the smattering of tall sea grass beyond the wall. Still, it seemed there were very few lights out on the water.

"I thought we had a guard dragon," Dimitri muttered, joining me.

He had a point. Flappy had stood vigil for us on numerous occasions, and done a good job too. Maybe we'd made a mistake trusting him.

Pirate snorted behind us. "Flappy's the best. When he's awake. But you didn't tell him to stay awake. So now, Flappy's really good at resting up for our next adventure. Flappy!" he hollered, right against the dragon's ear.

"Not so loud," I whispered. Not for Flappy's sake, but for ours. I didn't want to draw the attention of whatever was down on the beach.

In the meantime, Flappy didn't budge.

"Why don't you guard him while he sleeps?" I suggested to the dog.

Pirate stood with his tail rigid. "Oh, no. I'm fierce. You need me out front."

"I'll yell if I need you to attack," I assured him. No doubt he had it handled when it came to anything from the knees down.

"You got it." The hair on his neck bristled. "In the meantime, I've got things covered here, too."

"Good," I said, glancing to the darkened beach behind me. Given the choice, I didn't want Pirate anywhere near it.

Now that we were outside, I could sense the presence even stronger. "It's out by the water," I said to Dimitri. Almost as if I'd triggered it, a red glow appeared just beyond the sea grass. "There," I said, pointing. Red vibrations were given by dark magic, or something worse.

"I see it," Dimitri said under his breath.

I gave Pirate a loving stroke on his head with one hand, and hooked a chain to his collar with the other. He didn't notice. Maybe he was too busy guarding. "Good puppy," I crooned.

We didn't need him following us.

"Hey…" Pirate said, making his unpleasant discovery before I'd made it halfway down the stairs. "I've been had! I've been tied up! What am I? An animal?"

I ignored him, which was hard. He wasn't the type to suffer in silence.

Dimitri and I crept down to the wooden walkway. Me, in measured steps. My husband moving like the silent predator I knew him to be. The red glow had grown brighter by the time the path emptied out onto the shoreline.

The deep sand silenced our footsteps, but also made it hard to walk—or make a quick escape if we needed one.

We made our way through the rustling sea grass. The loud noise made it difficult to pick up any sounds between that and the ocean. Dimitri drew his knife, and I kept a hand on my switch stars.

Dimitri leaned in close. "You smell that?" he asked.

I wrinkled my nose. "Yes." The stench made me want to gag. Under other circumstances, I would think something dead had washed up on the beach.

The sea grass surrounded us on both sides and it occurred to me that the thick vegetation would offer a perfect cover for anything wishing to ambush us. Dimitri must have thought the same thing because he didn't even try to pull ahead. He stayed at my side, his movements practiced, alert.

I touched the emerald at my neck. Dimitri had given it to me shortly after we met. He had laced the teardrop-shaped stone with protective magic and hung it on an enchanted bronze chain. In the past, it had morphed into body armor when I needed it, tied me to a tree when I didn't, and fainted dead away at the sight of the Earl of Hell.

Smart necklace.

This time, it remained still. That worried me more than I would have liked to admit.

We broke out onto the shore and caught sight of a man about twenty feet down, on our left. I drew a switch star. At least we knew the origin of the red lights.

He stood like a shadow at the center of the crimson haze, his wrist manacled to a large wooden cage behind him. From inside came a loud *thud*, like a body smacking up against wood. The entire thing shook, and chains rattled. The glow around the edges grew brighter.

Dimitri snorted. "You have ten seconds to tell me what the fuck you have there."

He was right. We couldn't just stand here on a beach, exposed.

The man began to take a step forward. One glance at Dimitri and he changed his mind. "It's for you," he said, his voice garbled. As if he'd crossed dimensions, which he probably had.

Jumping Jesus on a pogo stick.

Still, his voice sounded familiar.

He reached into his torn jacket. I drew back, ready to fire my switch star. The man gave us a furtive glance, seemingly more afraid of what was in the cage than he was of us. He drew a marble-sized ball of light from his pocket and tossed it through the bars.

The snarling shadow of a black-furred, red-eyed beast shot forward and devoured the light with curved yellow teeth.

"That's it." Dimitri advanced, knife at the ready.

"Wait!" I started forward.

The man ducked his head and disappeared.

CHAPTER TWO

We stood alone on the beach, with a monster.

"What the hell?" Dimitri snapped. "What did he mean, this is for us?"

Chains rattled inside the large wooden box as a long snout shoved through the bars. Blood smeared along the side of the creature's jaw, as if it had been fighting the cage.

At least I hoped it was that, and not the remains of the last slayer who had received this trussed-up present. We had no idea what this thing was or what it could do, and the only person who might have had the answer had just zipped into the ether.

"Why'd you have to go and scare the guy?" I demanded.

Dimitri turned to me, shoulders back, braced for the fight. "It's called taking the upper hand."

And we could see where that had gotten us.

The creature had tusklike teeth and a flat brown nose that pulsed with every harsh, rasping breath. It caught a scent in the air and its entire snout rattled with a snarl. Spittle fell in steaming drops on the sand.

"At least it's in a cage," Dimitri offered.

"Truly?" That was all he had? I threw up my hands. "Next time, think before you get all testosterone-y."

Dimitri looked at me like I was the crazy one.

"Look how dirty it is," I told him. "I'm not having that in my house." I didn't know what we were going to do with it. "It's a mess and I'm going to have to take care of it." I always did.

Dimitri stared at me for a second too long.

"What?" I asked, straightening the T-shirt I wore, tucking back my hair, trying to get a handle on something…anything.

He cocked his head as if I were some strange phenomenon. "For a split second, you reminded me of your mother."

H-e-double-hockey-sticks. "I'm going to pretend I didn't hear that." In fact, I was starting to hope this whole thing had been a dream.

He grinned, despite himself. "What happened to always telling the truth?"

"I'm not so sure that works in real life." Besides, my mom was a control freak. I was just a girl who didn't want to stumble upon strange creatures in the middle of the night. "I mean did you see that thing? It devoured that ball of light like it was a Scooby Snack. What was that thing, anyway?"

Dimitri shook his head. "I've never seen anything like it." He eyed the spittle dripping from the creature's fangs. A red mist seeped out from between the bars. Dimitri held the knife as if he were tempted, sorely tempted, to end it all right now. "The only thing I can tell you is it's not from this dimension."

I gave it a sideways glance. "Thank God for that."

Dimitri pulled a flashlight out of his pants pocket and handed it to me. "I don't think it's going anywhere. Let's see if we can learn more about what happened."

"Right." We'd just leave it here, then.

For now.

I shook my head, muttering.

We knew the honeymoon couldn't last forever. Of course we were going to have to get back to our badass lives eventually. But this wasn't the way I wanted it to happen—dragged out of bed, confronted with a demonic beast, fifty feet from our new home, no less.

I hated the fact that leaving an evil creature on my beach was actually the better choice right now. We needed to determine who was after us, and what they wanted.

And then maybe we'd figure out what to do with ole snarly.

We backed away from the dark cage and began searching the predawn beach. What had been beautiful in the daytime felt ominous now. Shadows reached from the dunes and unidentifiable objects seemed to swallow the moonlight.

I stopped to check out a shadowy lump that turned out to be a tangled mass of seaweed. Dimitri got out a little bit ahead of me, toward the water.

"Take a look at this," he said, standing over a blackened circle of sand near the breakers. It looked like the remains of a portal. He bent down to take a sample.

Holy Hades. "Wait!" That could be black magic. I dashed across the beach, my toes digging into the sand.

His fingers touched the ashy residue and I had sudden images of it consuming him, killing him, transporting him to hell. I didn't know. I stumbled over my feet as it flaked away in his fingers, leaving nothing. He frowned, focused on the smidge of black on his pointer finger and not the fact that I'd been damned near ready to save his life, if not his soul. "This must be where he crossed over."

I rested my hands on my knees, insanely relieved to have him here, in one piece. "You gave me heart palpitations, touching the remains of evil."

He seemed almost amused at that. "I'm a griffin."

Hmm. Yes. Goodness and light. It would only get him so far. I was about to tell him that when the entire dark circle began crumbling apart. It was as if the varied parts of it decided to take flight at the same time. I felt the magic stir, the heavy weight lift as we watched it rise, bit by bit, and scatter to the wind.

"Dark magic always covers its tracks," I murmured. Grandma had told me that. Still, it creeped me out to see a live demonstration.

I wondered if the portal was still there. Maybe we simply couldn't see it. I braced myself and walked directly into the place where the dark circle had been.

Nothing.

I tested it with my foot, pressing my toes into the sand, bracing myself in case it gave way. I felt only solid earth underneath.

Okay. I stood for a moment, as if the portal would open up if I wished hard enough.

"You think it's still here?" I asked, trying to feel something, anything, in the air around me.

"God, I hope not," Dimitri said. The last portal we'd tried together had sent us straight to hell.

Right. "I'm going to try a spell jar," I said.

Dimitri backed off several paces. I tried not to take it personally. Last week, I'd shown Dimitri the supposedly "mild" wildlife enchantment spell Grandma had taught me. Unfortunately, it had made me wildly attractive to every bird, bunny, lizard, and ladybug for a five-mile radius. I'd felt like a princess in a Disney movie.

And we still had bunnies under the porch.

I pulled a jar out of my utility belt and held it up. "This one is supposed to flush out evil." If it worked right.

We both backed up several more steps. I glanced at him. "Relax. It'll work."

I gripped the slick jar. We braced ourselves as I heaved it directly at where the portal had been.

It didn't break. It didn't release any spells. It just landed with a *thunk* in the sand.

Dimitri eyed me, half cringing. "Good try."

Hmm. I rested my hands on my hips. "At least I didn't break any glass on the beach." I hadn't thought of that when I first tossed it.

Dimitri watched as I retrieved the spell. "Here," I said, screwing open the jar. I'd had it open when I mixed everything. The sludge looked like the same nasty copper-smelling stuff. "One more time," I said, trying this time to launch the contents of the jar at where the portal should have been.

The spell landed with a *splotch* at my feet.

Not very aerodynamic.

Worse, it just kind of sat there. Grandma's anti-demonic spell glowed really cool and would expose the tinges of evil in the air. It would also suck them up and give off this vibrant blue glow.

My spell just made a mess on the sand, not unlike a dead jellyfish.

I studied the gloppy pile. "It might need more goodness and light." Flowers could work. Botanicals did wonders for a spell. I nibbled at my bottom lip. I couldn't tell very well in the dark, but... "I think I saw a wild azalea on the way down here."

"Stop," Dimitri said, a little more forcefully than necessary. "You can figure it out later, when we don't have a creature from another dimension on our beach."

Good point. Cripes. I might be the Exalted Demon Slayer of Dalea, but I sucked at being a witch.

"Come on." He turned, his shoulders bunching in the moonlight. "The tide's moving in."

The water had already crept up on the remains of the entry point. We began at that spot and followed deep ruts in the sand.

The tracks twisted in spots, betraying the difficulty in transporting a wild beast. I ran a toe over one. "He had to be strong to make it this far."

"Or under the influence of something powerful." Dimitri used the flashlight to take a closer look at a particularly nasty gouge in the sand.

"I wish I could peg that voice," I said. It had been familiar, yet disguised. I didn't like it at all.

We pursued the tracks all the way back to our buddy in the cage.

Dimitri eyed the beast as it slammed its body against the bars.

The *thud*s I'd heard must have come from the creature smacking against the cage. The rattling came from the chains.

I shook my head. "That thing's going to brain itself."

Dimitri snorted. "Better it than us."

At least the cage stood far enough from the water to be safe from high tide. We didn't need our monster floating away. Now we just needed to worry about the joggers once the sun came up.

Dimitri studied the rattling cage. "Let's get it out of here."

"Right," I said. We needed to get a move on, and frankly, I was thankful to have my husband around. He had supernatural strength, while I still had trouble opening pickle jars. "We can hide it in the garage," I announced. I didn't see any other good options. We were living in a town house, for heaven's sake.

Dimitri chuckled. I couldn't tell if he was amused or what as he lowered his head and unzipped his black dress pants. Oh my. The realization hit me so hard, I forgot to even get a good look. Dimitri didn't intend to drag this thing, as our mysterious visitor had. He was going to shift.

I stepped back a few paces as thick lion's fur raced up his arms. Claws erupted from his hands and feet. He grew fast, transforming as bones snapped and muscles thickened. Red, purple, and blue feathers cascaded down his back and formed wings. In less than a minute, I stood staring at a beautiful griffin the size of a truck.

"I don't think I'll ever get tired of watching you do that," I told him.

He tossed back his eagle's head and stretched his wings out wide.

As a man, he was intimidating. As a griffin, he was something else entirely.

I gathered up his pants, and then located a large hauling rope in the utility shed under the deck. With the pants slung over my shoulder, I tied one end of the rope tight to the handle at the top of the cage and secured the other half around Dimitri's formidable lion's chest.

A light went on in our complex, just a few units down. The darkness still hid what we were doing, but dawn would be coming soon.

"Yikes," I said, double-checking my knots.

Dimitri pawed at the ground.

I hoped that any nosy neighbors couldn't see the actual cage. Otherwise, we'd have to come up with a good story, one that didn't involve mythical beasts and demons.

With a mighty flex of his wings, Dimitri took to the air. Soon, the cage lifted up as well. He carried it easily, past the shoreline and over our place. I followed, but hadn't even made it halfway before he'd touched down in the small parking lot behind our complex.

We'd done it. Together.

I just hoped the evil creature and its cage could fit inside our modest one-car garage.

Dimitri had shifted back by the time I reached him. The rope lay in a puddle at his feet, and he stood tall, looking quite wonderful naked. Too bad we didn't have time for me to show my appreciation.

I kissed him on the cheek and handed him his pants, like a good wife. "This feels so *Leave It to Beaver*," I said as I went to punch in the code to the garage door.

"What episode did you watch?" he asked, working on his pants while the door went up.

We'd already cleared the space for Flappy, so it was just a matter of moving some dragon toys, a blanket, and a small treasure chest that Pirate seemed to think his pet needed. Dimitri managed to push the cage all the way to the rear wall. Even still, the creature barely fit.

My husband cringed. "This is such a bad idea."

I couldn't argue with him there. The cage took up most of the narrow space. The heavy bars and red vapor were a stark contrast to our pretty yellow-painted garage.

"Too bad it's our only idea," I told him. Our nighttime visitor had been up to something. He left the creature here for a reason. We needed to figure out why, and how to defend ourselves against it. In the meantime, "I wonder what it eats."

"Lost souls and kitties," he muttered, shoving at the cage, trying to get it farther back.

Just then, I caught Pirate out of the corner of my eye. I fought back a groan. He bounded across the parking lot, dragging the remains of his doggy chain.

"What are you doing?" he called. "I know you found something. I barked at it! Did you hear me barking?"

Did his paws even touch the pavement? "How did you get loose?" I asked, intercepting him before he got too close. With skill born from years of practice, I caught him in mid-leap and scooped him up in my arms.

He wriggled like a caught fish. "I woke up Flappy and got him to chomp through my chain." He dug his cold, wet nose into the crook of my elbow, testing my grip. "I can't believe you chained me. Who ties up a dog?"

A strong breeze whipped over us as Flappy touched down outside.

I could feel the energy of the beast behind me. I glanced back. The rising sun shed light into the cage and onto the creature, revealing scraggly hair, massive paws, and even more teeth. It was built like a wolf, only bigger, and infused with pure rage.

Pirate managed to crane his neck around me and caught his first glimpse. "It's a puppy!"

It drew back and lunged, trying to bite through the bars.

"I stand corrected," Pirate said. "It's a watch dog!"

"No," I said, managing to keep a grip on my dog, despite his efforts to jump down. "We don't know what it is."

"Only that you need to stay ten feet back at all times," Dimitri added.

He might as well have been speaking Chinese, for all the attention Pirate gave his warning.

Pirate cocked his head, his ears pricking. "Can we keep it?"

As if on cue, a hairy snout poked out and a low, menacing growl echoed throughout the garage.

"He just doesn't like to be tied up," Pirate said. "Believe me," he said, raising his voice, his nails digging into my skin as he tried to scramble past my arm, "I know how you feel."

At least Flappy had some sense. The dragon crouched on the other side of us, snarling and baring his sharp white fangs.

"Don't be jealous, Flappy," Pirate ordered. My dog sniffed the air. "That poor doggy is just sad. And alone. We should call him Hairy."

"We're not keeping him," I said to Pirate.

The dragon began garbling under his breath. Black smoke curled from his nostrils.

I pointed a warning finger at him. "No fireballs."

We had to get this garage closed before Flappy spit flames or the neighbors saw what we had in here. Yes, we were in progressive California, but even liberals had their limits.

Dimitri gritted his jaw. "I'm thinking a demon sent it after us."

I shook my head. "Not in a cage."

He stood between the beast and me. Dimitri grabbed a flashlight off the wall of the garage. He shone the light inside and we saw lots of coarse gray and black fur.

"We have to figure out what this is."

And who had it in for us.

In the meantime...

At least our garage had a solid door.

CHAPTER THREE

That door had begun rumbling down when Sarayh, the head of our homeowners association, came ambling from between buildings two and three, right across from us. She waved, as if she wasn't surprised at all to find her neighbors gathered in front of the garage at dawn.

Frankly, I should have expected her. Sarayh walked her dog every morning.

She crossed the lot and headed straight for us, with Moxie the poodle at the lead. "You sure got an early start," she said, smiling at Dimitri. I took it as a compliment. My tall Greek husband was a sight to see.

Moxie made a mad dash for Pirate as they drew closer.

"Hello sweetness!" my dog gushed, going in nose-first and getting right up in her personal space.

She wagged her tail.

He turned back to me. "She's not much of a talker."

It took me a second to realize my neighbor stood watching me and not the animals. Because, of course, she couldn't hear what Pirate had to say. "Um." I scrambled to recover the thread of her conversation. "What were we talking about?"

Sarayh gave a knowing grin. "You, him, butt-crack of dawn, out on the beach..."

Yes. Well, I supposed it was strange for us to be outside the garage, with me wearing only Dimitri's shirt and him, standing there in a pair of half-buttoned pants, with his undershirt in one hand. "We just needed to grab something," I said, hoping she didn't ask what.

"Sure you did," my neighbor said, winking. "I don't mind. Newlyweds and all," she added, giving Dimitri an appraising look, "but I wanted to stop and tell you...I got a few calls about it."

"It's not what you think," Dimitri said. His face betrayed nothing, but there was a definite cringe in his voice.

She held up a hand. "I don't want to know. Just...try not to growl so loud. Or shine lights all over." She toyed with her brown ponytail. "You might also want to double-check your garage. I think something broke in there."

I looked to see where she pointed and saw a thin line of wetness coming from under the door and a faint smoke coming from the edges.

Oh, geez.

She frowned, the tanned skin of her forehead pinching. "I hope it's not coming from your recycling. You know how Stella wants everyone to wash bottles and jars before they go in your bin," she said, as if that were the only thing I had to worry about.

"We'll take care of it," Dimitri said stiffly.

"Right," Sarayh said. She tossed her hair back. "I mean I don't care what you do. Personal freedom and all. But don't get in Stella's way when she's trying to save the planet."

"Believe me, I understand." I had to try to save the planet more often than I cared to admit.

Meanwhile Moxie had wandered over to inspect the door of our garage. It rattled, sending the dog jumping back a foot.

"Raccoon," Dimitri said quickly.

Our friendly HOA board director nodded a few too many times. "Wow. Okay. I'll call wildlife rescue."

"No," I said quickly. "We've got it."

"Sure thing," she said, walking to pick up Moxie, giving an extra glance at the growling coming from the garage.

Why did I ever think I could have a normal life?

She forced a smile. "Don't forget about girls' night out. Craft beers and henna tattoos on the beach. It would be a great way for you to meet the neighbors and show them how nice you are." She winked.

"Thanks," I said, relieved when she began her good-byes. I didn't need to be making inane chitchat with a woman who may or may not think I just had sex on the beach.

Sarayh waved, and—after carrying her dog past our garage—she resumed her walk.

"You should go to girls' night," Dimitri said as we headed back to the vibrating garage.

"You've got to be kidding me," I said as Dimitri tossed his undershirt over the escaping drool. The shirt began to smoke. "There's nothing I could say to those people."

He wiped up the drool, careful not to touch the parts that were eating away at his shirt. "Hi. My name is Lizzie. I'm new to California."

I glanced behind us to make sure we were alone. "I'm a demon slayer," I reminded him under my breath. "The Earl of Hell tried to kill me at my wedding, but I managed to survive, thanks to my husband, who can strip naked and change into a griffin anytime he pleases."

He sat back on his heels. "Now you're just being difficult."

I don't know what universe he was living in. "Try realistic."

He shrugged a shoulder and stuffed the shirt against the small two-inch gap that had been the source of the leak. "This is your life now, and you're going to have to get used to living with non-magical people."

Um-hum. "Says the griffin who grew up on an estate in Greece."

He couldn't expect his undershirt fix to last for long.

"I do just fine." He straightened. "It's you I'm worried about. Don't try so hard to be a demon slayer, or a witch, that you forget about everything else."

"Let me handle things how I handle them," I said, almost wishing the garage would start leaking again, just to prove to the man that he couldn't fix everything.

I had Dimitri, the witches. My family at home now knew about my powers. That in itself was a big step. Yes, I'd cut myself off from all my old friends back in Atlanta. But I didn't know what to say to them anymore. It's not as if I could tell them about my new life. And if I'd invited them to my wedding, they might have been killed by a demon. These weren't normal problems.

We waited to see if his fix would work. It did, for now. Still, this was far from over.

I slid my arms around my husband—or at least I tried. His wide chest made it hard for me to fit all the way around. I leaned into him, enjoying his solid presence. "All I need is you," I said, reaching up to peck him on the lips.

"I'll let you get away with that. For now." He held me close, his chin resting on my head.

†††

A short time later, Dimitri and I turned toward the neat line of sand-colored stucco town houses. Stubby palm trees sprouted from the walkway leading to our bright blue front door. Everything seemed so *normal* on the outside. As long as you didn't count the mythical beast hidden in our garage.

Dimitri inserted his key in the front door and it made me glad to see at least one of us had decided to leave the house with pants. The sun had risen and chances were, if we'd had to sneak around back, we would have ended up greeting at least a few of our neighbors as they enjoyed morning coffee out on their decks.

I gave one final glance back. We'd left Flappy outside the garage, snarling, while Pirate kept him company.

"They're fine. If Flappy hasn't flipped out yet, he's not going to," Dimitri said, holding the door open for me. "Let's clean up and make some calls."

"I have Rachmort's new number," I said, heading inside the house.

Although my mentor had never explained why it changed.

Rachmort ministered to the lost souls of purgatory. He spent six months out of the year down there, coaxing wayward souls to give up whatever darkness they held and move to the light. The other six months he spent in Boca Raton, Florida. Or somewhere training slayers like me.

"That's not who I was thinking about," Dimitri said, locking the door behind us.

"He'd be better than the biker witches," I said, heading for the kitchen. My grandma's gang didn't exactly do things quietly.

Dimitri cleared his throat. "I'm talking about the only person we know who is part demon and also good with animals."

I turned to face him. "You've got to be kidding." No way I was bringing a half demon into this.

Dimitri had the nerve to look amused. "You said you liked her."

"I didn't kill her," I corrected. Big difference.

Shiloh McBride had lived a good portion of her life as a succubus, a special breed of demon who fed on sex and depravity. I'd let her live shortly after wiping out every soul-consuming demon in Las Vegas. She'd been spared because of her half-human side, and because she wasn't necessarily evil. Besides, when I'd gone to finish the job, I'd found her married to a demon slayer and running her own doggy grooming salon. Instead of a switch star, she'd gotten Pirate for a bath and a paw-dicure.

"She's the natural choice," Dimitri said, with his unfailing logic.

I leaned up against the edge of the kitchen table to think about it. Despite the fact that I really, *really* didn't like the idea, my husband had a point. Shiloh was on our side, and she may very well know what kind of beast we had on our hands. She certainly owed me a favor.

Dimitri rummaged through our junk drawer before handing me the card for the Pampered Paws Salon in Las Vegas. On the back Shiloh had written her private cell number.

"I can't believe I'm doing this," I said as I punched in the number.

Dimitri just smiled.

And wouldn't you know it, Shiloh answered on the first ring.

"Lizzie Brown!" Her voice sounded smooth, melodious, like a beauty queen—or a soul eater.

"Hey, Shiloh," I said, trying to keep my own voice even. "Long time, no…whatever." I cleared my throat.

"We have a situation. I'm putting you on speaker."
When I did, we picked up a noise that sounded like
dry-throated dogs snarling and barking in the
background. I didn't want to know, but I had to ask
anyway. "Are those hellhounds?"

"Only my two," she said. "They get excited when
the phone rings."

Right.

"We have a problem," Dimitri said, plowing
forward. He closed his hand over mine and gave me a
small squeeze. "A stranger showed up on our beach
today and left an aggressive creature behind. Frankly,
we don't know what to do with it."

"It's wolflike," I told her, "with black-and-gray fur,
curved teeth. It's crazy aggressive. Mean."

"Hmm," she said. The lid of a jar rattled and the
hellhounds started barking like crazy. "Does it have a
flat snout? Tusked teeth? Moon-shaped claws?"

"Yes," I said. "There's also a red vapor seeping out
around it."

"Aww," the half succubus cooed. "It sounds like
you have a fenris. Poor thing belongs in purgatory."

"Great," I said, not meaning it at all, even if I did
appreciate knowing where the thing had to go. "How
do we get it to purgatory?"

"No clue," she said. "The little devil's probably
scared to death. Be careful, though, because if its diet
is a little off, its breath might make you
woozy...unless he's a cave-dwelling fenris. He doesn't
have tiny little bat wings, does he?"

Of all the... "How the hell should I know?"

She ignored my tone. "In any case, it would be a
good idea to keep a fan going."

Wait a second. "We're not going to keep this
thing."

She sighed. "It's a living creature. With feelings."

I doubted that second part.

She cleared her throat. "Look, I'm not due in the shop today. I suppose I could run out there and help you get settled with your new pet. But you have to promise me you're going to take care of it."

No. Absolutely not.

For all I knew, it was part of some evil plan.

I sighed and made eyes at Dimitri. I didn't want to call her in the first place and now she wanted to visit and make me keep a fenris?

He shrugged. "It's not like we can let it loose."

"That's the spirit," Shiloh chirped, with that overly perky voice that made me wonder if I'd already died and gone to hell.

Dimitri couldn't hide his grin. He still looked rather amused after my somewhat awkward sign-off.

"What?" I asked, not liking it at all.

"Look at the bright side," he said. "At least we know what we have."

What to do with it was another matter entirely.

Chapter Four

"I'm going to go clean up," I said, heading upstairs. It's not as though I could greet Shiloh while wearing Dimitri's T-shirt and basically nothing else.

Sometimes, I actually felt like I'd gotten a handle on my life as a demon slayer. It hadn't even been two years since my powers had been thrust upon me. I'd gone from preschool teacher to kick-butt conqueror…with plenty of bumps along the way. But still, I'd survived. I'd saved many of my newfound supernatural friends and allies. I'd grown confident, strong. Then something like this happened and I realized I couldn't even imagine or anticipate half of what the world had to throw at me.

Maybe someday, I'd master it all.

I nearly tripped over the laundry basket at the top of the stairs. Grumbling, I shoved it aside with my foot.

Our room felt like a dark nest of chaos. I pulled back the curtains to let in some light. Outside, in the parking lot, Pirate and Flappy sat rapt outside the garage, staring at the door.

Maybe someday, I'd simply master my pets.

Don't count on it.

I undressed and ducked into the shower. Shiloh would take four hours to get here if she drove from Las Vegas. Surely we could contain the fenris for that long.

†††

Wonder of wonders, we succeeded. And roughly four hours later, Shiloh the half she-demon rang the doorbell.

Thank God.

Dimitri and I opened the door to the petite blonde. She wore pink capri pants, a white wraparound shirt, and a gold-and-white daisy necklace. It looked like the kind of outfit I would have worn a few years ago, before my change.

It didn't fool me for a second.

I, on the other hand, had dressed in my usual black leather pants and matching ass-kicker boots. I'd gone for an ivory bustier today, on account of my newlywed status.

"Hi," Shiloh said somewhat hesitant, raising her hand to wave and unbalancing the huge yellow Pampered Paws Salon bag she'd slung over her shoulder.

She blinked, as if I'd surprised her. Then she began staring at me. Hard.

"We appreciate you coming by," Dimitri said, but Shiloh wasn't paying much attention. Neither was I.

The half demon wet her perfectly-glossed Barbie doll lips. "You've gotten more powerful," she said, her voice breathy.

I could feel my power swelling inside me. "Thanks."

Her gaze skittered away, and she focused on a spot just past my left shoulder. "So," she said, as if this were a normal conversation, "where's your fenris?"

"Locked up in the garage," I told her.

"Poor baby!" Her eyes widened and her hand flew to her mouth. "We have to get it out of there. Fenrises are highly social creatures."

Dimitri towered over her. "It's dangerous."

Her eyes narrowed and she gave him a look from hell. Seriously. Her eyes flashed red. I had to almost admire her for it, seeing as she had to crane her neck up at one very big, intimidating Dimitri. "It's probably scared to death."

I doubted it. "No. Really. You have to see this thing," I told her, urging her down the path toward the garage. "It would have no problem eating you, me, any of the neighbors." It would make a snack of Pirate.

When my dog saw us coming, he rushed to Shiloh. "Hi! Remember me? Hi!" But the half demon didn't see him. I reached for him, but he ducked out of my way.

Shiloh adjusted the overstuffed bag on her shoulder. "Fenrises are high energy," she said, as if she were admitting a terrible fault, the only shortcoming of the huge, wolflike creatures. "But as with any animal, a little understanding goes a long way."

"You think so?" my husband drawled. "Check this out." Dimitri opened the garage door. As it rumbled up on its hinges, the creature immediately went insane, attacking the bars. It gave a stomach-curdling roar. The cage rocked from side to side.

"You see?" Shiloh pointed a petite hand. "It's terrified."

I shared a glance with Dimitri. He'd positioned himself between the cage and us. He didn't look convinced.

Shiloh opened up her hands, obviously adjusting her strategy. "Let's just take this in baby steps, okay? We'll simply move your fenris into the house, and—"

"Not in a million years," I countered.

She tucked her hair back behind her ears, clearly looking for an angle. "Does it have a name?" she prodded.

"Hell Raiser," Dimitri said.

Shiloh bypassed Dimitri and stood directly outside the cage. She held out a hand to the oversize, tusked-looking snout. Holy Hades. She was asking to get mauled. Its nostrils were as big as her entire palm, its teeth as long as her fingers. The thing showed two rows of those god-awful chompers. I wished I'd brought my phone to call 911. Then it hesitated, and gave her a wet sniff.

Naturally, she took it as a sign of love. "Aww..." she crooned, as the creature dripped steaming spit all over her hand. "You're just a big baby doll, aren't you?"

"What?" The question fell from Dimitri's lips, as if he weren't quite sure what he'd heard.

Shiloh glanced back at us. "First off, it looks like she's a girl and not a boy."

I didn't want to ask how she knew that.

"Second, when training an animal, you have to set expectations." She ran her fingers under its muzzle, as if she were the fenris whisperer. The animal gurgled and bit at the cage bars. "Isn't that right, sweetie pie?" Shiloh crooned. The beast let out a low, growly moan. Unbelievable. I figured Shiloh had a knack with animals, but this was ridiculous.

"I'm a sweetie pie," Pirate said, nosing up on her, but Shiloh didn't see him.

She straightened, wiping her hand on her pants, ignoring the red mist that rose up from them. She'd gotten a piece of doggy-sniffle in her hair as well. She didn't seem to mind. "Fenrises are a lot more delicate than, say, hellhounds or imps. We have to get Babydoll on a special diet or she's going to continue to be in a bad mood."

"Oh great," I mused. "Instead of eating my hand, it wants a custom evil diet?"

Shiloh wasn't amused. She turned to Dimitri, evidently deciding I wasn't in a listening mood. "You have a field fenris, from the barren plains of West Purgatory. You can tell by her purple tongue."

"We couldn't see past the snarling teeth," I said. I couldn't help it.

Pirate tried to ease past me for a better look. I picked him up instead.

Shiloh ignored us both. "Field fenrises are heavily pack-bound and have delicate digestive systems. No wonder she's a mess. Poor thing. They should never be kept as pets. They just don't thrive well in captivity. She needs devil's grass, from the barren plains. But if that's not available," she said, glancing back to me, as if I'd planned to stroll on down to purgatory in order to pick grass, "then I'd recommend alfalfa. It has the higher caloric count Babydoll is going to need to help her recover."

"As opposed to…" Dimitri began.

"Oat hay or orchard grass," she said happily. The fenris fought the bars to get at Shiloh. Instead of stepping back, she calmly slid her hand inside and let it mouth her hand like a puppy. She'd lose that hand if it bit down. But the she-demon didn't seem the least bit worried. "Babydoll needs a high-acid meal, something in the two to three range on the pH scale. Do you have any lemons?"

"Lemons," I said. She really was serious about all this. "For a fenris."

"I don't even get canned dog food," Pirate said.

She put both hands inside then, scruffing up the fenris's fur on both sides of its massive head. "I brought battery acid, but just looking at her condition, I think it may upset her tummy."

I really wasn't trying to be difficult—at the moment at least—but I felt obliged to remind Shiloh, "This morning, that thing wanted to devour us whole."

"And spit out our toenails," Pirate added.

Shiloh actually laughed at that. "Oh, no. Fenrises are vegetarians."

It didn't make any sense.

Dimitri shook his head, as if he were trying to reconcile it as well. "Why would someone bring us a fenris? Especially if it's a vegetarian and doesn't want to rip us into pieces?"

"I don't know," Shiloh said, saddening even as the beast tried to lick her to death. "She should be with her pack, or a family who loves her." Tears glistened in the half succubus's eyes. "That's why she's freaking out. And then you put her alone in a garage."

It's not as if we knew.

Shiloh nodded. "I'll see if we can find out where she belongs. I have a few...ah, *old associates* I can ask." She looked to us both. "In the meantime, let's get Babydoll into the house. I'll set her up there and then we can take a look at where she turned up on your beach."

No question Shiloh knew people and creatures we didn't. She also had a very different set of powers. Perhaps she could see something in the remains of the portal that I couldn't, but still. Shiloh's gifts came from a very dark place.

We stood in an uncomfortable silence for a moment.

Frankly, I was more willing to let Shiloh tap into her dark side than I was to let a fenris in my house.

I loved animals. In truth, her actions toward the beast had proven that she was a lot nicer of a person than me right now. I just hadn't seen it as a homeless animal that needed attention. Still, I lived in a community now, with full humans. I owed it to them to keep their little corner of the world safe.

As she reached for the cage opening, I had a responsibility, a duty, to ask one last time. "You *promise* it's not going to eat anyone."

"Never," she said. Her hand glowed red over the latch and she swung the door open. The fenris charged out halfway, and as soon as Shiloh unlatched the manacles inside the cage, she had a whole lot of crazy on the end of a chain. Not that she noticed. "She's feisty," Shiloh said, with the giggle of a mad animal lover.

Just when I wondered whether or not the beast would knock the dainty half demon on her rear, something outside caught Shiloh's eye. "Hi!" she said, waving to someone down the way.

I turned to see my neighbor Todd, running shirtless again. Yes, he had a hard body and I think he worked part-time as a male underwear model, but it was a bit terrifying to watch Shiloh's reaction to the handsome man. Her back straightened, her skin glowed, and I swore she grew an inch. She cocked out a hip, opened up a thigh. "Great day to run!" she said, her voice almost musical as she waved at the virile Todd.

He broke into a sexy grin and began a slow jog toward us. Another male, caught in a succubus tractor beam. "Nice dog," he said.

"Thanks!" Pirate answered.

But I saw where Todd's attention settled—on Shiloh's ample cleavage and then on the fenris going ballistic at the end of the chain.

Todd stopped close, way to close to Shiloh. "That's a big husky," he said, barely sparing a glance at the beast before his rapt attention returned to her.

"I know," she giggled, smiling up at him.

Yikes. He actually saw the fenris as an out-of-control dog.

And then suddenly, that wasn't our biggest problem. The fenris reared back and took out an entire shelf full of glass jars I'd set aside for spell work.

"Watch out!" Dimitri pulled me forward as they shattered into a million pieces behind us.

Shiloh and Todd didn't notice.

Her skin glowed with a golden sheen. Her hair blew softly, caressing her shoulders. Her cornflower eyes had gone deep blue and she licked her lips seductively.

"Go. I've got it," Dimitri said, moving to grab a broom and clean up the mess.

"Right." I took Shiloh by the elbow. Her smooth skin felt warm, flushed. "It's great to see you, Todd," I said, giving Shiloh a tug, "but we have to go."

It took quite a bit of pulling, actually, to get her moving.

Even when she came along with me, she craned her neck back at him. "What are you doing?" she asked me. "Bye!" she called out, giving him a wave.

"You're married," I reminded her.

"I'm not dead," she said, shaking off my grip.

"Even so, I don't want you feeding on the neighbors." I understood that her half-succubus side drew power from peoples' attraction to her, but she had to tone it down, at least in my neighborhood.

I never thought it would be this hard to blend in, especially where I lived.

"Spoilsport," she said, wrangling the fenris toward our front door.

I waved as a couple of our neighbors drove by in a beige Prius.

Nothing to see here. Just a semi-reformed demon seductress and a big crazy dog from the underworld.

I set Pirate down in the house, but Flappy wasn't allowed. The dragon zipped back to the deck, where he hunched, snarling, his nose pressed to our glass sliding door.

"Here," Shiloh said, handing me the chain.

She kept walking toward the kitchen and the fenris about pulled my arms out of the sockets as it leaped forward to keep up with her. "Down, boy!" I commanded. "Girl," I corrected. "Whatever you are," I said, fighting it as it dragged me into my kitchen.

Shiloh reached into her bag and pulled out a bundle wrapped in daisy-print cloth. The fenris went wild, nails scrabbling against my hardwood as it fought the leash. I tried to keep a hold on it as it turned and knocked over two of our kitchen chairs with its powerful haunches.

Flappy roared and stomped on the deck, rattling the entire complex.

"Wait, wait!" Shiloh laughed, unwrapping a bundle of green alfalfa.

The fenris shoved its snout into the heart of the greenery and immediately began chomping. Then it knocked over another kitchen chair with a wagging tail.

Shiloh dug a hand into the mess of fur on top its head. "That tastes like home, doesn't it, sweetie?"

"Okay, enough with the new dog," Pirate grumbled, as she stepped into his water dish. "I mean, did you ask her? I'll bet she's not even potty trained."

Babydoll gave the dish a sniff before she lumbered over to Pirate's doggy bed and plopped down on top of it.

Pirate's ears went flat. "Oh, no, you didn't!"

She fit maybe one back leg and a butt cheek on the bed. The rest of her made do with the hardwood floor.

Shiloh looped Babydoll's chain around our refrigerator and clamped it tight.

"If that's how you want to play," Pirate said, heading for a piece of alfalfa that the fenris had dropped. "I'll just eat this."

He gobbled it up and chewed. And chewed. And chewed. He winced, his shoulders hunching. But he kept on chewing.

"Poor Pirate," Shiloh crooned. "Would you like a doggy biscuit?" She pulled a homemade treat out of her bag. "I have one that I brought just for you." It was shaped like a bone and slicked with white icing and sprinkles.

Pirate's ears perked up. "Oh yes," he said, losing a bit of hay from the corners of his mouth. "Do you know how good I've been? You've been thinking about me, haven't you?"

Shiloh tossed the bone at his feet and just when he bent to see if he could get it into his mouth, Babydoll lurched forward and gobbled it in one bite.

"That's it!" Pirate spit out the hay. "It is on, bitch!"

Pirate lunged. The fenris cowered. I grabbed him. Flappy roared.

"Lemme go!" He scrambled against my hold. "This is between me and the bone stealer!"

"Pirate." I held him up so he could look me in the eye. "Babydoll is a guest."

He struggled to get away. "Not in my house."

"Do you want to go outside with Flappy?" I asked.

The dragon hovered outside the kitchen window, his snout pulsing, pressing heated circles into the glass. I'd have to clean every frigging window in this place—from the outside—if the fricking dragon didn't calm down.

As if on cue, the dragon sneezed—a wet, snotty one—right on my glass.

Shiloh joined me. "I'm so sorry, Pirate. Sometimes the fenris doesn't know better." She scratched my dog between the ears and he flinched. "You're older than she is." She patted him on the head. "I'll bring you another treat later."

Which meant *forever* to a dog. Poor Pirate.

"Let's all head outside and let everybody settle down," I said, taking my dog with me. Or else Pirate would try to jump the beast again. Babydoll had curled into Pirate's spot, across from the kitchen table, in view of the deck and the beach.

I opened the sliding glass door, and we all ducked out a second before Flappy came crashing back down on the deck. I slid the door closed. I swore these animals were going to tear my house apart.

"So what's the deal with the portal?" Shiloh said as I felt a headache coming on.

I tried to clear my head. *Get a grip.*

It was a warm, sunny day. We weren't battling for our lives. Not yet anyway.

I set Pirate down. He immediately dashed to join Flappy, and they both shoved their noses against the sliding glass door.

Shiloh and I edged past Flappy's pile of deck cushions and walked out to the railing overlooking the ocean. "We found the remains of a portal crossing down there on the beach," I said, pointing down and toward the left. Luckily, the beach was deserted at the moment. "Everything was fine yesterday. Or at least I didn't sense anything bad down there. But this morning, a guy came through with the fenris. Then he disappeared."

She thought for a moment. "So you think someone placed it there, specifically to get to you?"

In my world, things were never random. "It can only mean trouble," I told her. "But I have no idea who created it. Or why." I turned to her. "I know you can feel dark energies."

She cringed slightly. "I'm trying not to mess with that kind of thing anymore."

I got it. I really did. At the same time... "Is there anything you can do that won't compromise you?"

She gave me a look of dread. "You know how this works, right?"

"Not necessarily." That's why I was asking. "I mean, yes, as a slayer, I know to follow my instincts. I assume you're the same way, right?"

She chewed at her lip. "It's...different for me."

My stomach tightened. "Tell me if we're making a mistake." I didn't want to push her into anything.

"Let me try." She closed her eyes tight and held out her hands, as if she were feeling for energy. "Okay. I can see it," she murmured.

Her skin had that faint glow again, and it was impossible to miss the tinge of darkness that seemed to curl from her very pores.

Despite my better judgment, I had to ask. "Where does it go?"

Shiloh curled her fingers and brought her hands back to her chest. "There's only one way to find out."

Chapter Five

"Let's think twice about this," I told her. I didn't like how her skin was glowing. Even if it would be nice to know who or what was after me. I took Shiloh by the arm. She was ice cold. Not a good sign. "You don't need to tap into your demon tendencies for anyone. Least of all me."

She'd come a long way from her roots, and I didn't want to reward her goodness by shoving her toward the dark side.

Her blond highlights shimmered in the noonday sun. She watched me warily, expectant almost. "I can handle it."

Sure, because there was nothing wrong with tempting a recovering evil minion with a dark portal. It was like an alcoholic saying she could have just one beer.

Slowly, she extricated herself from my grasp. "It's not going to hurt anything to get a little closer and test the energy a bit. Maybe I can pick up a signature."

It was tempting. But, "This has 'bad idea' written all over it."

She studied me for a long moment. "Are you honestly turning me down?"

I watched the waves crash against the beach. "No." Truth be told, I needed her to do it. I wondered what that said about me, that I was willing to let her take that chance. "Shiloh—" I began.

"Don't overthink it." She took a deep breath, watching the portal like she wanted to devour it.

She turned and headed down the stairs toward the beach. Faster than any human.

Cripes. I headed down after her.

"Flappy, sit. Stay. Guard!" I tossed over my shoulder. But he wasn't paying attention. He trained his eyes on Pirate. My dog had his back arched and his tail up as he rolled a squeaky ball back and forth in front of the sliding glass doors, taunting the fenris.

As long as it kept them up on the deck and out of trouble.

No telling what Shiloh would find—or how she'd change.

I tripped over the last two steps and cursed under my breath. "Shiloh!" She was making a beeline down the wooden walkway. "Wait! I need to tell you something. It's urgent."

Thank God she paused. It bought me time. I picked up the pace.

Yes, I really, really needed to know whom we'd seen on our beach this morning. And if he'd be back. But not like this.

"What?" she asked, when I'd finally caught up.

I had nothing. "I just don't want you doing this alone."

She huffed out a breath and started walking again. Fast.

I jogged to keep up with her. "Why are you so anxious to get down there?"

Never mind that we were messing with a dark portal in the middle of the day. In public.

"I'm hungry, okay!" Shiloh shouted. "I'll just take a taste to let you know what you're up against."

Sure. Just like I could eat only one potato chip.

I hurried after her. At least it was a weekday. We didn't have tourists on this stretch of ocean. Just locals. Most of them seemed to be at work.

She slowed as we reached the beach. "I admit. A small part of me is…excited." She rubbed at her arms. "Still, I work very hard not to feed my minion side anymore."

I gave her a stern look.

"Much," she amended.

Lovely. "You need to calm down," I told her.

"It's always there," she said simply. She wet her lips and looked toward the invisible portal.

"What is it?" I asked. "Can you see it? Can you tell?"

She nodded, unable to take her eyes off it. "It's a temporary link portal," she said, breathy.

I didn't get it. "What does that mean?"

"It can be used again," she said. It began to glow red.

Even I could see it now, as the crackling red portal opened up. It was high tide and the thing was at least fifteen feet out into the ocean.

I watched it as it expanded, gained power. Shiloh had to be doing this. There was no other explanation. I understood it the same as I knew we had to shut this thing down. But first, I had to ask. "Will there be more visits?"

"I don't know," she murmured. "Oh, snap." Her breath quickened as the portal expanded, churning harder every second.

"That's it," I told her. "We've got to get out of here."

She braced herself, trying to get a handle on her urges. Her skin took on a glittering copper hue. "Have you ever given up cigarettes?" she blurted.

Not the time. "I had half of one in college," I said, trying to urge her along.

She wrinkled her nose. "That doesn't count."

Yes it did. It was nasty. "I tasted it for a week."

She shook her head. "You don't know. It doesn't matter, anyway." Her chest heaved as she gazed at the portal. "This is a hundred times worse." She drew a shaking hand over her cheek and down to her chin.

I reached for her. "Shiloh," I warned. "Now."

Without warning, she dodged around me and dashed for the water. Her skin blazed with copper, then orange, then red.

Holy Hades. I went after her.

I felt like I was watching my car roll backward down a hill and nothing I could do would catch it. Stop it.

She was faster than me, more agile.

The tide had moved in from where it had been early this morning. The water hissed as Shiloh splashed through the surf, excited—exalted.

I plowed in after her. The ice-cold water stung my ankles, my legs. Shiloh didn't seem to notice.

This was bad. I tried to run faster. I slogged in up to my waist. One minute the water retreated to my calves, then a wave would hit, knocking me off-balance.

It didn't seem to affect Shiloh at all.

She flung out her hands. "*Jo esperitum trucades ala teau esperitum!*"

Demon language. Hellfire. She was throwing herself directly at it.

A sound like electrical wires snapping pierced the incessant pounding of the ocean. It shocked me, shoved me back. It energized her.

Hellfire and damnation.

I shoved forward, into the surf. A wave crested at me, as high as my shoulders. I dived straight into it.

Freezing water tore at me. The salt stung my eyes. I could taste it on my lips. I surfaced on the other side. I'd gained on her. I could almost grab her.

Shiloh seemed to know exactly where she was going.

Then I saw it. The portal crackled and hissed less than five feet from us. It burned brighter with every step she took, as if it were drawing energy from her. I felt the suction in the water, the draw of dark power.

Without so much as a glance back, she burst through it. I drove forward, as hard as I could, as the portal swallowed her up, body and soul.

It was a horrible idea to fling myself headlong at a dark portal, but I didn't have a choice. I needed to get Shiloh out of there. She was only half demon. Her human side offered her nothing in the way of protection. If she somehow went bad, I'd have a demon on my hands—one I'd have to slay. I didn't know how I'd ever justify that to her husband. Or myself. Not when I'd led her down here.

The energy sucked at my very life force. The tide pulled me deeper. I dived forward again and surfaced, bracing myself to slam face-first into the dark portal.

But I felt the cold slap of churning water instead.

Cripes.

When I surfaced, I didn't see the portal anymore. I turned to look behind me as an icy wave slammed into my back and shoved me facedown into the water. Damn it. I opened my demon slayer senses, scrambling, tumbling. I slid my hands through the sand, searching, scratching them to hell on bits of shell and sand crabs.

Tendrils of dark magic pierced my psychic shield like hot needles, but it wasn't enough.

I spit water and scrubbed at my eyes so I could see something, anything. It couldn't just be gone. Not that fast. Another wave crashed over me.

No. I centered myself, tried to get a grip. I reached out again, harder this time. I could still sense it—dark and stinging. It wasn't anything I could get my hands around.

Okay, then. I wiped the seawater from my face. New plan. I dug my toes into the sand under my feet. It was shifting, unstable.

With great care, I forced myself to lift up, to levitate. The water sucked at me as my chest, my hips, my legs drew up out of the water.

A cold breeze plastered my leather outfit against me and chilled me to the bone as I hovered mere inches over the ocean and searched once more for any sign of the red portal. I craned to see any sparks, any hint of the darkness that hovered just beyond my grasp.

The water swirled below, unwilling or maybe simply unable to give it up.

It was *right there.* It had to be. I didn't know what to do.

I focused so hard on the portal that I forgot about the levitation until the second before I plunged back into the frigid water. It shot up my nose, stung my eyes. I tumbled blind through the darkness.

A chill washed over me. I didn't know what to do, what to think.

I found my way back up. "Fuck." I stood chest-deep in the Pacific in February. Alone.

It was frustrating. Ridiculous. Scary as hell.

"Fuckety fuck fuck fuck." I fought my way back to the place where I saw Shiloh disappear, for all the good it did. I could think of about a million things that could go wrong when sending a half-damned creature through a black magic portal.

She could be sent straight to hell and be punished eternally for cultivating her goodness. She could be sent to purgatory where she'd be isolated, exiled. Possibly attacked. She could be forced to bind herself to another demon—one that couldn't be defeated and would never let her go. Her husband the slayer would die trying to save her and it would be my fault.

And what would I tell her husband if she didn't come back? I'd never met the guy. He was a lone wolf. And probably a stark raving lunatic, considering he'd fallen for a half succubus. I mean, who does that? Truly?

I waded closer to the shore, trying to follow Shiloh's original path.

A jogger on the beach slowed when she saw me. No doubt wondering why I stood waist-deep in the waves in drenched leather.

She waved when she got close. "Are you okay?"

"I lost my earring," I told her.

It was better than the truth.

I hoped Sarayh wasn't up on her deck watching this. None of the neighbors had witnessed Shiloh's disappearance into the surf or they'd be down here for sure.

Maybe I was lucky enough to have nobody looking out their back windows. Or maybe they'd think I was eccentric. I didn't care at the moment.

The portal began crackling to life once more. I stayed where I was. It was too late to jump in. No. Now was the time to deal with who or what might come out.

I drew a switch star.

Please don't let her come back evil.

I really didn't want to slay the little blonde she-demon.

The energy expanded, going from orange to the color of blood. Then Shiloh burst through, running like a sprinter. She was actually on top of the water for a few seconds. Her eyes blazed red. Her hair was a mass of tangles. Her teeth had sharpened to razor points, and cripes—she had a double set. The ocean roiled around her. The portal snapped and hissed.

She ran straight for me.

She was crazed, wild. My fingers tightened on the handles of my switch star. I didn't want to use it, but I'd aim for the head if she attacked.

"Run! Run! Run!" she hollered, grabbing my hand.

What the—?

Her grip was like iron, her strength astounding as she dragged me away from the portal and onto the beach.

"What's coming?" I demanded, craning my neck to see, loath to turn my back on an opening to God-knew-where.

The portal crackled and began to fall in on itself. The energy suctioned at my very life force, like a black hole collapsing. We kept running as the gateway was swallowed by the waves.

Hell, it might have disintegrated altogether.

Shiloh released my hand and collapsed onto the sand, frazzled. Her hair was fried. Her skin flushed orange. At least her eyes had returned to a somewhat muted blue. She was back.

Mostly.

I half fell, half sat next to her.

I was wet and freezing and had sand in places I'd rather not think about. I sheathed my switch star, but kept a hand on it, just in case. "What happened?"

She blinked a few times, keeping watch on where we'd last seen the portal. She flexed her jaw and, yep, she had a double row of sharp dagger teeth. "The portal sucked me in and I popped up in the middle of some guy's office." Shock filled her voice, even as she spoke with a hiss and a lisp. "He was at his desk. Sleeping." She was shaking as badly as me. "He woke up and flipped out on me."

I supposed a stranger coming through a portal could incite that kind of a reaction. And Shiloh certainly didn't look like her usual alluring self, even to full humans. I was sure of it.

Okay. I shoved my frazzled brain into thinking mode. "Did you recognize him?"

With supreme effort, she forced her talons and teeth to retract. "Ow," she said to herself. She waved a hand in front of her face, fighting the sting. "No. He had dark hair. Tall. He had dark powers. Tasty ones. But then he had light ones, too. It didn't mix. It almost tasted like"—she tried to think—"oranges," she finally said. "Oranges and toothpaste."

I'd fought a lot of baddies, but I'd never had a bite of that. "What'd you do when he saw you?"

She used both hands to smooth her hair, to get a grip. "I thought about going out the window, but it was a window on the inside of a building."

Maybe she'd remembered wrong. "That doesn't make sense."

"I know." Her eyes locked on the place where we'd last seen the portal.

The portal remained still, inert. Shiloh's panic flared. "What will I do if he reports me? I don't want to be enslaved to a master demon anymore. I mean, he wasn't a demon master, but I could tell he knows one. Maybe more. I could feel it on him. Oh my gosh. Damien had a terrible time killing the last one." She gripped me by the upper arms. "That portal tasted so yummy. Even with that goody-two-shoes toothpaste flavor." She flung herself off me. "Oh, I am such a horrible person."

"Okay. Look," I said, needing her to get a grip. "Nothing's coming after you." I glanced back at the ocean. Yet.

I staggered to my feet.

"Flappy!" I called up to the dragon. He reluctantly turned from his vigil at the sliding glass door. "Flappy! I need you."

"Come on," I said to Shiloh, giving her a hand up.

The dragon moaned. Like the put-upon adolescent he was, Flappy took to the air and landed with a huff and a spray of sand.

"Guard the portal," I told him.

He yowled and looked back at the town house with the tasty fenris inside.

"Do it," I ordered.

Flappy *ker-snuffled* and set about positioning himself on the beach, right where the joggers usually liked to run. I let him stay there. It was rare for a non-magical person to collide with Flappy. More often than not, full humans would sense something in the air and detour around him. And if they didn't? Well, I had other problems.

Shiloh stood droop-shouldered, both arms crossed in front of her chest. "I'm a good girl," she said to me. I could tell she didn't quite believe it. She began repeating it to herself, "I'm a good girl. I'm a good girl."

"You are," I said, ushering her up off the beach. The portal was still dark. "There's nothing following you. And if something does come through, Flappy will let us know. He's the best guard dragon around," I added, hoping I wasn't adding to her worries—or stretching the truth too much. "Let's get back to the house."

She didn't resist at all as I got her to the house and into some dry clothes. My bathrobe and sweats didn't fit her at all, but she'd freaked out a little when I'd tried to give her leather pants.

"I need to calm down," she said as I deposited her on our living room couch. "Do you have any yarn and some needles? Oh! Yarn and needles!" Before I could react, she'd already begun scrambling for her yellow bag. "I think I have some." She tossed out a bunch of alfalfa, which got the fenris howling. "I always carry yarn for emergencies." She tossed out Kleenex, breath mints, and more lipsticks than I even owned. They clanked all over my kitchen floor. "Aha!" She drew out a skein the size of my head.

I watched her retreat to the couch. "Knitting?" I asked, as she tied off a knot and loaded up her needle. In the meantime, I unwrapped the alfalfa and tossed it to the fenris. I also picked up Shiloh's purse contents from the floor.

She perched on the edge of a cushion, furiously working yarn around the needle. "Oh my God, Lizzie," she said, "I liked it. What's wrong with me?"

"Nothing." Thank heaven. We'd dodged a bullet. "I shouldn't have asked you to get so close to a bad portal." At least we learned something.

She gave me a wide-eyed look of horror. "If you let me, I'd turn around. I'd walk straight back into it." She shivered. "How am I going to tell Damien?"

"Do you want me to call him?" Maybe he'd know how to help her. He'd pulled her over from their side in the first place.

"No," she started knitting furiously. "I'm a good girl. Besides, Damien is down in purgatory. He can't tell me more than that. Probably because I'm so evil. Damn it." She dropped a stitch as her hands began to glow orange.

Yikes. I eased down next to her. We didn't need Shiloh losing control. Chances were, Damien did some work that could put her in danger if she knew the details. I wanted to tell her that it would probably be the same for any wife, but I wasn't sure that was true. After all, I told my spouse everything. I settled for the truth as I knew it. "Damien loves you." We'd work out the rest.

She huffed out a nervous response while she attempted to smooth her hair with a shaking hand. "I'm just a little freaked out right now. Knitting helps me cope." She resumed her furious attack on the yarn. "Would you like me to knit you something? I can make you an afghan, or a scarf, or a poncho—or maybe you and Dimitri want matching vests?"

"Whatever you do best." I'd wear knit mukluks if it would keep her sane.

I heard the front door open. "Dimitri?" I called. I sure hoped it was him.

"Yeah," he said, still shirtless as he entered from the hallway. He stopped cold when he saw us. "Are you two all right?"

I glanced at the she-demon. "I think so."

"I'm knitting," Shiloh said.

"Sure," he said, eyeing me for an explanation. "What do we have on the portal?"

"Shiloh went in." As for the rest, "I think we should let her tell you."

"It led to an office in this dimension," she said quickly. "I don't even think it was far." Shiloh hunched her shoulders and worked faster. "That's what's so strange. It's coming from northeast of here. All that yummy dark power. I could probably even be there in twenty minutes. But I'm not going to," she added, with way too much forced cheer.

Wow. "I can't feel it," I said. It could be that it was too far away. Maybe Shiloh was more sensitive than me. "Can you think of anything specific that could give us a location?"

Shiloh shook her head. She already had about four inches of pink and orange and yellow knitted. "There was a flask on the desk. I stay away from vices. I'm a good girl."

I tried to tune in and failed. She hadn't given me much to go on.

"We should be okay," Shiloh said, refusing to look up from her knitting. "There wasn't anything Egyptian in there."

"I'm not following," Dimitri said.

Shiloh kept at it. "No temple of the moon. No tombs. No line in the sand."

"And those things are bad," I said, trying to understand where she was going.

She shuddered. "Very." She glanced up at me, afraid. "I shouldn't even be telling you. But before you burned up all the sex demons in Vegas, they were working with a really powerful demon. They were feeding him power, and wow, it was intoxicating the way he was growing stronger."

Dimitri stood over her. "In what way?" he pressed.

Shiloh swallowed, intimidated. She crushed her work in her hands and didn't even notice. "It was changing our vibration as a group. We could feel him all the time." She shook her head. "We weren't the only ones. There were others. Again, we could feel it." She said it as if sensing demonic creatures were as natural as knowing a family member was in the next room. "If and when he gathered enough soul ties to rise up," she said, squaring her shoulders, "we were going be rewarded quite generously."

I wasn't sure I was following. "What do you mean soul ties?"

Shiloh bit her lip. "They didn't let me do it. Not that I would have. I'm only a half born. But I think they get mortals"—she took a deep breath—"people to bind part of themselves to the demon."

"Voluntarily?" Dimitri asked, as if he couldn't imagine it.

I couldn't either. "What was the demon going to reward you with?" I asked. "People?"

"Oh, no." She looked from Dimitri to me, as if she were afraid of how we'd see her, that we wouldn't understand. "Black souls," she said, meekly.

I exchanged a glance with Dimitri. Black souls were trapped spirits—too bad for heaven, too good for hell. The demons would capture them and use them. These were nasty entities. But still human. Some could even be redeemed. I could see why they'd be quite tasty to succubi.

"You don't hate me, do you?" Shiloh asked.

I wasn't crazy about her past. Or what she was. But, "We get that you're on our side," I told her. "It's your husband's side too, right?" Not only had she turned her life around, she'd probably broken some dark code by telling us what she had.

Dimitri sat next to her. "How did you learn about the signs?"

She winced. "We wanted to know when the dark lord would come. He forbade it, of course. But patience was never one of our nest's virtues," Shiloh added quickly. "Our second in command had the gift of sight. It's rare." She gave an embarrassed laugh. "Succubi tend to live in the moment." She shook off her rumination. "Anyway, our seer looked into the future said the demon's rise would come to pass with the appearance of a fenris on Earth, a temple reborn, and from the power generated from the tomb." She looked from me to Dimitri. "Still, we can't get too carried away. I mean, a fenris is just a fenris, right?"

Dimitri studied her.

Her eyes took on a reddish hue. "It's not Babydoll's fault she's here."

"Hey," I told her. "Relax. We're not going to do anything to Babydoll." Unless she tried to eat someone.

Dimitri didn't look so convinced. He stood. "Let's check it out. We'll head northeast and see what we find."

"Agreed." We'd better hope we didn't uncover any temples, or tombs, or other kind of trouble. I was still trying to wrap my head around it. I mean, "Northeast of here, that's Beverly Hills." Land of building codes and round-the-clock security. Designer shops and mega-mansions.

What could go wrong there?

Chapter Six

"Are you going to be okay, here by yourself?" I asked the she-demon. Most of her second row of teeth had retracted and she'd stopped glowing. That had to be a positive sign.

She gave me a long look before hastily gathering up her knitting. "I've been through a lot worse." She lowered her hand and began a new row of stitches.

I didn't doubt it. "Fine. I'm going to go get ready, then."

While Dimitri scrounged up a shirt, I changed into a dry pair of black leather pants with a matching bustier—all the better for butt kicking—and added silver dagger earrings and a chainmail choker that Grandma had given me as a wedding gift. My usual black work boots were soaking wet, so I slipped on a pair of higher-heeled ones that zipped up past my knees. Sexy. My hair was drying into crinkles from the salt water, but there was nothing to be done about it. I brushed it out and looked forward to covering it with a motorcycle helmet.

When I came back downstairs, Shiloh had two more inches of knitting done, and had also gained a dog in her lap. Pirate curled up with his head under her arm.

"Pirate," I said, half expecting him to ignore me, "are you sure you're not intruding?"

His head popped up. "This is called up-close guarding."

More like needy dog syndrome.

"He's fine," Shiloh said, reaching down to stroke him between the ears. "And I like how comfy he is in my lap. When I hold my hellhound, it's like having an electric blanket going."

"Gotcha." Not that I'd ever touched a hellhound. They were damned creatures, after all. But I did hear they ran warmer than most animals, seeing as hell was so frigid. "We shouldn't be gone more than a few hours," I said, making sure I had my keys. "I'm going to have my grandma check on you."

Shiloh gasped. Her back went ramrod straight. "The biker witch? She's not going to smite me, is she?"

"No," I said quickly. "Relax. You're my guest." If anything, Grandma might come bearing a spell to settle Shiloh's nerves. I'd have to tell her to leave her flask at home.

"The worst has to be over, right?" Shiloh said, glancing toward the beach. She gathered Pirate in her arms and began stroking him. Hard.

"Oh yeah." He leaned back into her. "Now get my ears."

He was such a shameless hussy.

I double-checked my weapons. "If something comes out of that portal, blast it. Or run. Do whatever works for you."

She nodded, and I took comfort in the fact that her incisors looked a little less pointy.

"Don't worry," Pirate said, giving her access to the soft furry spot under his neck. "I'll watch her. I'm a better guard dog than that thing in there." He cocked his head at the fenris, who lay on her back, legs straight up, sleeping.

I hated to leave the she-demon here. Alone. But Shiloh had fought her dark side with strength and courage. And it wasn't as if we could ask our neighbor Sarayh.

How sad was it when I counted a semi-evil succubus as my best dog-sitting option?

"Call us if you need us," I said. "There's food in the fridge. You have my cell."

As if on cue, my hunky husband sauntered down the stairs looking particularly handsome in black pants and a pink button-down dress shirt.

"You're going to wear that on a motorcycle," I said, more impressed than questioning.

He grinned. "I've worn this while fighting an ogre."

"I don't think I've heard that story yet," I said, kissing him on the cheek. Grandma was right. He'd never fully conform to biker witch standards. I slid my arms around him and leaned into him, enjoying his solid presence. "You ready to head out?" We had to learn where that darkness was coming from, and hopefully, what was behind it.

"I'm yours," he said, holding me close, his chin resting on my head. He held me like that for a moment and we simply enjoyed each other. He broke away first, a rueful twist to his lips. "Let's go."

†††

We fired up our Harleys and headed for the 405. It gave us the most direct northeast route. Cars and trucks crowed five lanes of solid traffic, but I didn't feel anything else off-putting as we drove through West Los Angeles and exited at the Santa Monica.

As we inched through the city, sparse vegetation and fast-food joints gave way to towering palms and high-end shops.

I'd only been down this way once before, in search of a doggy salon for Pirate.

It hadn't gone well.

In the first few years I had Pirate, he went all the time to get his hair done and his nails clipped. But now that he could talk—and give his opinions on scented soap and rhinestone collars—that took some of the fun out of it.

Maybe Shiloh could talk him into a paw-dicure.

She'd better not teach him how to knit.

I shook my head as I slowed for a stoplight. My rational mind still couldn't quite believe that I'd left a she-demon back at our place, not to mention a dragon guarding a portal and a fenris chained to my fridge. At least the dragon had stopped nosing up my windows. I gripped my handlebars tighter and ignored the smell of exhaust from the bumper-to-bumper traffic on Santa Monica Boulevard.

Sure, Shiloh wanted to be good, but still, I'd brought a creature of darkness into the neighborhood and told her to make herself at home. Her clothes were in my washing machine, probably on the spin cycle by now.

I went ahead and called Grandma's cell while we waited for a red light. It went straight to voice mail, so I left her a message telling her where we were headed, and asking her to check in on my guest.

The traffic opened up a bit near Century Park West and that's when I started feeling it—a pinging against my demon slayer senses. It had nothing to do with the ten-dollar latte bars or the woman in the lane next to me, wearing an all-gold jumpsuit. I sensed a shift on a spiritual level.

Dimitri glanced over at me. It amazed me sometimes how sensitive he was to my mood shifts. No doubt it had to do with the power we'd shared in the past, and the fact that we were married both legally and spiritually.

I nodded to him. *Shiloh was right.* There was something here. I just wished I knew where it came from.

The sun faded under the horizon as we snaked closer and closer to the city. With each passing breath, I felt the walls close in on me. The air felt thicker. The greenery dripped with shadows. Amid the brightly lit shops and glittering signs, darkness lingered, just out of reach.

We passed the lush green confines of the Los Angeles Country Club, the bronze-plated exterior of Cici's Couture. One minute, the inky blackness lingered, the next, it vanished. It scattered itself like buckshot.

With a jolt, the energy got worse as we passed the gold-lettered sign at the corner of Santa Monica and Moreno and entered Beverly Hills. Holy smokes. We followed it, making a right onto Burton Way. It didn't even bother to hide anymore.

Did it want us to follow? It could be a trap.

Or was it simply too overwhelming to hide anymore?

At least I knew one thing—I could shut down my bike and fire a switch star in 1.2 seconds or less. I looked forward to the opportunity.

My switch stars felt heavy against my hip as we traced down a smaller street, and then another. I didn't need Shiloh to pinpoint the location. I just had to follow the darkness to Saint Lucia Boulevard.

Ah, Saint Lucia, who was set on fire and then stabbed with a sword. I hoped my day would turn out better.

I turned one last corner and hit the brakes hard. The evil of this place screamed at me, and I realized with a start that it came from an old 1920s art deco movie house. It stood at the end of a small square. The stucco facade had been painted a strange orangish-pink, which should have looked gruesome, but appeared quite arresting instead. Parts of it almost seemed gold. A white and gold sign read: Salvation of the Hills.

At least it didn't say Temple of the Moon.

The building seemed to glow from the inside in a way that made me very, very uncomfortable.

I kicked my bike into low gear and took it slow. The rose-gold double doors were a work of art in themselves, with carved lotus flowers climbing twisted vines. A golden griffin presided over the gilded ticket booth to the right. I saw another similarly ornate window next to it, and a matching pair on the other side.

Posters advertising "spiritual beauty" seminars covered the glass. A broad awning shielded the entryway and above it, two arched windows stared like eyes. At the top, a slash of molded architecture thrust out, reminding me of something out of a Batman movie.

Dimitri had stopped a little ways ahead of me. "This keeps getting weirder and weirder," he said when I reached him. He pointed to a placard by the front doors. In bold, black letters, it read:

Looking for a sign? This is it.
Services 24/7.
Change your life NOW.

"It's a church," I said, not quite believing it. The place creeped me out.

"Feeling spiritual?" Dimitri asked.

"I might have the bug." In a *let's slay some demons* sort of way.

We headed across the street to a small park and found spots for our bikes on the other side. I could feel the dark powers streaming from the so-called church.

"Leave it to you to dress for the occasion," I said, easing off my bike. When I'd first met Dimitri, he'd had a hankering for tailored slacks and good-looking suits. He might have gone more casual lately, but given the choice, he liked looking slick. I'd gone from flowered sundresses and straw sandals to biker witch chick. It turned Dimitri on something fierce and I liked how it made me feel. Comfortable. Powerful.

Of course even I had never worn black leather to evening services, but hey, there was a first time for everything. I looped my helmet over my handlebars and began rooting around in my saddlebags.

"What are you doing?" Dimitri asked, as if he were afraid of the answer.

I held up two handfuls of baby food jars. "Spells. I made them myself."

"Because they worked so well this morning," he said drily, watching me stuff them into the pockets of my demon slayer utility belt.

"Have a little faith," I told him. I'd followed Grandma's spell recipes to the letter. I had two jars of Explosive Escape, one Lose Your Keys spell (you never knew when that would come in handy), and a jar with a live Mind Wiper spell inside. That one came out a bit flat. Or at least it didn't have the long, swirly look of Grandma's Mind Wipers. The black-and-silver blob of a spell had flattened itself against the glass, glittering, as if begging me to take it out and let it play.

Dimitri studied it. "It looks funny."

I tried to shake it down into the jar, but the little guy held on for dear life. "Maybe it has its own personality."

Live spells were more like creatures than enchantments. They behaved for the most part; at least, they did exactly what they were bred to do. Mind Wipers rendered a person or creature unable to focus on anything other than their one secret wish. They were great for neutralizing an enemy and I'd be willing to bet they'd work on security guards.

"I named this one Max," I said, tucking it into my belt. Max was a demon hunter I knew who had only one, suicidal, wish—to slay as many demons as possible. I found him quite charming in that way.

Dimitri frowned. "Because you can always count on Max not to go nuts, rebel and conquer everything in sight."

"Jealous much?" I asked as we started off across the park. It was no secret Max and Dimitri didn't always get along. "Listen," I said, shifting gears, "let me know if it gets dicey for you in there." It wasn't only me who found Dimitri tasty. Griffins radiated strength and light—and they attracted dark creatures that liked to feast on it.

He gave me a dark look. "Let's both be careful." He glanced at the glittering church. "I've got a funny feeling about this."

Yeah, I did, too.

Shadows flitted over the empty park benches. The palm trees rustled. We weren't alone in this park.

We kept walking.

"We'll be okay." I hoped. "We don't even have to pick a fight. As long as they think we're just here for some religion."

Unfortunately, when you're a demon slayer, there's always a catch.

CHAPTER SEVEN

I tried to keep the clanking of my jars down to a minimum as we approached the polished gold entry doors. "I don't know how the biker witches do it." At the very least, it made for a distraction. I needed to focus.

"Act natural," Dimitri said, holding the door open for me.

"Thanks for that." There wasn't anything "natural" about this.

A small crowd had gathered inside the art deco lobby. I breathed the scent of floral perfume, which was nice. Of course, it didn't hide the acidic stench of evil that permeated the walls.

At least we were in the right place.

My heels clicked against the marble entryway. Dimitri fit in perfectly with this crowd. I didn't.

In fact, I realized with growing dread that we had started to gather a few looks. I lowered my hands, resting them casually in front of my jars. *Nothing to see here.*

It didn't help that most of the women wore skirts or dress pants. Many of the men had dressed up, like Dimitri. Not everyone wore expensive clothes. Far from it. But nobody, it seemed, favored leather.

Part of me wished I could hightail it out of there.

If we hadn't been awakened by the visitor on our beach, if Shiloh hadn't followed a dark magic portal that led to *this place*. If we had any other way of figuring out what was happening in this pseudo church... I'd say we should go. But as it stood, this was our one shot. If we didn't tackle it now, my life would just get stranger. And somebody was bound to get hurt.

I nodded at an older woman with blond frosted hair and a broach on her blazer the size of Vermont. She couldn't seem to tear her eyes away from my over-the-knee boots. Her slack-lipped stare traveled slowly up my body. I wished I'd thought twice about the low-slung leather pants with the little silver skulls on each hip. "They're new," I said, trying to be pleasant. "Those too," I added, when her gaze fell to the jars clanking together on my utility belt.

At least she couldn't see my switch stars. I didn't want to freak her out.

She nodded slowly. Good. Because frankly, I couldn't think of anything else to do or say to make it better.

She gave a faltering smile while eyeing my bustier. "My granddaughter says corsets are good for your back."

Props to her for keeping an open mind. I couldn't help but grin. "Is she a biker?"

She considered the question. "I think she might own a Schwinn."

Ah, well, you couldn't win them all.

In the not so distant past, I would have been petrified to be wearing skintight leather around anyone, much less this church lady. Heck, I'd freaked out when my mother discovered I preferred bustiers to button-downs. But I'd loosened up a bit. I liked the new me, and it was liberating to do my own thing instead of trying to fit into someone else's world.

I just had to figure out a way to make it work here.

Dimitri and I moved on. "The church members themselves don't feel bad or evil," I murmured to him. "A little repressed maybe…"

My husband barked out a laugh.

I looked up at him. "What?"

"Nothing." He grinned as if he were in on some joke that totally eluded me. "I love you."

"You'd better," I said. Let him have his little joke. "You're stuck with me for the rest of your life."

He wrapped an arm around my waist. "Good."

I leaned into him. To keep up our cover, and because it simply felt right.

Beyond the chattering crowd in the lobby, two pairs of gold doors opened to what appeared to be a theater-turned-church, complete with a stage. More animated voices collided inside.

We headed that way.

"This place draws quite a crowd," I said, low enough so hopefully only he could hear me.

"At seven o'clock on a Monday," he said, his grip tightening on my waist.

I wondered what these people were really here to do.

They appeared human, only they felt too *good*, too pure. I didn't understand it. There was no mistaking the evil of the place. Malice, destruction, had seeped into the very walls. Every step we took felt like walking into an ever-darkening, ever-shrinking cave.

"I sincerely hope this isn't like Vegas," I said.

A shiver ran through my husband.

We'd run into an entire coven of man-eating succubi there. Griffins were one of their favorite snacks. We'd learned that the hard way.

He was guarded, his casual air precise. "Act natural," he said, low and close, as we neared the doors. "We're surrounded."

I nodded. We couldn't fight. There were too many of them. We had to blend in if we wanted to learn the truth about this place.

Ha. Me—blending. I'd laugh if it wouldn't torpedo our cause even more.

Don't mind us. Just a biker chick and her *GQ* date, wandering through a church that may or may not be from the devil.

I could almost hear the crackling of a portal nearby. If it wasn't on this floor, it was definitely on the one above it. I could barely make it out, like the low hum of a bug zapper on a warm summer's night.

It gave a sharp pop and I jumped. "You hear that?"

He scanned the room, not even risking a look down at me. "I'm not picking up anything."

So it was only me. Again.

Darkness had a way of easing into your heart and your mind. It could capture you before you even realized. My powers gave me a reasonable defense, and a way to fight back. But griffins like Dimitri fought the darkness with teeth and claws. His human form left him vulnerable. He might not even know if he'd been compromised.

We'd have to stick close.

A stunning woman with long braided hair waited by the door that led down into the theater. "You're new," she said, her voice deep, warm as molasses. The beads decorating her braids clicked together. "Mimi," she called to a woman just beyond the entrance, "could you come on up?" Her large almond eyes roved over us with abject curiosity. "Mimi is on our membership team."

"Great," I said, hoping she didn't see the thin sheen of sweat I felt breaking out on my upper lip. "We're all about membership."

Real smooth, Lizzie.

The woman gave an uncomfortable smile. "Are you a member of a church now?"

"Heck, no," I said automatically.

Truth be told, talking my way into evil fortresses made me uncomfortable. I preferred sneaking or blasting in—anything that required the least amount of small talk.

"Hello!" A voice said in a heavy Eastern European accent. Right next to me.

This new woman had short, teased-out hair dyed an unnatural yellow, and lipstick on her teeth. Despite that, she looked dazzling, lit up from the inside. "I am Mimi Monroe." The odd little woman gave me a squeeze. I swore I could feel her bones. "And you are?"

"Confused," I told her.

She smiled wider. "Then you have come to the right spot." She linked arms with me and I couldn't help it. I sidestepped right into Dimitri.

Mimi leaned closer. She wore an ankle-length linen shift with way too much embroidery at the neck, along with a half dozen strands of costume jewelry black pearls, and she smelled...dusty. "I don't want to scare you, but this truly is life-changing." She stared at me until I nodded. "Now first things first," she said. "We must get to know each other."

"We'd rather just check out the service," Dimitri said.

"You're interested too?" Mimi grew even more excited. "I love it. Two new members!" she announced loudly. A smattering of applause went up and to my dismay, a crowd began to gather around us. "Just step this way," she said, ushering us toward the far back section of the lobby. At least a dozen church members trailed behind. "You don't know how happy we are to have you here," she continued. All the while, she didn't let go of my arm. Maybe she needed it to stand up, although she seemed to have a lot of spunk. "You seem like perfect candidates."

"For what?" I asked.

"Change." She gushed. "Illumination!"

Mimi reminded me of an Old Hollywood starlet—in a *Sunset Boulevard* kind of way.

I sincerely hoped she didn't take us to see her dead monkey.

The top of her head barely reached my shoulder. She held on tightly, though. Like a pull line I couldn't shake. Dimitri walked on the other side of me.

"Now tell me your name," she prodded.

I stared at her, from her wrinkled dress to her black plastic pearl earrings. I couldn't tell her that.

"Starr," I said, trying to act natural as it kind of fell out of my mouth.

I sucked at lying.

A low moan rumbled from below. If it wasn't so vicious, I'd have thought it was Dimitri groaning— which he probably was. Damn.

I concentrated, trying to locate the source of the noise, but it ended too fast.

Mimi's gaze never wavered and I realized she wanted more of my name. My mind raced for something familiar. Something I could remember.

"Pirate," I said quickly, as if that were the solution to everything. "My last name's Pirate."

Dimitri let out a choked cough. "Starr. Pirate." he repeated slowly, as if he couldn't quite believe I'd said that.

That made two of us.

Mimi Monroe was going to think I was a porn star.

"I'm a rock star," I said quickly. That got a gasp from a few of the people behind us. In for a penny, in for a pound. At least it explained my outfit.

My husband cleared his throat. Some of the people in the crowd were pulling out cell phones.

"No photos!" I announced. *And please don't try to look me up.*

"A heavy metal babe. Isn't that nice?" Mimi said, as if she were used to crazies. Or maybe she could just speak the English language way better than I could at the moment.

Starr Pirate. I mean, really?

"Perhaps I have heard some of your songs, yes?" she prompted, as if she were truly interested.

"I'll bet you have," I said. If she'd stood outside my shower lately. Damn. I had to sell this. Fast. "I'm part of the whole eighties hair-band resurgence. Very underground stuff. Think Def Leppard meets Pat Benatar. With a dash of Twisted Sister." Mimi nodded, as if she'd heard this sort of thing all the time. "In fact, my hair used to be purple," I added, "but then during my world tour in Russia, I couldn't find my regular dye so I went black and told everybody I'd started a dark period."

I'd have to post some pictures when I got home.

"Fascinating," she gushed. "I must admit we have never had a rocker."

"He's my manager," I said, lobbing it back at Dimitri, hoping my husband could make more sense than me.

Besides, we needed to get him talking. If he clenched his jaw anymore, he was going to have a monster headache.

"I keep track of her when I can," he said, matter-of-fact. Hopefully I was the only one catching the

dangerous vibe radiating from him. He held out a hand
to Mimi. "I'm Dimitri." He paused almost
imperceptibly, as if he couldn't quite force himself to
say it. "Dimitri Pirate." Oh, our dog was going to love
that.

And, hey, Dimitri had a choice. He could have
hightailed it and run. Instead, he'd married into our
little brand of crazy.

Mimi led us deeper into the back of the building.
There were at least a dozen more churchgoers behind
us, now that I'd outed myself as a rock star. Cripes.

I tried not to stare at the warrior designs on the
walls or the sunbursts in the corners. The place was
entirely too...hieroglyphic.

Oh, hell. Egyptian was bad, at least according to
Shiloh.

Dimitri paused to check out an image of a two-
headed cobra spitting flames. It was a symbol of the
underworld. Above it hovered a circular orb.

Shiloh said the she-demons anticipated the arrival
of a fenris, the rise of a temple of the moon.

"Is that a moon?" I murmured.

"Hard to tell," my husband said under his breath.
"Stay alert."

"Come now," Mimi said, leading us farther back.

Even if that hadn't been a moon, this place felt
wrong. I rested a hand on my switch stars. The walls
were painted gold. Marble graced the floors, but on a
soul level, it felt no different from a shadowy prison.
Ornate Tiffany globes clung to the ceiling, giving off
broken, inconsistent light.

A sharp bang sounded directly below me,
reverberating through the floor, and this time, I knew I
heard something growl.

I stopped cold.

Mimi shook her head, her expression one of both pity and excitement. "I used to live my life confused, afraid. You don't have to be that way anymore."

"It's part of my job," I said.

The crowd behind us murmured in excitement as Mimi led us to an elaborate alcove that housed a statue of a creature with the head of a crocodile, the body of a leopard, and the backside of a hippopotamus.

"Ammut," Dimitri said, low under his breath.

Ah, an Egyptian demon of the underworld. Word had it she liked to eat hearts and basically condemn anybody she deemed unworthy.

I'd never met her personally, though, and I truly hoped she wasn't real.

Just then, a current of energy snapped underneath us. I jumped, startling Mimi and myself. Holy Hades. We had to be standing right above something powerful. I dropped her arm, glad I hadn't yanked it out of the socket.

It didn't feel like a portal. I didn't know what it was. Every demon slayer instinct I had screamed at me to go find it. Only I knew I'd never make it that far. Not right now, at least.

Mimi's wrinkled brow furrowed some more. "Are you all right, darling?" She studied me. "You have a little tic-tic going on right above your eye."

I tried to shake it off. "I think I'll be fine after a little saving."

Mimi perked up. "That's the spirit."

She slipped a key into the side of the statue, and a small gold door in Ammut's bulbous posterior swung open.

"This is new," Dimitri muttered.

"Prepare to be amazed," Mimi announced, working the crowd. She touched a withered hand to her chest. "Behold, a gift from the spirits."

"I can't wait," I said. *Tell me about your pseudo-church. Reveal your demon scum secrets.*

Mimi held her hands out in front of her. "But first," she said, in true P.T. Barnum-style, "we require a gift."

Oh, hell.

I glanced behind me. We were walled in by people. It would be tough to get out of here if things went bad. And I didn't want to pull my weapons. No doubt the place was evil, but these people felt *good*.

Mimi kept talking. "Many people come to our church because they feel there's more to life than what they see. I come to this country when I am barely seventeen and everyone says, 'Oh, you are so beautiful.' And I find glamour," she said, getting excited, "but as I grow older, I learn there is so much more than that.

"What we do here, it is about opening yourself," she said, growing more animated, "finding an honest connection." She wrapped an arm around me and turned us to face the churchgoers. "Talk to me, Starr. Tell me one thing that truly frightens you."

Just one?

I knew better than to bullshit her on this. The lady was punch-drunk on this connection thing. It was a small price to pay, and an honest answer could get me in. I glanced toward Dimitri, then back at Mimi.

"My greatest fear is probably losing control," I said. "Half the time I don't know what I'm doing, and if I mess up"—I paused, trying to put it into words— "failure just isn't an option."

Our eyes locked and for a moment, I sensed a real opening between us. It was the last thing I'd expected from this woman, in this place.

She beamed. "Thank you for that." She gave me a hug. It was awkward—at least on my part. Then she turned to Dimitri. "What about you, my darling?"

It had to be the first time anybody had called the six-foot-six hunk of a griffin "darling."

Dimitri ducked his head and went for total honesty as well. "Losing someone I love," he said simply.

I gave him a kiss on the cheek.

"Aww," Mimi purred. She took one of his large hands in both of hers. "You have made my day. My year. There is nothing more humbling than opening yourself to us, here in this sacred space." She released him. "Now we will amaze you and show you how special this church really is."

The churchgoers gave a collective *oooh* as Mimi reached into the statue and withdrew a gorgeous jeweled box. It reminded me of a Fabergé egg.

Behind me, a woman drew in a sharp breath. "I remember the first time I touched it."

"Best thing that ever happened to me," a man's voice said.

"I want to be her," murmured another.

If she was talking about me, that had to be a first.

Mimi paused for a pregnant moment. She had the crowd exactly where she wanted them. I hoped for something basic, but was prepared for a moon symbol, a tomb fragment, maybe a demon's mark.

With a grand flourish, she opened the hinged top.

We all leaned forward, Dimitri and I included. It was beyond my control at that point. I needed to see what as in that box.

I took one step forward, then another. This was it. Their big secret, nestled in red velvet.

Mimi beamed.

I stood, dumbfounded. The object in front of me wasn't magical. It wasn't a relic or a treasure or anything that pointed to a dark and evil demon. I hated to break it to her, but, "It's…a rock."

Chapter Eight

Truly.

It wasn't sharp. Or old. It wasn't even all that big. In fact, it looked as if it came out of someone's planter box—if that person liked to decorate with flat tan rocks.

Mimi acted as if she were displaying the Hope Diamond.

"I don't get it," I said, flatly.

Was I the only one?

No. I was pretty sure Shiloh wouldn't get it, either. Neither would demons or imps or black souls. Over the past two years, I'd met more dark creatures than I liked to think about, and none of them had cared about rocks.

Dimitri frowned, his attention on Mimi as she drew a pair of delicate gold tongs from the back of the case. She handed the display case to another church member. Then she extracted the rock.

With all the solemnity of a priestess, she carried it to us. "Hold out your hands very carefully."

Clever. If she meant to make it tough for me to use my weapons.

Dimitri caught my eye. "Me first," he said.

Good call. If there was any kind of a threat, he could shift and I could go for my weapons. I took two steps back, a hand on my belt, as he cupped his palms toward her.

"Prepare to be amazed," she said, breathless.

The presence below us felt heavy. The air itself seemed to vibrate. Whatever was about to happen, I was ready.

Dimitri tensed as Mimi pressed the rock into his outstretched hands. "Yesss," she hissed. "This is it."

I watched, afraid to blink as he held the stone for one second. Two.

Mimi slung the tongs over her thumb, pressed her fingertips to her lips, giddy with anticipation as the roundish, mostly flat rock in Dimitri's hands…sat there.

"It's not doing anything," I pointed out.

It made sense, really. We were talking about a rock.

I drew in a breath of heavy, energy-laced air. I was just glad we hadn't gotten attacked. Then again, we hadn't made much progress, either. I glanced at the faces behind me. Good. They were confused, too.

A tall, thin woman touched my arm. "Is it the right one?"

"You have more than one?" I asked her.

"No," she said, wide-eyed.

Then this was it.

Dimitri remained focused on the stone in his hands. "I don't feel anything."

"Try again!" someone else suggested.

He flipped it into his other palm. "There."

This was so fricking weird. No doubt this place was evil, potentially part of a prophecy, but either these people weren't any good at evil machinations or they were hiding something even they didn't understand.

"Let me see," I said, moving in next to him.

"Wait—" Mimi fussed, fumbling with her tongs.

Dimitri leaned in close to me. "I'm used to Skye stones," he said, under his breath, mentioning the magic of the griffins. Mimi would never know. "But this isn't doing jack." He dropped it into my hand.

It lay there...like a rock.

I turned it over a few times. "It's a little sharp on one side." That was really all I had. I held it up to the light. "What's the secret?"

Mimi looked almost frightened. "Give it back," she urged.

Sure. No problem. "It's not like I'm running away with it." I felt a rumbling in the air, almost like a Harley engine. "Here," I said, holding it out to her.

"Not like that!" She dropped her tongs. "Oh heavens." Half a dozen people scrambled for them.

Dimitri cursed under his breath. "We're screwed," he said, distracted from the melee in front of us. He focused on the front door.

Jesus, Mary, Joseph, and the mule. I heard a Harley engine.

Sure, at times, the roar of motorcycles meant the arrival of the cavalry. But I didn't need saving at the moment and certainly didn't need any senior citizen witches showing up and calling me Lizzie.

Thankfully it sounded like only one bike.

Even so, a single biker witch could be difficult to handle on a good day, and I'd be screwed if it were one of the more flamboyant ones, like Ant Eater, or...

"Helllllllooooooo?" a chipper, smoke-roughened voice echoed through the lobby.

"Frieda," I muttered.

The blonde witch strode into the lobby like a woman on a mission. Of all the people in the world, she reminded me of Flo from Mel's diner. Naturally, Frieda considered herself much more trendy.

Today, the biker witch wore KISS-style platform biker boots, a black catsuit and pink feather earrings that dangled down to her shoulders. Her bouffant hairdo glowed like a halo against the bright lights behind her.

If the entire gang showed up, they'd for sure blow our cover. Frieda alone would be enough to do it. She wasn't exactly subtle.

"Lizzie!" She scrunched her nose as she squinted at the crowd. "There you are!" She pointed directly at me.

Five seconds. It had to be a new record.

Mimi drew back. "I don't think we have a Lizzie here."

Frieda grinned and strode on over. I had to give her credit. Frieda made platform heels look easy.

Mimi bit her lip, confused. "We have a Laurie," she said, nodding to a woman at the back.

"Hey, sweetie!" Frieda gave me a big hug. Lovely.

"Do I know you?" I asked.

Mimi began to fret. I drew her aside. "I get crazy fans." I leveled a look at her, as if she understood these things from her years in Hollywood. "This happens all the time."

Mimi's brow furrowed. "Fans were much more genteel in the 1950's."

At least Frieda seemed to be the only witch. For now.

Maybe I'd get lucky and the biker witch would buy into my hair-band story. Although Frieda lied about as well as I did.

Dimitri took her by the arm. "Can I help you?" he said with forced cheer.

"No," she drew out the word, as if she were finally understanding there may be more to this than met the eye. "I'm here to help you. Grandma sent me." She took a quick look around, giving extra attention to the rapt church members, and Mimi with the tongs. "Yeek. This place feels creepy."

I pasted on a smile. "We're applying for membership," I said, emphasizing that last word when all I really wanted to say, "Don't screw this up."

"I need the stone back." Mimi pressed forward, tongs out.

I'd almost forgotten I still had the rock.

Mimi started to get flustered. Her hair had gone even more wonky, her breath came in hard bursts, and she'd completely lost any of the "membership committee" suave she'd had. In fact, in a second, she'd need to start breathing into a paper bag. "Give me the rock," she said.

"This one?" Frieda asked, taking it out of my hand.

Energy crackled from the stone as soon as she touched it. It bit my hand like a super powered static electricity charge.

Frieda grasped the stone. "Shit on a biscuit." The power ripped through her and she looked thrilled—ecstatic.

My God. I didn't know what it was doing to her. "Drop it," I ordered.

She let out a raspy breath. "Fuck that, honey," she said, holding it tighter. Blue light shot out from between her fingers. She reveled in it. "This is heaven!" She threw her head back. She was completely at its mercy.

I grabbed for the thing. How it had gone from zero to full power, I had no idea. Whatever it was, Frieda had no defense. I hoped I still did. But it didn't matter. I had to get it away from her. She'd been too good a friend to go down like this.

"Stop it." She shoved away from me, clutching the stone.

I landed hard on my butt.

Dimitri caught her, held her. I scrambled to my feet as finger by finger, he pried the rock from her hands. It throbbed with blue light. "This. Is. For. Your. Own. Good."

She elbowed him hard in the ribs.

"Ha!" Dimitri grabbed it away as more hands reached for the rock.

It stopped glowing the moment he had control of it. He held it out of the reach of anyone else as he went for Mimi. "Come here." Dimitri seized her tongs, placed the rock in them, and then handed them back to her.

She stood shocked for a moment. Then retreated to her helper, who stood with his mouth open, holding the ornate case. She eased the stone back inside. "Go. Everyone. Now." she cried with her back to us.

Frieda breathed hard, as if she'd run a mile in those platforms. I took her by the arms, afraid she'd fall over. "Are you okay?"

She let out a low chuckle. "That was better than sex."

Mimi whipped around. "This is a church!"

Frieda cocked a hip. "Then sign me up, sugar."

"I—" Mimi turned back to her rock, which was now closed in its case. She held it protectively, practically stroking the thing. "Please. Stay back while I put this away."

I glanced behind us and saw that the church members had obeyed orders and had backed away. No wonder she was worried.

"I'm not going to reach out and take it from you," I said. If anything, I'd swipe it on the sly.

Dimitri advanced on her. "What kind of power does that thing hold?"

She shoved the case back into the statue and locked the door with shaking hands. Smoothing her dress, she faced him, chin out. "We don't need to understand in order to believe."

He took another step forward. "Then tell us why it's important to the church."

She straightened. "I'm afraid not." She swallowed hard. "That was a test." She gave a shaky laugh. "Usually, everyone passes, but you didn't."

Wait. Evil lairs had never come with entrance tests before. "What do you need me to do?" I asked.

She looked sad all the sudden. "Make it glow." She paused. "I'm sorry. You can't be a member of our church."

Wait. "We got rejected?" From a cult. "There's got to be something else I can do." This couldn't be it.

"Those are the rules." She took my hand. "You are unusual. That's not bad at all. But it's not mine to decide."

Cripes. She was even nice about turning me down.

Maybe the rock was some kind of tool. Maybe it sensed we were there to fight whatever force had corrupted this place.

In that case, Frieda should have gone down too, but she didn't. "What about her?" I asked, pointing at the biker witch, who was currently unwrapping a stick of gum that she'd taken from her bra.

Mimi gave a shaky smile as she eased around Dimitri. "Yes. I'm sorry. The testing today...threw me. And then our unexpected guest..." She turned to the biker witch, addressing her. "You did wonderfully, my dear. Of course, you're in."

"A biker witch," Dimitri said, as if he couldn't quite believe it.

She fought evil as much as we did. But the rock lit up for her.

Frieda slung a hand on her hip. "I don't know, sweetie," she said, chomping on her gum, "I may have to try that test again."

Mimi laughed, a real one this time. "You kids," she chided, as if Frieda wasn't pushing sixty-five. "Actually, you get to come back and see the tomb. Maybe even meet the pastor."

"Oh, no," I said, startling them both. They had one. They had a tomb. That must have been a moon symbol Dimitri and I saw earlier. Which meant Frieda had no business going in there alone.

"Is the pastor single?" Frieda asked.

Did she not understand she was in danger? Or was she just playing along?

Of course Frieda didn't know the whole story, or that there was an active portal somewhere in the building.

Mimi gave me a vapid smile. "Good-bye. Have a blessed day." She motioned to Frieda. "You come with me."

"See you kids on the flip side," Frieda waved, following Mimi.

Absolutely not. I straightened, causing the spell jars to clank around my waist.

Frieda was smart, experienced. She knew how to defend herself, but she didn't have what it took to fight a rising demon. And if she hadn't picked up any of the threats in this building, she was going in blind.

Dimitri touched me on the arm. "Calm down." He locked eyes with me. "It's okay, Starr. Let her go. She can take care of herself."

"No." Frieda could walk into an ambush and not even know it. Hell, this could be one right now.

I tried to laser it into her with my eyes. But I didn't have those kinds of powers. All anyone else could see was me tipping into the land of raving lunatics. I didn't care.

Damn it all. She was my friend. I appreciated her help. But if she thought I'd leave her alone in this "church," she was out of her mind.

Slowly, stealthily, I pulled out a jar. Inside, the Mind Wiper spell hovered like an eager puppy. Grandma designed Mind Wipers to incapacitate, not to kill. They rendered a person incapable of focusing on anything other than their secret wish. So in terms of *knock you on your ass* spells, these were kind of nice. Subtle.

We'd be in trouble if Frieda's one desire was to join this freakish cult, but the spell shouldn't affect her. Just my target. Mimi.

Dimitri's eyes widened as I cracked the lid on the jar. The silver blob of a spell bounced up and down inside. These people really shouldn't have messed with a biker witch wannabe.

Of course that's when everything went to hell.

CHAPTER NINE

The spell shot out in a wave of sparks and got a whoop from Frieda. "Go, Lizzie!"

Dimitri pulled me back. "Watch it."

The Mind Wiper slapped flat against Mimi's left temple. Her black plastic earrings swayed as she brought a hand up to touch where it hit. She tried to speak, but nothing came out. Meanwhile, the spell wiggled out from between her fingers like crazed Silly Putty.

I drew a quick breath. They usually just...disappeared.

This one tumbled sideways and went straight for Frieda.

"Duck!" I hissed.

Frieda didn't listen. "Hey, now. I've got it." She reached out.

Missed.

The spell smacked her in the side of the neck. She stumbled sideways, tossing a glare at me. Like it was my fault she didn't get out of the way. "Did you use the toenails of a *happy* fox?"

Sure. Because small animals love to have their toenails clipped. "It wasn't exactly smiling." What did she expect? "Now chill out." We didn't need to be drawing any more attention.

Frieda slumped backward. I started for her, but Dimitri got behind her first. He caught her against his chest. "Jesus, Frieda. How do you feel?"

"Like I just had a shot of Jack." The blonde witch let out a small croak. "Make that three."

So much for saving Frieda. Dimitri and I watched in horror as the spell slithered down her neck, leaving a glittery trail in its wake.

We had to be smart about this. I turned to Dimitri. "Drop her if it goes for you."

"Hey," Frieda protested.

"Move," Dimitri said, as the spell pulled away from Frieda with a pop.

I took two steps back, trying to figure out how to stop this thing. It was going to turn into a spectacle, if it hadn't already. Besides, Frieda should have a few tricks. Her coven invented spell jars and live spells and whatever we were dealing with right now.

The biker witch started giggling.

Aw, hell.

I couldn't switch-star it. I couldn't exactly start throwing other spells. No telling what those would do. I smiled at a group of church members who were, quite frankly, staring at us.

The spell hovered for a moment before it zipped away, heading toward the back of the building. I watched it go, shocked. Grandma's Mind Wipers never ran away like that.

I didn't even know if I could catch it. Or how to trap it. Frankly, I was kind of glad it didn't attack Dimitri or me.

I went to stand at Dimitri's side, away from some of the crowd. "I followed the recipe exactly," I whispered, not at all pleased at how my voice cracked.

He didn't look so convinced.

"Stop—" He brought a hand up to his forehead. "Stop trying to be a biker witch. As for the spell, we'll get it later. Soon," he corrected when I opened my mouth to protest. "Your grandma can trap it."

"I can't help who I am." Anything I could do to learn spells would only help us. Usually. We watched the Mind Wiper round the corner.

In the meantime, this could be our chance to figure out what was going on in this church. I turned to Mimi. The membership guru looked a little worse for wear. Her shoulders slumped, her face looked mottled, and her hair had gotten all mashed down on one side.

I bent down in front of her. "You okay?" I asked. Mind Wipers were all about taking people into another reality. "It's time for you to tell us what's really going on around here."

Mimi let out a low chuckle, shaking her head from side to side. I felt a twinge of guilt. Still, it wasn't as if there was anything dangerous in the spell.

"You..." She reached out and dragged a lazy finger down my forehead, between my eyes. "You have no spiritual vibrancy whatsoever." She flung her head back. "And I haven't felt this way since the cast parties after *Hair* the musical." She lifted up, her eyes hazy. "You see that one? Naked penises flapping everywhere. It was glorious."

I didn't know what to say to that.

Mimi didn't care. "Now mind you"—she pointed at me—"I didn't get naked for parts like that. I did get naked for a few directors. Hugh Marlowe was the bee's knees. But I'd have done that for nothing."

Dimitri scrubbed a hand over his face. "Tell us about the church," he insisted.

Mimi giggled. "You couldn't even make the rock glow," she said. She shook her head. "I mean, it's a rock."

"Tell me about it," I muttered.

Frieda wobbled over, like an inebriated giraffe on stilts. "Lizzie's too uptight. Wouldn't know a happy fox if it bit her." She made it over to the wall next to Mimi and slammed her back against it. "Lordy, I could go for some Doritos right about now."

Dimitri watched Mimi, calculating as ever. "You said you'd take us back to learn about the church."

She gave a long, slow blink. "I wish I could, darling, but you failed the spirituality test. We can't do anything if you don't have the inner oomph." She considered it for a moment. "Maybe you just need to be purified."

Frieda braced her hands on the wall behind her. "Oh my God—yes."

"Show us," Dimitri said. "Maybe then we could join."

Mimi thought for a moment. "I've never tried it that way."

Dimitri cocked a grin. "Think of how great it would be if this turned out to be a new way to get members."

She nodded slowly. "Yes. The pastor would be so pleased. And he's always looking for new members." She paused. "We'd have to go to the sanctuary, though."

"Well, you know we'd love to see that." Dimitri took her arm in his like an old-fashioned gentleman.

He led her toward the back while I hung back to grab Frieda, who was busy running her hands over the gold-plated sunbeams on the wall. "Are you coming?"

She turned her gaze on me, eyes wide. "I hate to tell you this, Lizzie, but this place feels wrong." She blew a lock out hair out of her face. "Have you ever thought we shouldn't be here? That you failing is a sign to get the hell out of Dodge?"

"No." The signs were lining up. That meant I had to press forward.

"Okay," she said, an octave higher than normal.

Church had ended. We passed groups of people chatting to one another and laughing. They flung out white-hot energy that made my eyes water and my entire body warm. It was like dashing out of a dark room into the light.

We caught up with Mimi and Dimitri at the doors down to the old theater. The same usher stood guard, positively beaming. "Welcome to the church!" She practically glowed from the inside out.

I gave her a wave and dragged Frieda inside with me.

My pulse picked up when I saw they'd replaced the movie screen with a large mural of the full moon. It had been drawn so that rays of moonlight seemed to reach out to the rows and rows of theater seats. Mock torches lined the walls.

"Here we are," Mimi said, picking up speed as she approached a curtained-off enclosure at the front. Her presence here seemed to give her energy, or at least eliminate the effects of the spell I hit her with. It was wrong.

Darkness radiated from the curtained area. The heavy drapes matched the purple velvet of the theater seats. Silver beads glittered down between the folds. She turned to us. "It's usually just one at a time—"

Frieda whipped open the curtain. "Let me at it."

Oh, geez. "Wait up!"

Silver metallic fabric lined the inside of the space. It was small, with enough room for a battery-operated fountain, and a set of wooden stairs that led up to a tomb.

I shared a glance with Dimitri.

The stone burial chamber reminded me of the ones I'd seen at museums, or in *National Geographic*. It was constructed from of a single slab of cut and polished stone. The corners were rough. The lid was immense, decorated with a raised image of a bird. The sides were carved with a language I'd never seen before.

I approached it slowly. It was ancient. And evil. My demon slayer senses screamed at me to destroy it. End it.

If only I knew how.

It was cool to the touch. Crammed with inscriptions. My finger tingled as I ran it over a series of markings at the center of a large sun-like disk. They read:

सीजननी जन्मश्च '

जन्मभूमिर्गादश्च स्वपि गरीयसी'

गरीभूमिय

स्वर्गादरीयसीपि ग

My powers had given me the ability to translate texts before.

I tried to unfocus my eyes and concentrate. It was harder than usual. The sarcophagus emitted a slow pulsing energy that grabbed at me, tried to scramble my signal. I tried harder. It fought me at every turn.

"Darling?" Mimi touched my shoulder.

I shrugged her off, not necessarily wanting to explain my ability to read ancient languages, yet extremely grateful for it all the same.

Then I felt the words resonate deep in my chest. Underneath the swirling text, I could almost *see* the translation.

I squinted, ignored the icy thrum of the stone, until the words were clear. *Guard my soul...*

It appeared as if it were written in red script underneath.

Lift me up
I am yours
Mighty one

My temples pounded. It was never this hard to translate. This thing didn't want to be found out.

I yanked my hand away and gathered my thoughts for a moment. No way I could translate the whole thing without passing out. Even if we did have time.

"Who's the mighty one?" I asked, wondering if anyone in this so-called church even knew.

Mimi frowned. "Our Lord, I suppose." She fussed with her robe. "At least that's how the pastor explains it." She gave a small smile. "We're nondenominational."

No they weren't. They were dangerous.

"It's so Egyptian," Frieda said, sliding past me, reaching for it. "And if it feels anything like that rock, I'll take two."

I grabbed her arm and pulled her back. "No touching."

"It's okay," Mimi said, too pleased for her own good. "Everyone loves it. It cleanses our souls." She scrambled to the foot of it and pulled the lid back, as if it were on rails. "Yes, it's a sacred sarcophagus, but that's the point. We're dead when we lie down inside of it, but then it gives us life. A new hope!"

Dimitri moved between Frieda and the artifact. "You don't mean literally dead," he asked, studying it.

Mimi lowered her hands. "Of course not."

"Just checking," he muttered.

She ran a loving hand over it. "This will show you the true beauty of the church."

"Oooh…" Frieda clapped her hands together.

Again, I wondered just what this cult was about if Mimi had no clue.

Shouldn't the evildoers know if they're working for a dark lord? Shouldn't they be tainted some way? When Mimi touched the artifact, the darkness should have impacted her. It had to. There was no way they should be able to remain in this building for any length of time without the darkness seeping into them.

"I'll try it first," Dimitri said, approaching the tomb as if it were an attacking animal. God, I hated to see him do it. He didn't look too thrilled, either.

"Where did it come from?" I asked, wondering if Mimi even believed in other dimensions.

Mimi seemed inordinately pleased at my question. "It was a gift, brought to us by our pastor. He's such a lovely man. I can't wait for you to meet him."

"Me neither," I muttered.

"Once you pass the test," she added. "It stands to reason, once you're purified, the rock will glow with no problem."

Sure. Yes. But first I had to watch my husband lie in a tomb that a reformed succubus had warned us about.

We were so screwed.

Mimi backed off. We all did, as Dimitri climbed the steps.

My breath hitched as I watched him climb into the coffin. I don't know what I expected—an evil spirit, a dark cloud, a portal that would zap him away.

It was creepy all on its own.

Gingerly, he lay down in the tomb. Mimi moved to the foot of the ancient piece. He braced himself as she began sliding the lid closed over him.

"How are you strong enough?" I asked her, with growing dread.

"It's a mystery of the church," she said, gleefully. The lid closed over my husband's hips, his chest. "It's one of the many beautiful things that happen here," Mimi continued. She was burying him alive.

Dimitri's shoulders were almost as wide as the tomb. He moved his hands to touch the stone on either side of him as the heavy lid rolled completely over him. It locked into place with a low boom.

Mimi clasped her hands together and let out a happy sigh.

This was one sick cult.

"How long?" I asked. "Dimitri?" I called, for my own assurance. And his.

He didn't answer.

Mimi didn't catch, much less comprehend, my worry. "Believe me, he's in heaven!" she gushed.

Not too soon.

"Dimitri." I pressed my hands against the stone, feeling the weight of the darkness. This was a mistake. "Get him out of there."

Mimi's mouth opened. Closed. Opened again. "It's not doing anything."

Yes it was. It was smothering him.

"It should be glowing," Mimi protested. She reached out and the rock warmed to a soft amber where her fingers touched. "Yes. I feel it." She shot me a look. "These things really don't work on him."

Something had happened if he wasn't answering. I raced up the steps. "Get him out."

"Yes. All right." She moved to the back of the casket like a hummingbird. "You don't have to be rude about it."

Slowly—much too snaillike for my taste—she pulled back the lid of the coffin.

I saw his head. His eyes were closed. "Dimitri!"

They popped open. "I'm fine," he said, voice hoarse. He sucked in a deep breath of air. Dimitri rose, anxious to sit, even though the stone lid was still at chest level. "I hate small places."

Thank God. "Did you feel anything?"

"Nothing." He shot a caged look at Mimi. "Unless you mean that glowing it did when I was in there."

He was usually a better liar. He must have been freaked out in there. Or he was getting his tips from me.

Mimi didn't buy it for a second. "I'm sorry, darling," she began.

I reached for Dimitri's arm, but he'd already leaped out and over the side like a cat.

"Let me try," I said to Mimi. We didn't need to get kicked out twice. I could rig this thing. I mean, it had to be just a larger version of that little stone we saw outside, right?

I stared at the claustrophobic space inside. It was a bad day when I was trying to talk someone into closing me inside a tomb that may or may not be from a demon.

But I had a plan.

I could make this thing light up. Even if I wasn't a natural, like Frieda, I had powers that would at least piss it off.

Then once I got in this fricking cult, I'd drag my rock-and-roll manager along for the ride.

Piece of cake, right?

I just wish it didn't smell like dust…and death.

Mimi took her place at the end. "I think you can do it," she said, eager to get me in the box. "Ready, darling?"

Like I was ready for a hole in the head. "Can't wait," I muttered. I stepped one foot in. Craving a little comfort, I touched the emerald at my neck. It didn't warm like it used to. Not since the day the Earl of Hell had attacked me and forced a knife into it.

It had healed itself. A soft line ran through it where the gash had been. It would never be the same. The Earl corrupted everything he touched.

I considered the loss a tragedy, not only because it had been a one-of-a-kind piece but also because I really could have used some extra protective magic right about now. I eased my other foot into the tomb. This was it.

Dimitri watched me, as if he could make it better though sheer willpower. "Be careful."

I nodded and sat. I could swear I felt the thing lurch under me. Fight me. The blackness hissed from it like a snake coiled and ready to strike.

I tried not to think about that as I lay down inside the tomb.

Stone walls surrounded me. I curled my hands into fists and centered my power as the lid began rolling up over me. I felt the light inside me churning, itching to escape. Every fiber of my being wanted to lash out at the terrible evil surrounding me.

I felt hate, vicious aggression. It pierced my skin like a thousand needles. The air grew heavy as the lid passed over my face. My lungs tightened, breathing in salt and dust and despair as the stone tomb trapped me, closed me in until only a single shred of light shone through.

With a resounding boom, the lid shifted, sealing me inside the pitch-black tomb.

The stone walls pulled at me; the darkness swallowed me whole. I couldn't get enough air. I pressed my hands against the lid and felt another wave of hate. It grated at my skin. It wanted to imprison me forever.

What if this was a trap?

This afternoon, I feared the very existence of this artifact, and now I'd willingly climbed inside of it.

H-e-double-hockey-sticks.

The dark power that resided in this tomb had helped Mimi lure me in. What if it didn't let me out?

I tried to breathe. To keep my head. *Focus.* I'd make this thing glow and we'd get in the cult and we'd be happy.

My hands tore at the lid.

Okay. Power. I needed my power.

I reached inside myself for that churning, otherworldly strength. Cold fear skittered through me when I couldn't find it. It was there. It had to be there. It had been so angry before. I'd felt it right in my gut, behind my stomach and my backbone. It had wanted out. It had demanded to attack this evil. And now?

I tried to find any small sliver of light, but only felt a heavy, dark pit of a hole.

Had the casket somehow blocked my powers?

Why weren't they letting me out?

I resisted the urge to scream. Loud. Damn it all. I'd fought demons and dark lords. Once, I'd even killed a demon on my toilet bowl. I could find my power in this casket.

Or die trying.

I battled for that spark of light. I demanded it. I searched and I pulled and I forced it to come out. Fight, damn it!

It glowed low and deep, and that wasn't good enough. I pounded the sides of the casket. *Get it! Hate it! Fight it like it fights you.*

It shoved me down hard, knocking the breath out of me. I wheezed for a few seconds, then kicked back hard. I pushed out every bit of strength and fear and love until it began to rise up inside me. The power grew, twisting in my gut, racing out through my hands.

Yes, yes. *More.*

I held it, grew it until it churned molten and eager. I fed it, held it until it burned bright and strong. It wanted out. It wanted to be heard. But I held it back just a little bit more. Teased it. Sharpened it.

"You want out?" I hollered. My fists punched against the stone. My legs pounded. "You want this?"

Yes! It screamed. It begged.

"Ha!" I let it loose. It flowed from me in a single hot burst.

Then I saw light. I saw fire and white-hot liquid energy. It was beautiful. It surrounded me, seized me with purity and strength. Goodness.

The tomb rumbled all around me. Ha!

I shoved harder, drunk on my own power.

A fissure opened up in the rock above my head. Cripes! I pulled back, toned it down. Too late. The power had been trapped in the stone. *Crack.* My feet dropped into empty space as—holy hell—the entire bottom of the casket crumbled and dropped away.

Oh, no, no, no.

I couldn't break this thing. I needed to blend, to learn.

Desperately, I tried to reclaim my energy, to suck it back in, to do *something.* But I had no idea how.

I'd never even considered holding back before.

The fissure above my head deepened, spread down the side of the casket. I pressed against it, as if that would meld the pieces together again. I couldn't even feel the power of the tomb anymore. I only felt the overpowering thrum of my own energy.

It rumbled. A large crack split the heavy rock above my head. I rolled sideways, curled into a ball to protect my skull as chunks of gravel-sized rock rained down on my hips and side. The casket groaned and lurched as the entire front wall fell off.

Rock shards dug into my hip and arm as the bottom crumbled under me.

Cool air turned my sweat-sheened skin ice cold. I choked on the dust. Pieces the size of gravel pelted my head and hair.

Mimi screamed. Horror flooded her voice. "What did you do?"

"Nothing," I hollered, trying to get a grip, to hold back my powers that fought to flow freely. I pressed my fingers against the rock-strewn bottom of the coffin. A crack splintered it. I couldn't let her see my complete and utter lack of control. I had to figure this out.

"You broke the Tomb of Kebechet!" Mimi said, her shrill tone piercing my ears. "How did you do that?"

"I barely touched it," I said, shifting to ease out the front. My knee accidentally hit the back or maybe I breathed wrong because that part crashed over, with all the subtlety of a sonic boom, taking one of the purple curtains with it.

"Damn it!" I rolled all the way out. My legs were shaky. I had dirt in my mouth.

Mimi let out a strangled squeak. "Pastor!" she hollered. "Help! Someone get Pastor Xavier!"

Dimitri wrapped an arm around me. "Can you stand?" he asked, bracing me against his side. "Because we may need to make a run for it."

Tears flooded my vision. My hands were shaking something horrible. I felt drained. Tired. I didn't know how fast I could move. "We may need to hit them with a spell."

Dimitri groaned. "So you're saying we're fucked."

Footsteps pounded down the aisle. "In here!" Mimi yelled.

"Stay back!" A man wearing blue suit pants ripped the curtain back.

Dimitri cursed.

I knew it was bad. But when I looked up and saw the pastor, it got even worse.

There, wearing a blue suit with a conservative red tie, stood the man I thought I'd never see again. The man who'd walked out of my life. The one I swore I'd never chase down.

"Dad?"

Chapter Ten

He'd let his inky black hair grow, making his sharp features even more pronounced. He stood about six feet tall, although he didn't come close to Dimitri. It troubled me to note that since I'd seen him last, Dad had lost even more weight off his lanky frame.

Hands still shaking, I gave a pathetic wave. "Hey," I said.

Because that's what you say when your estranged father walks in on you destroying a demonic tomb.

Hellfire. I couldn't believe he was in charge of this place.

My throat was parched. My knees wobbled. I never expected to see him again. He was a fallen angel. A real one. He'd abandoned me long before I was born and I'd never even seen him until a year ago when he'd searched me out and asked me to save his eternal soul.

I'd risked everything for him. I'd saved him, given him a new start at life. He'd paid me back by walking out on me. He'd said he wasn't interested in being a dad. He wasn't the type, whatever that meant. I sighed. At least he'd been honest with me, even if it had hurt like hell.

Now he stood here, mouth open, eyes wide. At least I'd caught the king of bullshit off guard.

He stared at me like he'd never seen me before.

Clearing my throat, I glanced back at the pile of rubble. "Sorry about that."

I was. Now we'd never know what the demon was doing with it. Unless I could get it out of my dad.

Dad didn't say anything, which was a first. Instead, he approached me slowly, picking his way through the rubble.

"Huh," Frieda said.

Great. Even the biker witch didn't know what to say.

Dad folded me in an awkward hug. I swore I could feel the bones of his back through the fine wool of his jacket. He pulled away first, studying me as if I were a new kind of bug in his garden. "I never expected to see you here."

That made two of us.

Dimitri stood stiff-shouldered, wary. Dad pretended not to notice. "And you," Dad said, with the casual air he'd made into an art form, "I remember you."

A muscle in my husband's jaw twitched. "You should. I helped save you from demon possession." He seemed to grow taller, infusing the room with his presence as he spoke. "I killed the banshees that hunted you. I fought the Earl of *Hell* for you."

Dad adjusted his tie. He pasted on a smile, teeth clenched. "Not in front of the help."

We were gathering a crowd of startled churchgoers.

Dimitri didn't care. His voice took on an even harder edge. "I was there for your daughter after you abandoned her."

The stab of truth made me wince. I'd been a fool.

Dad grew twitchy, as if he wasn't quite sure how to react. He cleared his throat and turned to his minions instead. "The man is right about one thing," he said, with the wave of a hand at Dimitri. "This is my prodigal daughter." He said it without affection or joy.

"The rest is an inside joke. And a very bad one at that."
He shot me an aw-shucks grin, as if he actually cared.
"My little pumpkin's glad to see me, isn't she?"

He'd never called me a pumpkin in his life.

Mimi fretted with her dress, her hair. She had the
nerves of a hummingbird as she moved to stand behind
my father. "I'm so sorry. I had no idea you even had a
daughter."

Exactly.

I wanted to tell Dad in no uncertain terms that I
wasn't overly thrilled to see him, but screw that. I
wasn't a sullen child. Any kind of games I played only
gave him power.

He'd made his choice. He didn't want me in his life.
As awkward as this was right now, I was here on
business. I'd figure out a way to make this work.

"Honey bun?" Dad prodded.

Sweet Jesus. He actually wanted an answer.

I didn't get it. Was it all about image with him?

Painfully enough, I had no clue. I didn't know
enough about my father. And I refused to look at
Dimitri.

If you're going through hell, keep on going.

I wiped some of the grave dust from my arms.
"Sure, Dad. It's nice to see you." *Even if you'd never
choose to see me.*

"Now what are you doing here?" Dimitri finished
the thought.

My dad's slick smile was back. "I discovered a
powerful relic, a direct line to God," he added in a
hushed tone, for the benefit of his followers. "I had no
choice but to spread the word and found my own
religion."

"Naturally," I said. It happened all the time.

Behind him, Mimi had tears in her eyes. "She broke
the Tomb of Kebechet."

"Yes," Dad said, with the sobriety of a true politician, "that's unfortunate." He directed a tepid smile at his followers. "We must all pray on it. This is a test, you know."

Absolutely not. He had something up his sleeve. I'd bet anything.

Mimi shook her head, wiped her nose on her dress. "That rock is ten times denser than quartzite. It was forged in the fires of Mount Thinis. It rested for three millennia in a dimension beyond our dimension," she said, as if reciting holy text. "It is infused with powers we can't possibly understand." The membership chair pointed at me. "She. Broke. It."

I stiffened. I knew where this was headed.

We didn't need anyone questioning my humanity.

"It was old," Frieda said, in my defense.

Dad looked a little pale. He hadn't expected that. Yes, he controlled his congregation, but I wondered how much of that had come from his great and magical tomb.

"If it's any consolation," I said to him—and to the rest, "it was a total accident." It's not like I did it to be a jerk. I didn't even know how I managed to split a stone in the first place.

Dad blinked, trying to get a handle on himself. "It's done, though, isn't it?" He tried to shake it off. "Things happen." He ran an unsteady hand through his hair. "Trust in me and in this church," he said to his congregation. Then, turning back to me, "I suppose this is what it's like to be a parent."

Right.

"Come along," he said to me.

I cringed at the thought.

Still, Dad may be a jerk, but he was a first-class bullshitter. And if he was in charge of this place, that in itself was valuable. If I could stand being in the same room with him.

I glanced to Dimitri. "I'll be fine." We needed to know Dad's angle, and he'd be more likely to talk to me without Dimitri there, pushing his buttons.

He gave a short nod. "Frieda and I will wait."

Which was shorthand for *investigate and get into trouble, probably steal a few pieces of the broken relic.*

Dad had no idea whom he was dealing with.

I leaned closer to my husband. "Whatever you do, find out what's down in that basement."

"Gladly," he said, already plotting. I had no idea how he was going to do it, but he'd figure out a way. It was one of the things I loved about him.

Meanwhile, Dad had focused on Mimi. "Pick two helpers," he told her. "Wrap the remains of our artifact in the velvet cloth. Please. Capture every last fragment." He fiddled with his lip as his gaze traveled over the ruined Tomb of Kebechet. "I may know someone who can fix it."

My husband leveled a glare at him. "I shudder to think."

Dad's eyes flicked up. "Watch it, young man. You're addressing your father-in-law."

Dimitri let out a snort.

I was more shocked than anything. "How did you know?" The last time I'd seen Dad, Dimitri and I weren't even engaged. He'd left and hadn't wanted anything to do with me or anyone in my rather small social circle.

Dad squared his shoulders as we headed out to the hallway "You're both wearing rings," he said, as if it were obvious we must be married to each other. "Plus"—he tilted his head—"your adoptive mother stopped by to see me."

"Hillary?" I said, dumbly. Of course. There was only one, thank goodness. My adoptive mom may be a size-four socialite, but she was a bulldog when it came to standing up for the people she loved. I hadn't shared the gory details of my dad's rejection. And of course she would assume my bio dad would make me happy. Ha.

He walked me out toward the lobby. "Now that is a fine-looking woman. She even took me out to lunch at the Ivy. I'm surprised she didn't mention it. She was quite taken with me."

In his dreams. The dull realization settled over me. "She tried to fix this."

I was going to kill her. She never could leave things alone. And now, it seems she'd hunted down my biological father the same as she'd snared a set of live pink doves for the wedding toast.

My dad hit me with a megawatt smile. "I told her I wasn't up to being a dad, not even for the free booze." His face fell when I didn't share in the joke. "Lighten up. I was teasing."

About my life and my wedding. This was one battle I was glad Hillary had lost.

As we made it out into the lobby, Dad continued, as if we were discussing the weather. "You didn't want me to show up. It would have been awkward as hell to walk you down the aisle."

"My other dad did that," I told him. Cliff wasn't exactly the warm and fuzzy type, but at least he cared.

"Exactly." He stopped in front of a small elevator with gold doors. "Much better all around." He spared me a glance. "It *is* good to see you."

"For real?" I didn't get why he was acting so friendly.

The elevator doors dinged open. "Sure." He ushered me inside.

It was an antique model, with wood paneling and a metal cage that closed in front of the more modern doors.

Dad glanced down at me. "We could use you around here."

The lights above us flickered as the carriage lurched up. Ah, so that's why he'd been so chatty. He needed something.

The small carriage shook and I felt the low crackling of a portal.

It was on this floor.

Of course it was. My dad was behind this entire thing. I could feel it stronger as we drew closer and closer. The vibrations reached out to me, settled low in my stomach. I winced as it gave a hard pop.

Dad leaned closer. "You okay?"

"Never been better," I muttered.

We exited into a small hallway with antique wood-paneled walls. Two doors stood directly opposite each other. Red vapor trickled from the one on the right, spilling out over the white marble floor.

I stopped, bracing myself as the cold trickle of evil caressed one of my ankles. "You want to tell me what that is?"

"Have a little patience," he said, as if he were the put-upon one in this relationship. Dad inserted a key into the door on the left. "I'm not your enemy, Lizzie."

That remained to be seen.

His office was in the old projection room, with a bank of glass at the back, overlooking his church. Talk about being the king of the castle.

The glass had been tinted, treated no doubt so that Dad could see out, but no one else could see in. I looked down at Mimi and two of her helpers, scurrying to make some sense out of the mess we'd left behind.

Dimitri and Frieda were nowhere to be seen.

Built-in bookshelves lined the right wall of Dad's office. They were curiously free of books. Instead, stone statues and bits of rock crowded the shelves.

A carved wood desk stood at the center.

The skin on the back of my neck prickled. "What is this place, Dad?

He tossed his keys on the desk. "It's the latest in joint ventures—a whole new way for people like you and me to help others."

I shoved off the wall. "You've made it clear there is no 'you and me.'" The last time I'd seen him, he'd been extremely matter-of-fact about ending things between us.

Before that, we had no relationship at all. He didn't even come to see me after I was born.

"I admit I'm not the father type," he said, moving behind his desk. He motioned for me to take one of the matching red leather seats across from him. "I'm not going to lie to you about that. But there's no reason we can't be friendly when we run into each other." He tugged his pants legs and sat. "In fact, I think I may be in possession of contacts that could help you."

True. Dad was a fallen angel. I doubted we ran in the same circles.

I took my time making my way over to him, arms crossed over my chest. "The last time you offered your help, you ran and hid while we battled."

The biker witches had told me all about it afterward. I'd been so busy fighting, I hadn't stopped to consider what my dad was doing.

He didn't even have the decency to look ashamed. He clasped his hands on the desk in front of him. "You can't blame me for that. I was fighting my own darkness at the time. But now, I'm clean." He leaned back in his chair. "I'm happy. And it's because of this place: the Salvation of the Hills."

He sounded like an infomercial.

I took a seat across from him. "There's a dark portal in your church, Dad. Some freak used it to drop a fenris on my beach."

"No, no." He rapped on the mahogany. "That was me."

"What?"

Dad stood. I followed.

"I have a portal." He moved around his desk to an open area next to a shelf lined with canopic jars. "See?" He raised his hands and a crash of electricity erupted into the space.

It was ten times worse than before. It pounded against me, sizzled over my skin. It felt like we were right in the room with it.

Dad merely grinned as a churning red portal opened up in front of him. It swirled with power, radiated with dark energy.

I realized with a jolt that I hadn't sensed it since he'd come into the room with the rock. Was he intentionally blocking me? Or was it an accident? There was no way I'd ask. I didn't trust Dad.

"This one's all mine," Dad said, as if he was showing off a new car. "I set it to go anywhere I need."

"Like our beach." It made sense, even if it was the last thing I wanted to hear. "Don't tell me that was you personally that I saw early this morning." The man had been shrouded in a cape, but he'd been tall, lanky.

Cripes.

Dad clapped once and the portal disappeared. "I can explain."

"No, you can't." Nothing he said could be good.

Dad paused, as if trying to figure out a way to say it. "I made a deal with the Earl of Hell," he admitted.

"Jesus Christ on a cracker."

Dad held up his hands. "No. Listen. This time, it works. The Earl is okay now. He knows he can't come up and walk the Earth."

This was insane. "He tried to kill me at my wedding!"

"And that was a mistake," Dad said, talking over me.

Ya think? "Listen to yourself!"

But he was too busy talking. "The Earl needs power, right? And, yes, he wanted yours. But it's good that he didn't get it because now we're working a new angle. It's all good now."

"You don't get it. I can't save you every time." We'd barely made it the last time he'd gotten caught up with the Earl, and that time, Dad's immortal soul was in danger. Now he didn't even realize he was in trouble, and God knew what he'd already done. "You're working with the Earl of Hell," I said, trying to get it through my head, and his.

Dad nodded like a salesman on speed. "He needs darkness, despair, hate, loneliness. Even hopelessness. All of the things that we have to live with on Earth."

"Because he's a demon!" This was insane.

He kept talking, as if he could make me see reason. "The Tomb of Kebechet takes that despair and gives it back to the Earl in hell, where it belongs."

"I broke it," I said, my voice an octave higher.

"The Earl made thirteen," Dad said. "That's the great thing. What I said down there about praying? That was bullshit. The Earl can give me another one."

"Of course he can. You are part of his evil plan. He's doing something to these people. God knows what. Open your eyes and take a good look for once in your goddamned life!"

"Listen to yourself," he shot back. "You can't imagine that for once you don't know everything. You just walk in here and assume."

"Yes. Yes, I do." In this case, I was right.

"We are very well equipped," Dad went on, as if I were somehow going to say, "Oh sure. Now I get it. Let's partner with a demon." He glanced out over his church before turning back to me. "We help people feel better. It's so simple. They come here and they let go of any darker emotions, any baggage, anything that holds them back. It goes straight down to the Earl and leaves each of the members of our congregation feeling light, free—happy! It's also a potent anti-ager. Some in our congregation are actually aging backward!"

"By feeding a demon in hell," I said slowly.

"Well, we're hoping he can make it up to purgatory soon," Dad said.

"Are you insane?" Purgatory was an in-between place, and way too close. No wonder the people felt good, while this place was so evil. So hateful. It was unnatural, scary, and wrong on about a hundred different levels. "You don't honestly believe the Earl is going to stop in purgatory."

He waved me off. "The emotions he's getting from us aren't enough to feed a second coming."

That was a lie wrapped in bullshit—the Earl's specialty. I couldn't believe Dad fell for it. I crossed my arms over my chest. "You said you needed me. For what?"

Dad eased his suit jacket off, as if it had suddenly gotten warmer in here.

"Does it have anything to do with the fenris on our beach this morning?"

He moved back behind his desk and hung the jacket on the back of his chair. "The fenris was a...complication." He paused, his fingers caressing the fabric. "We've had some side effects with the transfer of dark emotions." He found a particularly fascinating piece of lint. "Sometimes things show up from the other side."

"Jesus." I rubbed at my eyes. They were scratchy. Cripes, I'd been up since the fenris showed up on my beach in the middle of the night.

"It's mostly under control," Dad said quickly. "I can usually send things back, and when I can't, I find them homes." He brightened. "Like that fenris. I know you like dogs. I figured you'd take good care of it."

He basically dumped a large devil dog on my property and expected me to adopt it. Hell, I had. But that wasn't the point.

"You could help me with other things," he said, as if it were the best idea in the world.

"Let me guess," I said. "You had a succubus pop up this afternoon."

"It was so freaky," he said, as if we were old girlfriends, "but I handled it."

By screaming like a girl.

Enough. "Dad. If you won't stop this, I will."

"Don't you dare," he shot back. "I'm in hock to the Earl for sixty-three more years. You saving me didn't change that."

Then we'd just have to take out the Earl. I was done pussyfooting around this. That demon had proven time and time again he'd kill me if he got the chance. I hadn't vanquished him yet because, frankly, I didn't know how. He was the most powerful entity I'd ever come across. But now he was way, way too close to the surface. It was clear that locking him away had done no good.

Oh frig.

I'd figure it out this time. I had to. And if I played it right, Dad could be my unwilling accomplice.

CHAPTER ELEVEN

I ran a hand over the squat statue of Ammut on the desk. "If I'm going to be any help, I need to see more of what you do." Like what was growling in the basement.

Dad leaned back against his desk. "Not going to happen, sweetie." He shot me a grin, as if we were colleagues in on a joke. "Do you realize how pissed the Earl is going to be now that I've brought a demon slayer into this?"

I watched him. "You don't look too worried."

He kept his face carefully neutral. "The Earl needs me." He rapped his knuckles on the desk and pushed away from it. "He's still going to chew my ass."

"Don't tell him." I really couldn't see any advantage to letting the Earl of Hell know I was onto him. I'd just as soon he forget about me until I shoved a switch star through his heart.

Dad gave me a level look. "The demon's not stupid. Who else besides, well, *you*"—he flung a hand at me— "can break the Tomb of Kebechet?" He paced in front of his bookcase full of artifacts. "Besides"—he gave an involuntary shudder—"the Earl knows everything about me. Total transparency," he added. "It was the only way he would trust me." Dad paused in front of a statue of a screaming man. "He can crush my soul with a thought."

I didn't want to know that.

It made sense. Demons didn't trust anyone. And they were assholes when it came to demanding loyalty. There was no way the Earl of Hell would let my dad have free rein up here. Especially when he had a daughter like me, even if I wasn't in the picture.

This was too much for anyone to bear, and for that, I was sad.

"I'm sorry this happened to you," I told him. No one deserved to be used that way—to be controlled. It was worse than joining the mob. At least the Godfather couldn't read your mind, or tear holes in your soul like tissue paper.

Dad nodded. He stood stoic, determined. "I'll be fine," he said simply. Scarily enough, he actually seemed to believe it. "I just have to keep feeding him," he explained. "We'll make it through this. We'll get a new coffin."

Yes, because that would solve the problem.

I tried to reach out. One last time. Maybe I was a fool to do it, but something in me hoped, thought, prayed, that maybe Dad wasn't as far gone as I feared.

He had to see that it didn't need to be this way. "You could have come to me earlier," I told him. "I might have been able to get you out of hock for that sixty-three years you said you owed." We could have taken a different path. "There still might be a way now."

Dad shook his head slowly, as if the suggestion were foreign, absurd. "Don't you get it? I'm happy here." He turned his back on me in order to look out over his church.

It was over.

It hurt more than I thought it would. More than I wanted it to. There were so many things that we could have been for each other.

Stop. I blew out a breath. I had to stop wishing for that and look at the reality of this church, this cult—this man and his demons.

I watched his rigid back, his practiced control. I couldn't save him anymore. If Dad didn't have the sense to put an end to it, I would. I'd play along, learn more, and then stop him cold. I approached him slowly from behind, my heels echoing off the wood floor. Casually, I took my place at his side, overlooking the worship area.

The way I saw it, I had one major disadvantage. Unlike the Earl of Hell, I couldn't peer into Dad's mind before we started down the primrose path. Then again, Dad wasn't on my team. He never had been.

Together, we observed Mimi and her assistants as they frantically tried to salvage the demon's artifact. Poor Mimi crouched over it, attempting to piece the thing together with her bare hands.

"Let her know it's okay to quit," I told him. It was a useless endeavor, and a sad one to watch.

"No," he said, his tone reflective. "It gives her a purpose."

Irritation ground in me like glass. These church members looked up to him. He had a responsibility to treat them like people with feelings, dreams, *living souls*.

Keep it down. Or I'd explode with it. The only way to change things was to keep my cool.

I might not be able to save Dad, but I could halt Earl's hold on Dad's unwitting congregation. The churchgoers were the real victims. They felt whole, blessed, and so they'd assumed this place was good.

When I finished, it would be.

I glanced at Dad. It was so tempting to straight-out ask him how it worked. But, no. That wasn't the right question. "What do you need from me?"

Besides salvation?

Only I'd offered that to him once. I'd earned his freedom. And he'd squandered it on this.

"Truly?" he asked, his face a profile, as if he were afraid he'd give away his thoughts.

"I'm not going to offer again." I had to be in charge of this or it wouldn't work.

He turned to me. "You don't know how glad that makes me, sweetie."

I tried not to cringe.

He approached me, hands spread. "I found a way to improve on the process."

I hated that tone.

Dad gave a slight wince, but I had a feeling he did it for show. "You have to understand how much power we're sending down to the netherworld. We have to take something back or it disrupts the flow. The entire portal will collapse."

It made sense. But I didn't like where this was going. "What are you pulling out of purgatory?" I asked. I had to learn exactly what we were facing.

"Rocks," he said innocuously. "Trees," he added, misreading my frown. "I know what they say about foreign plant life, but they really were harmless. We burned them in my new fireplace at home."

Sending the ashes...everywhere.

I held back that thought. "You have a new place?" I asked, keeping the conversation going.

He fingered his collar, as if it had grown too tight. "I've made some improvements."

Lovely. There was quite a profit to be made in salvation. Dad certainly wasn't the first purported holy man to discover that. When I'd decided to hold back, to draw out the information, I'd underestimated his ability to piss me off.

I worked to set aside my feelings about his greed and his lack of regard for life on our planet. Even more worrisome is that he'd talked about those rocks and trees in past tense. I rested my hands on my hips, fighting the urge to finger a switch star. "What are you pulling out of purgatory now?"

Dad glanced at me warily. Hell, he should realize I'd be chewing his butt this way to Sunday if I weren't trying to learn more.

"Gold," he said, innocently, moving away from the window. "Jewelry." He shook his head dismissively. "A few minor artifacts. Those who are incorporeal don't need their valuables anymore," he quickly explained. "Still the adjustments I made to the power flow meant that a few...undesirable creatures...have also managed to sneak through."

Greed and a complete lack of foresight—two of my dad's finest qualities. "Of course you haven't told the demon," I added.

"I almost had to do it." He walked over to the bookcases to the right of his desk, fingered a volume on public speaking. "You can't hide that sort of thing forever. But now you're here," he said, brightening.

I hated that look. "You want me to fix it."

"I love you," he said, solemnly.

"Don't push it." He wanted to use me. We both knew it wasn't love. It was cruel of him to pretend. "But fine." We'd use each other. As long as I didn't throttle him first. "If you want my help, give me access. Show me exactly where you're drawing from."

I wasn't going to give if I didn't get anything in return. That was how Dad's world worked, didn't it? Besides, he needed me, not the other way around.

He hesitated.

"Or don't," I told him. Frankly, I was sick of this entire thing, of him.

Sure, it might be easier if he gave up his secrets, but at that moment, I was done being the same room with him. I turned and walked out the door.

He gasped. "Lizzie!"

I slammed the door behind me. God, that was liberating.

No more games. No more lies.

There was a certain freedom in being pissed the hell off, in not caring for once. I headed for the elevator. I should have done this the minute he told me about the fenris.

He needed me more than he was willing to admit and if he didn't see that, I was done. I was done trying to save him. I was done trying to fix him. I couldn't be held responsible for the kind of life he'd chosen. I wanted him to be good and strong and all those things a dad should be. But he wasn't and wishing for it was useless. And exhausting.

He'd told me enough. I'd find another way to stop the Earl of Hell, and if my dad went down with him, I didn't care anymore.

Red mist poured from behind the wooden door near the elevator. Ah, yes. I placed a hand on the knob, drew a switch star.

"Lizzie, wait!" Dad stood in the hallway, terrified. "Not that one. The demon will know you're here for sure."

I turned my back on him and kept walking.

His footsteps were frantic behind me. "I can't show you my operation. You're a demon slayer. Just stop. Give me a minute. Let me think about how to get you involved."

I punched the elevator button. "I'll buy you a clue. Stop leaving creatures on my beach."

"Loud and clear." Perspiration dotted his upper lip. "I'll figure something out. I promise."

He didn't get it. This whole "being finished" thing? It felt too good. I'd had my taste of freedom and that was all it took. "I'm done. You want to be in it this deep? You want to lead? Go for it. Let 'er rip. Be the best goddamned cult leader on the planet. Just leave me out of it."

Until I send it all crashing down on your head.

The elevator doors dinged open.

"Sweetheart—" he pleaded.

I walked inside the small car, turned to face him. "Don't you dare," I said, pointing a finger at him before he could step inside.

The doors closed on his startled face.

Even his surprise pissed me off.

That he'd think, dream, imagine I'd let him run the show again. I'd trusted him once. I'd redeemed his soul. And it wasn't enough. It would never be enough.

He was incapable of change. Now I just had to figure out a way to stop him.

The doors opened and I headed for the exit.

I turned the corner into the lobby and saw two burly guards manhandling Dimitri and Frieda.

Fancy that. It looked like they got something done while I was gone.

The brutes were as big as werewolves and rough, too. The smaller one had Frieda's shoulder in a vise grip. He shouldered open one of the doors at the front and hustled Frieda out onto the sidewalk

The larger one had Dimitri by the arm. The guard gave a sharp exhale, even though my man walked easily next to him. Dimitri must have given him a bit of trouble earlier. Go hubby.

Dimitri was sweaty, and a little wrinkled, but none the worse for wear. He shook off his handler and opened the door for me as I approached. "You look pissed," he remarked.

"You look hot," I answered.

We left on our own power. Mostly.

Frieda stood on the sidewalk, straightening out her zebra-print top and glaring at the back of the security officers as they left.

"You okay?" I asked her.

"Sure, sure," she mumbled. "This ain't my first time getting tossed out of a place." She paused and glanced back at the building. "Maybe the first time in a church."

At least it appeared that the Mind Wiper had worn off.

But the trouble wasn't over yet. Dad had caught up to us. He thrust open the doors. "Wait."

The guard threw an arm in front of Dad, as if we were dangerous. "Security breach, pastor. The man and the old woman tried to get into the basement."

"Who are you calling old?" Frieda shot back.

Dad looked truly pained. "You can't ever go there."

"Yeah, I got that," Frieda said, holding up a hand. Her palm was swollen and red. Burned. She shrugged when she saw the alarm on my face. "The locks were enchanted."

We'd talk about it later. When we didn't have an audience. "Let's motor," I said, as Dad watched helplessly.

We headed across the street, toward our Harleys.

Unlike Frieda, Dimitri appeared unscathed. Still, they could have used something magical back there and that could hurt him worse than physical force. "You okay?" I asked him as we walked

He shot me a lopsided grin. "I may have a few new scratches on my back."

He was happy. They'd discovered something. "Did you have fun?"

"I'll tell you soon," he said. "After we get out of here." He turned to Frieda. "Where'd you park?"

She pointed to a chrome-and-steel beauty under a tree. Dimitri and Frieda shared a glance. "We gotta bring the witches in on this," she said.

"Agreed," he told her.

I wasn't going to argue. "Okay, Frieda. You get everybody together and bring them over to our place."

In the meantime, we'd stop off and grab a certain she-demon. I had an idea of how to crack my dad's defenses. With any luck, Shiloh would be more help than she realized.

CHAPTER TWELVE

When we arrived home, I found the she-demon in my kitchen, making a mess. Yellow mixing bowls competed for space on my already-overcrowded counter with a three-tiered cooling rack and assorted cookie trays. She'd taken out every piece of Tupperware I owned. Some of the containers were filled and stacked. Others were scattered over the counter. A large hunk of dough clung to the base of the KitchenAid mixer that I hadn't even gotten to use yet. It had been a wedding gift. Never mind that I'd had half a year to take it out of the box.

In the middle of it all, Shiloh worked like a woman possessed.

Boy, I sure hoped she wasn't.

"Is everything okay in here?" I asked, moving slowly, sharing a *what-the-frick* glance with Dimitri.

She'd tied her hair up in a messy ponytail and flour dusted one of her cheekbones. "I suppose," Shiloh said, both hands digging into a bowl. Her voice kicked an octave higher, her movements stressed. "No more creatures, no more threats." She held up her dough-caked hands. "I'm making homemade dog treats." She broke out into a genuine smile.

"Because I'm special," Pirate added, practically sitting on her feet. Oh my Lord, Pirate wore a sweater.

Yellow and pink squiggly stripes, with four legs and a tail hole.

It was flat-out ridiculous. Which was when I decided Shiloh's culinary way of coping had to be better than her knitting a matching sweater for me.

I bent down and held a hand out to my dog. "Hey, remember me? The one that feeds you?"

"Yeah. Science Delight Light." He reluctantly dashed over for a quick pat on the head. "That stuff is better when I hide it under the couch for a week, but it's still nasty."

"What are you storing under my couch?" I asked, but he'd already returned to his sugar mama. I saw how it was.

Dimitri, on the other hand, looked like he was about to start laughing. I didn't get it. This was serious here. I had a demon issue and, it seemed, some housekeeping problems as well. He opened his mouth, closed it, all the while taking a few steps backward. "Why don't you stay and talk to Shiloh?"

"Oh, come on." I wasn't looking forward to asking her to get more involved. Besides, as soon as Frieda assembled the witches, we were out of here.

But Dimitri was already moving toward the sliding glass door off the deck. "I'm going to do a quick perimeter check," he said, flicking the lock, "just to make sure."

Um-hum. "You do that." I was all for a walk around, but let's be honest—I could hear him bust out laughing the minute he slid the door closed.

And, geez Louise—the fenris was eating one of my sunflower dishtowels.

I went to take it away from her when I noticed one of my cobalt-blue mixing bowls—another wedding present—licked clean next to the massive wolflike creature.

"I thought Babydoll was supposed to eat hay," I said, recovering the bowl. On second thought, she could keep the dish towel.

"I made her a special nutrient mix," Shiloh said, glancing over her shoulder at the beast. "It'll help her feel better. Pretty soon, she'll be running all over the place."

Oh, boy. "That sounds terrific."

Shiloh nodded, but as she worked the dough, I could see tears forming at the corner of her eyes. "Hey," I said, wanting to get closer, but not so sure if I had the right. "What's wrong?"

She shook her head, even as the tears grew fatter. "Nothing. I hope." She swiped at her eyes with a flour-dusted forearm. "It's silly, really."

"Is it?" I highly doubted that.

She tried to smile and hiccuped instead. "My husband and I have a standing call. Whenever he's on the road, even if he's deep undercover, he calls me on Saturday nights." Every word held the weight of her worry. "Last night, he didn't call."

That was bad. Truth be told, though, it could be any number of things. She'd said her husband was working on a classified project. "Maybe he had an emergency."

She tried to look hopeful and failed. "When that happens, he always sends a text."

I didn't know their dynamic. I just knew that it would be hard for me to make a calling commitment to someone. Life had a way of altering your schedule when you were a demon slayer. "What was he working on?" Maybe they sent him someplace where he couldn't catch a signal.

She shook her head. "I don't know. He wouldn't tell me."

"Right." I planted my hands on my hips. This actually fit into what I wanted to talk to her about. I wished I could figure out a way to cage it, but my mind drew a blank, so I just said it. "I'm going to be meeting with the Red Skull witches."

Shiloh let out an involuntary gasp.

I pushed on. "It turns out you were right about the church and the tomb."

She drew her doughy hands up over the periwinkle apron at her chest, her eyes red-rimmed and frightened. "This is terrible. Do you understand how bad this is?"

I did. But we couldn't afford for her to lock up. We had to press on. "The witches excel at seeing the truth in situations." It was as good an explanation as any for the crazy-ass ceremony we were about to do. "Come with me. You can help us learn more."

Her hands were shaking. "I told you what I know."

I didn't sugarcoat it. "We could use you to connect to that succubus seer energy." There. I said it. "We'll also ask about your husband."

She chewed on her lip. I really hated to bribe her like that, but I wasn't about to lie to her about what we were getting into. Besides, if there was any chance she could make a difference, we had to do it.

She nodded weakly. "I'll go."

"Good girl," I said, wishing I could pat her on the shoulder, not so sure I should.

A flash of surprise crossed her dainty features. "Nobody's ever called me that."

I shot her a grin. "There's a first time for everything, right?" At least there was in my line of work.

My iPhone chirped and I fished it out of my coat pocket. A text from Frieda popped up.

Witches out and about. No idea where. Let's meet/plan at first light tomorrow.

"No," I snapped at my phone. Pirate's ears pricked. "Not you," I said to him in a gentler voice as I typed a response:

Get the witches NOW.

I had Shiloh. I had a bead on my dad. What part of demon infestation didn't these people understand?

I scraped my hair away from my face with my free hand. And truly, if we were going to wait forever and a day, couldn't we set a time that had more to do with clocks instead of sun schedules? This wasn't the Middle Ages.

Shiloh shook her head. "I need a drink. You want one?" She opened my lower cabinet and pulled out my blender. "I can make piña coladas, rum runners"—she planted the blender on the counter—"watermelon daiquiri?"

She had to be kidding. "I thought you were ignoring your vices."

Her perfectly white teeth found her plump bottom lip. "Mostly."

My phone chimed as Frieda's return text came through:

Nobody here. Tomorrow at sunup. I'm turning off my phone.

Of all the… My fingers tightened on my own phone. "She can't do that."

My father was in league with a demon. I'd destroyed the Tomb of Kebechet. We were in fricking emergency mode here. Frieda and the biker witches had been on my team from the start and no way I would accept "tomorrow" as an answer. I hit redial and found she had indeed turned off her phone.

Grandma did too.

And Ant Eater.

And every other witch I had on speed dial.

"Son of a..." I saw Pirate, looking up at me with big, innocent doggy eyes. "...biscuit eater." No sense corrupting the dog.

Still, what could possibly be more important than this?

I shoved the phone into my pocket.

The witches had better be mixing a batch of volatile spells or battling a legion of dark wizards or rescuing kittens. I didn't know what else would make them unavailable. They'd never ignored my call to arms before.

"Drinks it is," Shiloh said, moving to the cabinets near the refrigerator. "Where do you keep your alcohol?"

I leaned a hip against the counter. "If I haven't yet, I wanted to thank you for telling me about the moon symbols and the tomb." Shiloh dug through my cabinets as I talked. "You were right on both counts." I crossed my arms over my chest. Of course it appeared as if we weren't going to discover anything else until tomorrow morning.

She turned around, rum bottle in hand. "Did you see a line in the sand?" She focused on the over-tight lid to the bottle, as if she were afraid of my answer.

"No," but now that she mentioned it, I wondered if the ultimatum I gave my father was the line in the sand.

Shiloh headed for the blender and nearly stepped on Pirate, who was right at her feet. "Oh my..."

He jumped back. "Hey. Whoa! A little warning, please."

Her face fell. "Ohmigosh!" she said, completely ignoring Pirate's role in getting stepped on. She planted the rum bottle on the counter and went for her mixing bowls. "I'm so sorry, sweetie!" She dug out a heaping scoop of doggy biscuit dough and fed it to him.

He ate it happily, and quickly—considering she'd given him about two biscuits worth.

"If you're going to do everything my dog wants, we have a whole other kind of danger on our hands," I remarked.

Shiloh gave a faint smile. She wiped her hands on a towel. "Do you really think the witches can help me find out if Damien is safe?"

"Yes." I wouldn't have told her if I didn't believe it.

Shiloh gave a simple nod.

Dimitri slid open the glass door. "Everything looks good out there," he said, wiping at the corner of his eyes. "Flappy hasn't seen any action on the portal."

"It went dark about a half hour after you left," Shiloh said.

"At least it's safe for the neighbors." I didn't like introducing too many supernatural elements to the block, said the woman with the half demon and the fenris in her kitchen.

Shiloh abandoned the rum and retreated back to her cooking while I told Dimitri about our delay with the witches.

He groaned and glared at the floor, before he brought his gaze back up to mine. "Fine. I believe things happen for a reason." He held up a hand. "And not because the witches are out to drive you crazy."

Funny. That would have been my assumption.

Shiloh made dog biscuit dough circles. She placed each one on a wax paper-lined cookie sheet. "Actually, you know, that means maybe we could go to the party," she said, feigning innocence.

Now? Hardly. "Where'd you get that idea?"

Shiloh placed the new batch of biscuits in the oven. "While you were gone, a very nice lady named Sarayh stopped by. She said to tell you that you were welcome to bring a girlfriend to the bonfire on the beach." She gave a small shrug. "It would be more fun than drinking by ourselves."

I'd forgotten about that. With very good reason.

"You should go," Dimitri said, in that tone that suggested he was up to something. "You could stand to relax."

That was rich. "You want me to dance around a bonfire while a demon rises up in Beverly Hills?"

Shiloh squealed. "There's going to be dancing?"

I turned to her. "*That's* what you choose to focus on?"

"Think about it," Dimitri prodded, in that annoyingly logical way of his. "There's nothing else you can do tonight. You need to take a step back, or you're not going to be as good when we do need your head in the game."

Maybe so, but one of my strengths was that I was on-target 100 percent of the time. I lived for it.

Shiloh stood in front of the oven, absently playing with her wedding ring. "Sarayh seemed very nice. She invited me, too. You know, in case you felt more comfortable with a friend along."

Sure. The she-demon had offered me booze and now she wanted to go to a party. I didn't feel comfortable at all. Besides, Shiloh wasn't my friend. She was technically a creature of the night.

She dropped the act. "I could use this, Lizzie. I really could. It'll help me focus better tomorrow."

So we'd moved from bribery to blackmail.

Dimitri placed a hand on my shoulder. "Relax. Be with the normal people." I felt myself stiffen at his words. "Just because you're different doesn't mean you can't have fun. We made a lot of headway today." He gave me a light squeeze. "If a crisis comes up, we'll handle it. But for now"—he shrugged, as if he couldn't figure out why I found it so hard— "go make some friends."

"It'll make you feel better," Shiloh agreed. She took a few steps toward me, and then stopped. "I could use some human contact, too," she added.

Now I knew her angle. "Don't you dare feed off those people," I warned her.

Her forehead pinched. "I can get a lift from happiness as well," she said, an edge of defensiveness in her voice, "just like anybody else."

Pirate nosed around my legs and I picked him up. I couldn't believe I was even considering this.

A quick glance out the window showed they were already setting up for tonight's party. Sarayh and some of the girls from the homeowners' association were out there, stacking wood for a bonfire. Other women in bright shorts and festive skirts were carrying orange and green coolers down onto the beach. And it appeared as if they had some wireless speakers out there as well.

Shiloh washed and dried her hands, making extra sure she got all the dough out of her ring. "Come on. I have an extra sundress. We'll get you changed."

"I don't want to change." If these people wanted to get to know me, then they were going to meet a leather-clad goddess.

Girl power.

"Ever get sand inside of leather?" Shiloh asked.

"Yes. This morning." And it hadn't been comfortable. I ran my hands down my rather tight bustier. I didn't want to ruin more cowhide. Not to mention the fact that my heeled boots would sink into the beach like tent stakes. "Fine. I'll go put on something else," I told her, "but I'm wearing my own clothes." I didn't need help fitting in. There were bound to be some of my old dresses in the spare bedroom.

The sun had begun to set.

"Come on," Shiloh said, directing a dazzling smile at my husband. "Let's get cleaned up. Dimitri can handle the kitchen."

He shook his head. "You know what, I will," he said, in the miracle of the year. He must really want me to go have fun. I glanced back at my hunk of a husband, standing in our disaster of a kitchen, giving me the shoo motion.

Pirate stared up at him, no doubt willing to clean up any mess that fell onto the floor.

Let's face it: I was outnumbered. I took a quick shower and spent a few extra minutes drying and curling my hair. I wasn't sure whom I was trying to impress, but I found a cute strappy sundress in the spare closet. My mother had picked it out and brought it along for the week of my wedding festivities. I think she'd worried about me not having anything properly feminine—her definition, of course. In this case, it had been nice to have her take charge. I'd always liked the simple yellow dress.

I made it downstairs as Shiloh leashed up a drooling, excited fenris. "Let's take Babydoll. She could use a run."

The beast's nails scrabbled against our hardwood floors, reminding me once again why we'd kept her in the kitchen.

"Pirate can stay with me," Dimitri said. "We can have a boys' night."

My dog's ears perked up. "Will you let me bark at the dishwasher?"

"Sure, buddy," my husband said. "We can also order a pizza."

"Yes!" Pirate spun hard, and almost hit the side of the counter.

"He's so cute," Shiloh cooed.

I may have grunted. I reached down to pet Pirate and got a wet nose instead. At least someone was going to have a good time.

Dimitri had already started on the dishes. I gave him a sweet kiss on the cheek.

"Have fun," he said.

"I'll try," I said, leaving.

Shiloh was already out on the deck. I was bringing a half succubus and a fenris to a bonfire on the beach. With alcohol. While the Earl of Hell planned a second coming.

What could possibly go wrong?

"Just watch it," I told Shiloh. She seemed to have a handle on the overgrown brute, but it made me uneasy all the same.

Waves pounded the beach. The night was clear and warm, beautiful really.

Babydoll raced out as far as she could without strangling herself on the leash. Still, she half dragged Shiloh as we made our way to the path leading down to the water. The sun had just begun to set over the ocean, casting gorgeous pinks, oranges, and blues over the horizon.

Shiloh took a deep breath and then glanced at me. "Do you even know how to have a good time?"

Ouch. "Yes." My girlfriends and I used to go out all the time. Of course I hadn't seen them since I'd become a demon slayer, and now I wouldn't even know what to say. It's not as if I could admit what I was. They'd never believe it. And even if they did, I'd just be putting them in danger.

The last few years hadn't exactly been full of free time for hanging out with the girls anyway. Truly, there had to be about a hundred better ways for me to spend my time. I could be mapping out Beverly Hills, maybe researching moon temples or Egyptian mythology. Old stories had a strange way of pulling from fact. Or maybe they'd started off true and—

"No offense, but you remind me of a demon I knew once."

"Except I'm good," I reminded her.

"Well, yes," she said, "but the point is, the guy is a serious workaholic. If he has a project, that's all he thinks about."

"Then he's smart," I told her. Which is why I had to work just as hard. Chances were, I'd face him eventually.

She stole a glance at me and quickly looked out toward the beach. "That's the thing." I could hear her cringe. "He thinks he's being smart, but he's not. If you can't take a second and pull back—breathe—then you don't have the perspective you need to really see a situation for what it is."

Oh Lordy. "Can you at least pretend you're still talking about your friend the demon?"

"Fine," she snapped. "In case you're wondering, I'm trying to help you. Obsession isn't good."

"Thanks, Dr. Phil."

At least nothing had come out of the portal. Flappy sat on the beach, in front of where the gateway had gone dark. Babydoll reached him first. Her cold nose found the dragon's backside, causing the adolescent dragon to jump.

The dragon let out a *rwaaar*. Smoke curled from his nostrils. Babydoll slunk behind Shiloh.

"That's not nice," she told the dragon.

Flappy snorted, but he didn't attack.

Oh, look—progress.

I reached up to pat his head, but he wasn't interested. He blew a few small flames out his nose and tossed his head at a group of ladies in possession of a bowl of popcorn. Lucky for the ladies and their snacks, Flappy wouldn't leave his post.

"Watch this," Shiloh said, tossing a stick into the water. She cut Babydoll loose and the crazy animal dashed into the waves.

"Stay away from the portal," I warned.

"I thought it was closed," she said, as the fenris ran back to us, wet and happy.

Didn't mean it would stay that way.

Babydoll shook off, hitting us with a spray of water. I ducked as it hit my cheek. Shiloh laughed.

Sarayh waved and began trotting over with some red plastic cups, while the music kicked on. It was a classic. "Wipe Out" by the Surfaris.

I'd almost forgotten what it felt like to listen to anything other than the rock songs Grandma and the gang favored. I found it surprisingly pleasant, given the tang of salt water in the air and the sand at our feet.

"I'm so glad you came," Sarayh said, her hair tangled around her shoulders. She wore a grin as wide as Texas. "Have a Sex on the Beach."

She winked, as if Dimitri and I had been doing that on the beach earlier, which we hadn't. Well, at least not last night.

We'd been capturing my dad's fenris from purgatory, which was a much better excuse, although not as much fun.

Shiloh grabbed the first drink. "Thank you. This is so neat," she gushed. "I love the bonfire and the music. I've never been to a beach party before."

Sarayh seemed charmed by that, although she wouldn't be if she knew why. It took me a second to realize my neighbor was still trying to hand me a drink. Right. "Thanks," I said, not really wanting to take it.

Sarayh waited for me to say something else; what, I couldn't imagine.

"Okay." My neighbor smiled. "We have snacks on the table and we're going to be roasting s'mores later," she said, as if that were as much fun as roasting a demon.

She left us, which made sense because we probably weren't very good company. I glanced down at my cocktail like it was a foreign object. I wasn't even sure what was in a Sex on the Beach. It was cold, though.

Shiloh tossed another stick and I was tempted to walk out into the waves and see if I could feel any trace of the portal from this morning.

"Let's walk over to the party," Shiloh said, as Babydoll ran back with the stick.

"And leave the portal?" Flappy wasn't guarding it anymore. He had his head in the waves. Make that his entire body. I should probably warn him to keep his eyes peeled and his teeth snarly.

Shiloh stood in my line of vision, her pixie face a mask of determination. "Look, honey, you've got to let it go for tonight. The portal is dead right now. Finito. Ended. Do you get it? It's not even interesting to me."

No kidding? Maybe Dad listened to me and shut that part of his operation down. I smiled to myself. Ha. As if he'd be that smart. I'd certainly need more proof than an inactive portal.

Flappy dashed out of the surf with a huge chunk of driftwood. Oh, great. He was going to play, too. If he didn't brain someone first.

"Let's get another drink," Shiloh suggested. That first one sure went down fast.

I tried to hand her mine, but she refused. Instead, she took my hand and dragged me down the beach like we were in college or something. It had been fun back then, but those days seemed really far away.

Torches crackled in the sea breeze. This part of the beach smelled like smoke and dried seaweed. A girl with pigtails manned the cooler.

"Whatcha got?" Shiloh chirped.

The girl grinned. No wonder. She guarded all the goodies. "We have tequila, vodka, and rum. Mixers are in the orange cooler. Or you can help yourself to a beer."

"Beer," I said. At least I was used to that.

"Oh, no," Shiloh said, slamming the blue cooler with the beer. "You need another Sex on the Beach."

"I haven't even had one," I said, protesting as Shiloh motioned for me to try it. I did and it was actually pretty good. Sweet and easy to drink. I had another sip.

"That's the spirit," Shiloh said, opening up the coolers and mixing herself another drink like a pro.

I had to admit these were pretty tasty. I wasn't a big drinker, so I tried to slow down, but the cup was empty way too soon. Shiloh made me another. It hit the spot.

The bonfire was a huge, spitting mass of gorgeous flames and a bit of welcome warmth. Shiloh and I drew closer and watched the sparks fly up into the night sky. The crackling of the fire blended with the rush of the waves.

Then someone switched the soundtrack to the "Macarena" of all things. "I actually know this one from college," I told Shiloh.

She giggled at the mishmash of lyrics. "What are they saying?"

"No clue. That's not the point," I said, as our buddies around the fire started breaking out the dance moves.

Shiloh handed me her cup. "Teach me," she said clapping her hands together.

"No," I said, taking a sip of her drink. Mine was empty.

"Please?" she begged.

Oh, Lordy. "Watch," I told Shiloh as I joined in.

I surprised myself when a giggle escaped me. Maybe it was the silliness of the dance, or the squishy feeling of my toes digging into the sand. It was probably because Shiloh grinned at me like a wild child.

She caught on fast. It wasn't as if the Macarena was complicated. I think she liked the butt-grabbing part best, or maybe it was just that she looked so ridiculous doing it. Either way, Shiloh rocked the dance area. We became goddesses of the line dance. In our own minds, anyway.

"Repeat," I hollered after the last note sounded, which got everyone else going.

They didn't play our song again, but they did blast out the Electric Slide. I taught Shiloh that one as well. She was built for dancing, with those long legs and swingy hips. I liked how she improvised. We made up our own twists on the moves, because that's how we rolled.

I smelled popcorn, but I didn't want to stop dancing.

When it came time to grab another drink, I poured Malibu rum and pineapple juice for myself and a neighbor I'd never met from 14B. Christie had long brown hair, wore a cute maxi dress over her curves, and had two small kids and a baby at home, which was why we both agreed we hadn't met yet. Too busy. Right?

She never got out of the house. I gave us each an extra pour of rum and we toasted to a night out. To fun.

Then the "Cha-Cha Slide" came on and Christie insisted we had to go dance to that.

"Why didn't my clan do this in Vegas?" Shiloh hollered into the night.

"Because you were too busy trying to be sexy," I said, bumping into her as she bounced in place like an excited six-year-old. Stars lit the sky behind her.

Her head found my shoulder. "I'm always sexy. That's my problem."

"It's what got me in this mess," Christie agreed. "Can you believe my husband wants another one?"

"Tell him he's in charge of the night poop," Shiloh suggested. We busted out laughing.

It was so stupid. And kind of true.

Okay, I had to admit, I'd needed this. I'd needed girlfriends.

We danced until we could barely see straight. Or maybe that was the alcohol. Kidding. We weren't that drunk. I hoped.

S'mores were a challenge with everyone well into their cups, but somehow they still tasted good in spite of getting a little sand in them. Eventually talk around the bonfire swung into "girl talk" territory, and we got to chatting about our various sex lives.

Shiloh was surprisingly reticent for a succubus, but I couldn't believe some of the things I freely admitted about Dimitri to the group. Sometimes, you've just got to brag on what it's like to have your guy rip your leather skirt off. And there was the time we did it in the garden and Dimitri had to kick my underwear behind a bush when we almost got caught. The girls broke out in a chorus of screams. Apparently quite a few women had been admiring my husband on his morning jogs.

They had good taste. "Too bad, girls. He's mine." My face hurt from grinning.

My announcement was met with a bunch of groans and a marshmallow lobbed at my head.

I deserved it. I was taunting them. But damn, it felt good to get out. To appreciate what I had right here, right now.

To be alive.

Sarayh started in on a story about her ex and I realized exactly why she'd been so understanding when she thought she caught Dimitri and me on the beach this morning. Plus, she had some tips on how to go about doing the deed with minimal sand chafing.

"Are you taking notes, Shiloh?" I asked, mainly to watch her blush more.

"Come on, peeps," Sarayh said, clapping her hands. "I promised the good people of LaVista Townhomes that we'd be off the beach by eleven."

We answered her with a chorus of awws, which unfortunately didn't make a difference. Our HOA board president was a hard-ass when it came to schedules. I had to admire that.

Flappy had fallen asleep right where he'd been guarding the portal, so we left him there as the group started breaking up and everyone said their good-byes. Babydoll had amassed a small nest's worth of sticks and was curled up in the center. I let Shiloh leash the fenris as I headed toward a group of women clearing and folding the snack table.

Sarayh stood at the center, instructing. "Thanks," I said to her, genuinely meaning it. "I had a great time."

She smiled. "Good. Now take a cooler up."

Shiloh and I each grabbed an end and headed up from the beach, with Babydoll trying to break the land speed record for a fenris running uphill. I took the lead. Shiloh kept getting dragged by the beast, then bumping the cooler up against my legs, which cracked me up for no reason at all. Then laughing at something so stupid was somehow just as funny.

I wobbled my way from the beach with a permanent grin on my face. A stillness settled over the night. We listened to the soft rhythmic rush of the waves.

Sure, we could still hear voices of the cleanup crew behind us, and the lights up ahead, but it was quiet here. Peaceful. I hardly recognized it.

"That was fun," I admitted. It had been what I'd needed.

"Yeah," Shiloh said, nudging me with the cooler. "Friends?"

It wasn't a strange question, but it caught me off guard all the same. I didn't know what to say. "I guess."

"Good," she said, her voice sweet and clear in the silence of the evening. "I don't have any friends."

That struck me as unbearably sad, until I realized that since I'd left Atlanta, since I'd become a demon slayer, I'd suffered a complete lack of girlfriends as well. Yes, I had the biker witches. But as far as secret-sharing, silly-dancing, laughing-for-no-reason friends? I didn't have any either. Until that moment, I didn't realize how much I'd missed it.

The weight of the cooler pulled at my shoulder and a soft breeze blew off the ocean and tangled my hair in my face. "Friends," I said simply.

I felt it more than I saw it, but I could swear Shiloh smiled.

I did too.

CHAPTER THIRTEEN

The next morning came too early. As in, my head felt like Flappy had been using it as a beach ball.

I sat up in bed, my skull pounding in time to the *beep-beep-beep* of our alarm. It was five fifteen in the morning. Because, you know, we had to be at the witches' headquarters at sunrise. Of all the dumb ideas... I silenced the alarm with a heavy *thwack* and scrubbed a hand over my face. "I'm never going to drink again."

Dimitri flipped on the searingly bright bedside light and got up as if he had all the energy in the world. "I tried to tell you the nightcap was a bad idea."

"You fixed me more drinks?" I tried to give him a withering look, but it was hard to hate a guy who wore nothing but sexy plaid sleep pants and a smile.

He shrugged a broad shoulder. "I went to bed," he said, heading over to the closet. "You and Shiloh had margaritas and danced to Abba."

Yikes. "I do like 'Dancing Queen.'"

"Good," he said, pulling out black jeans and a T-shirt, "because you appointed yourself president of their fan club."

No kidding. My head hurt when I tried to remember. "Can I do that?"

"I wasn't going to question you." The corner of his mouth curved up. "I'm glad you had a good time."

"I did," I admitted. I didn't want to repeat the alcohol part any time soon, but I had enjoyed getting out and relaxing for an evening. Sometimes, it was easy to forget to take a second and just breathe in the midst of everything that needed to be done.

My entire body protested as I lurched out of bed. Meanwhile Dimitri had gone into the bathroom and turned on the shower. Even that sounded loud—high-pitched in a way that rattled my skull.

I'd just have to make a point to hunt down a few Advil. My husband didn't take over-the-counter drugs. His system metabolized them so quickly they didn't do any good. I rarely got sick. This was an aberration.

Which meant we probably had no drugs.

Served me right.

If I didn't feel good, I'd at least look good. I stumbled to the closet and pulled out a pair of black leather pants and a blood red bustier.

Too bad my skin was puffy. And it hurt to brush my hair.

I tossed the clothes onto the bed. This morning called for extreme measures. Or at least a huge honking glass of orange juice.

After a harrowing trip down the stairs, I found Shiloh curled up on the couch, reading an *Us* magazine. She had every single light downstairs blazing. It was brain-piercingly bright. I started turning them off while she popped up like she had a spring in her butt.

"Look at this," she said, flipping a lock of perfectly coiffed blond hair over her shoulder. "Stars are just like us. Here's Matthew McConaughey eating a pretzel."

"I'm happy for him." Bread sounded good. I needed something to settle my stomach. It felt hollow and tender at the same time. "Did you hear from your husband yet?"

She chewed at her lip. "No. I've been up all night reading magazines, trying to distract myself. But you said the witches will have answers, right?"

"I hope so." Despite her worry, she looked good. Too good. "How do you feel?" She was smaller than me, and a pitcher of margaritas was, well, a lot.

She crossed her arms over her chest. "A little nervous about the witches."

That was understandable. But her skin looked clear; her eyes were bright. She wore a pink fitted dress. Dang.

I, on the other hand, felt like my head had been stuffed with cotton. And rolled down a hill. I searched the fridge for orange juice and came up with an old can of root beer, rough with fridge crud. Better than nothing. "You handle your booze like a champ," I said, popping open my A&W.

Shiloh's eyes widened. "Oh, I'm sorry. You're hungover!" She said it as if it were the discovery of the year. She clucked. "I forget sometimes because alcohol doesn't affect me. I mean, I feel it, but then poof—it's gone."

I leaned against the counter, bracing the cool can against my head. "Must be nice."

"Don't move," she said. "I can fix this." She pulled the blender out from under the sink, then started rooting around in my fridge. "This used to be part of my job," she said over her shoulder.

Great. "Listen." I had to make one thing clear, even if my brain felt like mud. "Don't worry about the witches. They just want to help, same as you do."

She chewed on her lip and nodded. "It's just that the biker witches have a"—she searched for the right word—"reputation."

"So do half succubi." I gave her a wink, which made her smile.

I paid for it when my right eye started to twitch. Son of a bitch. I was falling apart.

Shiloh didn't notice. She was caught up in her own thoughts. "No matter how scared I am, it doesn't matter," she said, as determined as I'd ever seen her. "If I can get some kind of word about Damien, just to know he's okay, it'll be worth it."

Good for her.

Shiloh was as efficient as a master chef as she filled my blender with an overripe banana, a handful of strawberries, two blackberries, a glug-glug of apple juice, and some kind of herbs from her big yellow bag.

She hit *puree*. Then as the whirr of the metal blades gouged a hole right between my eyes, she searched through the cabinets above the sink.

Just when I was ready to curl up on the floor and call it a day, Shiloh poured a purple-pink concoction into one of my large red wineglasses. "Drink," she said, handing it to me. "It's the super hangover smoothie. The wineglass just makes it look pretty."

If you'd asked me five minutes ago, I'd have told you I'd never drink out of a wineglass again. Good thing this particular libation smelled both fruity and delicious.

I held it up in a mock toast. "If it doesn't cure me, may it at least put me out of my misery," I said, bringing it up to my lips.

Oh, yum. It tasted like berries and bananas with just a hint of zing. I tried it again. It had a definite citrusy flavor, but I hadn't seen Shiloh use any oranges or lemons.

She nodded her head. "It's good, isn't it?"

Truly, it was. But more than that, the sweet, refreshing infusion seemed to travel from my mouth, directly up into my head. The throbbing in my temples ceased. My thoughts cleared. I felt grounded, awake. Peppy, even. I could feel it, soft and sweet, traveling down my body, easing the aches and infusing me with energy. Amazing. I held up my empty glass. "What is this stuff?"

Shiloh beamed with pride. "Oh, it's a little succubus secret, handed down generation to generation."

"You should bottle it," I said, only half joking.

She snorted. "Believe me, it's been tried." She took the glass from me, holding it up to the light, no doubt admiring my ability to drain every drop. "It loses its effectiveness in two point three minutes." She rinsed the glass in the sink. "I was going to warn you, but the way you were downing it, I didn't need to."

"I know what I like," I said, spinning on one foot, trying a karate chop, feeling like a million bucks. Amazing. Little tendrils of energy zipped through my veins. "I'm queen of the world."

"You *are* something," Shiloh agreed.

I grabbed the blender, ready to move, take on the morning, or at least help her clean up the mess. Then it hit me with a jolt. My happy morning zing started to ease a notch lower.

Oh my.

My head felt clear, my energy shot sky high, and the tingle in my body had gone from zingy to downright sex-ified. I curled my hips, unable to stop myself as sparks of desire shot down my spine. I felt empty. Needy. My breasts chafed against my sleep shirt. The pleasure of it cut through me, concentrating into a heavy throb between my legs. It was all I could do not to press my thighs together to intensify the urge.

I thudded the blender back onto the counter as I battled a raging surge of pure lust that I hadn't felt since the time Dimitri and I made love for the first time in that little roadside motel. Or the time he stripped me bare and had me wet and ready as he plowed into me on that warm desert rock. Or the time I climbed on top of him and rode him hard by the ruins of an ancient altar on his family's estate in Greece.

We really should do it in a bed more often.

But right now, the man was upstairs—naked in our shower.

I rolled my hips and was rewarded with a streak of pure rapture.

Get a grip. I had to meet the witches, not jump my husband. Even if he was six and a half feet of raw Mediterranean heat and power. Even if he did growl every time I licked that sexy hollow right where his collarbone met his neck.

My fingers clenched at the marble countertops, when they should have been sliding down his shower-slicked skin. "Shiloh," I gritted out, "you want to tell me more about this potion?"

She reached past me to grab the blender. "Isn't it great? It's also an aphrodisiac."

I could picture him under the spray of the shower, the water droplets clinging to his hard pecs. "Why didn't you tell me that?"

Her shoulder hitched as she rinsed out the pitcher. "Sometimes you don't like to have fun."

I tried to ignore the heat coursing through my body. "I don't have time this morning." Although I did have to shower. And since Dimitri was already in the shower...

She shot me a look over her shoulder. "Lizzie." It came out as an accusation. "I wouldn't give you something that would mess you up." She placed the blender on a towel to dry. "I timed it out. We don't have to leave for twenty minutes. You won't be late as long as you don't dawdle." She turned to me. "If you have your man safe and whole, be thankful." The corners of her mouth lifted in a sad smile. "Take advantage."

She had a point. We were involved in a dangerous business. There was no telling what tomorrow might bring.

Shiloh wiped her hands on a towel before tossing it on the counter. "In the meantime, I still have half my magazine. I think I'll go read out on the deck with Flappy and the gang. Maybe I'll get Pirate's opinions on 'Who Wore It Best.'"

"Great," I said, heading for the stairs. I was going to do it. I was actually going to go attack Dimitri in the shower. Still, I forced myself to slow, if only for a moment. "Shiloh," I said, pausing halfway there, "thanks."

"You're welcome," she said, blushing a little as she slipped outside.

The shower blasted hard upstairs. Dimitri should have been finished by now. He didn't normally linger. Unless he was taking care of something.

I doubled my speed up the stairs, and once I made it to our bedroom, I closed the door and quickly stripped down into what God had given me.

The bathroom door was closed. I could feel the warm steam escaping.

The urge to barge in, to take what I wanted, was overwhelming. Instead, I fed my curiosity. I eased the door open.

He stood under the spray, one hand clutching the top of the clear glass shower door. His arm looked massive in that position, the firm, hard muscle flexing down over his ribcage and curving at his hip. He was built like a Greek god, a magnificent work of art.

His head was thrown back, water clinging to his spiky black hair, water trailing down his neck, over his chest, down to where he pumped a fist between his legs.

His cock thrust long and hard, his fingers curling around it, touching it the way he liked. The way he taught me. He circled the head, hissed as he drew his fist down the length and back up again.

Every corded muscle, every tendon, was locked tight, focused on his pleasure.

He was beautiful.

And he was mine.

I crossed the room and opened the shower door. He jolted, shocked out of his trance, then treated me to a wicked smile as I joined him.

The warm water sluiced over me. I breathed in the moist air, the heat, the soapy aroma of freshly washed male. "Sorry I'm late." I ran my fingers over his chest, down over his nipples and lower.

He inhaled sharply. Tilted his head down, the water clinging to his broad jaw. "I was just thinking of you."

He kissed me then, a harsh, demanding, all-consuming kiss that left no doubt as to what he had planned for me.

Thank heaven.

He pulled away. "You feeling okay?"

My fingers curled in his wet hair. "Never better." I kissed him hard, my tongue tangling with his, breathing him in, giving myself over totally.

His mouth trailed over my collarbone. His thumb flicked my breast and I gasped, drawing a leg around him, desperate to urge him closer. But as much as he looked like a statue of a god, he was also as hard to move. He took his time, circling my nipple with his thumb, watching it bead as if it were the most fascinating thing he'd ever seen.

"I was thinking of this," he murmured, his Greek accent thicker with desire. He drew his thumb down over my breast, lingering on my belly button, coasting even lower. "And this," he said, dipping into the cleft between my legs.

I thrust against him, struggled to make him go faster. He had to feel how slick I was, how ready for him.

A smile tickled his lips as he drew his fingers over my wetness. His thumb lingered on my clit, sending shocks of pleasure straight through me.

"Did you think about going faster?" I gasped as he rasped his thumb in a slow, achingly delightful circle.

"No." He pressed close, his chest scraping over the tips of my breasts. "I'm enjoying every fucking second."

This was it. He was going to kill me.

He brought his mouth down to mine for a biting, eating kiss, his fingers working magic between my legs, his body teasing me, torturing me, wrapping me up in a fury of need and want and white-hot fire until I couldn't think beyond the next moment, the next touch.

My body screamed for him. His cock felt hard and hot against my hip. I closed my fingers around him, reveling as his muscles clenched. He pulled away with a moan, both of our mouths wet from the kiss and from the water beating down over us.

"Not that way," he said, even as I drew my fingers down his length, found his balls tight and straining. "This way." He turned me against the back of the shower, and lifted me in one motion until the head of his cock found my entrance.

I tried to think of something to say and might have succeeded if I hadn't been so focused on my thighs spread over his hips, his cock at my entrance.

It was beautiful.

This time, there was no teasing. No hesitation. We both cried out as he drove deep inside me. He filled me so tight, so good. His breath rasped harsh against my ear. "You're so fucking wet."

I nipped at the hot skin of his neck, licked it. "Only for you."

A shiver ran through him. I could tell my words excited him. And they were true. This was the only man I wanted to be with. The only one I'd ever loved. And I would show him that until the day we died.

His grip tightened. He let out a strangled moan as he pumped his hips into me. I tried to roll with him, to keep up as he thrust.

He was my world, my North Star, my everything.

He kissed me hard, slid his lips down my jaw, over to my cheek. I tried to kiss him back, but my thoughts centered on the sensations that radiated from where his cock filled me. Every down thrust, he scraped my clit. Every piston of his hips, pleasure erupted everywhere my over-sensitized skin touched his.

He began losing it too. His motions became more and more erratic. His breath came in wet pants against my cheek.

I wanted to scream in triumph that I'd brought this rock of a man into a state of pure desire, of lust. My fingers dug into his shoulders, my body clenched as I reached for it, felt it. I tumbled over the edge as the pleasure turned supernova.

He shouted, or maybe that was me. It echoed off the tile walls as he erupted deep inside of me.

For several long moments, I clung to his neck. Pressed against the wall, surrounded by him. I felt safe. Loved.

He stirred, his fingers touching my cheek, nudging me up to look at him. "I love you, Lizzie Kallinikos."

He didn't need to tell me. I could see it in his expression, the warmth in his chocolate-brown eyes. But I loved hearing it all the same. "I love you too, stud."

"Stud," he laughed, his chest rumbling against mine as he helped me slide down the wall and regain my feet. "I like that," he said against my ear. "If you ever need a reminder, just let me know."

Chapter Fourteen

I was in a much better mood as we set off to see the witches that morning.

Shiloh drove her Miata convertible while Dimitri and I rode our Harleys. I didn't even take it personally when Pirate opted to ride in the open car. Yes, I could give him motorcycle-style wind to blow back his ears and shoot up his nose, but I suspected Shiloh had also packed him a few homemade doggy biscuits.

Dimitri led the way, even though I'd been to the witches' new hideout more often. Chalk it up to the Y chromosome. Or maybe I simply felt extra mellow.

At least we were early enough to avoid traffic on the 405.

We headed in the direction of Beverly Hills once more, but this time, we exited onto Pico Boulevard before I could detect any of the darkness that had invaded the city itself.

I took it as a good sign, although I wasn't naive enough to think we'd been given a reprieve. Tentacles of evil slithered outward with every vibration of energy captured, with every soul "saved."

At least we were about to do something about it.

The Pico Boulevard exit took us down into an older neighborhood of squat 1940s-era buildings, mixed in with strip malls and restaurants. A yellow-and-orange sunrise colored the sky overhead.

This place reminded me of some of the older, more comfortable neighborhoods back in Atlanta. The urban sprawl seemed to go on for miles.

The witches had holed up in an old motor inn just past the white-and-gold painted facade of Eddie's Guitar Heaven. Grandma claimed it felt like home the first time she saw it. I didn't want to argue, because their last home had been a beat-up biker bar off the New Jersey Turnpike.

We pulled into the lot behind the Cocoa Cabana, a U-shaped assembly of motel rooms made to look like beachfront bungalows. Only they were painted brown, and they were all attached, and we were in the California desert. I glanced up at the dried bundles of white yarrow hanging from the pointed rooftops. It warded off hexes, so I'd heard.

"I always figured they'd end up living over a place like Big Nose Kate's," I said to Dimitri as we shut down our Harleys. Most of the other Red Skull hangouts had been along the highway, or at least more rough-and-tumble.

He hitched a leg over his bike. "They have a new life now," he said, careful not to step in a lavender garden, "just like we do."

I glanced at Shiloh, who pulled up to a spot under a palm tree. Pirate danced around in the front seat while she untied the yellow-and-pink daisy scarf she'd used to tame her hair.

What if Dimitri was right?

What if the witches and I had grown apart, without my even realizing it?

I didn't like it. After all, the gang had always been around for me when I'd needed a hand. They usually showed up before I called. Half the time, I didn't even want them there. This time, I'd had to wait for *them*.

To be fair, I hadn't been hanging out with them as I used to, either. Dimitri and I had invited them over a few times. But we'd been focused on our own place.

But dang—the witches had been busy. They'd taken this goofy little motor inn and made it their own. Every small plot of land between the parking lot and the rooms had been turned into gardens. They'd planted spearmint and chamomile, hyssop and larkspur, and dozens of other herbs and flowers I couldn't even name. Half of them didn't even grow in the desert climate of California. Most people's gardens around here consisted of rocks, scraggly palms, dead grass, and the occasional rattlesnake. Nothing like this. There was definitely magic afoot.

Pirate sniffed among the plants, his tail poking out of the foliage. "No other dogs around here. That's nice."

Dimitri studied the dirt. "They've got crystals planted around the roots of these plants. Looks like they're staying."

"It must help them survive the arid climate." I'd have to ask. The Red Skulls had also replaced their room numbers with rune symbols, guaranteeing that they'd also spelled whoever managed this place.

"What do the runes mean?" Shiloh asked, hovering close.

"I'm not sure." First, I needed to master spell jars.

It didn't matter. The coven had been expecting us. Maybe they didn't need me the way they did when I had to save them from a demon, but they had always had my back in the past.

I knocked at the door in front of me, with a symbol that reminded me of Pac-Man. Nobody answered. I moved down to the door with a crazy-looking *B* symbol.

Nada.

Pirate stood up on his hind legs and pawed at the door. "Are you sure they're home? I don't hear anybody."

"They have to be. They're expecting us." We moved down another door. Then another.

Dimitri stood at the rear, not because he planned to go in last, but because he needed room to shift if something went wrong. That alone told me volumes.

I started to worry as well. Yes, the Red Skulls could take care of themselves, but this wasn't like them.

We moved to a door with a squiggly pear-shaped rune. This time, I didn't knock.

Perhaps announcing my presence wasn't the best idea.

Not when I had another way.

"New plan," I said, reaching into my utility belt. Shiloh watched, riveted. Dimitri didn't look so happy. "It's answer time," I said, turning to them. I held up a fat red spell about the size of my thumb. A Lock Eater.

Grandma had worked on this spell personally with me. Lock Eaters were one of the easier and more practical live spells available. They were small, portable, and able to wriggle inside a lock and disable it in ten seconds or less.

The witches tended to keep theirs in Ziploc sandwich bags, calling it the cheap and easy solution. But I had mine housed in a Ziploc snack bag, because you really didn't need full-sized bags for Lock Eaters. See? I was making improvements.

A muscle in Dimitri's jaw twitched. "You know how I feel about this."

Yes, you couldn't exactly call me a witch. We were both aware of that. But how crazy would it be for me to limit my power and abilities while a demon tried to rise up in my new home city?

Shiloh, on the other hand, gave the proper "Ooh…" response.

"His name is Houdini," I said, holding him up like a little worm. He was kind of cute, if you liked live spells.

Pirate licked his chops.

I was careful not to drop the spell as I pointed what I hoped to be the creature's nose end at the keyhole. Lock Eaters would chomp key card entries, too, but in this case it was fortunate the old motor inn hadn't updated. I didn't like the idea of smushing him flat. And real keyholes had to be tastier.

"Show us what you've got, buddy," I said, as it wriggled right in.

His backside had barely disappeared inside the lock before we heard a high-pitched *teek* from inside the door. I counted one second, two, before the tumblers fell and the lock clicked open. "Lookie there!" I said, mostly to my doubting griffin husband. "Go, Houdini," I said, as I gripped the doorknob.

It came off in my hand. Whoops.

"Is that supposed to happen?" Shiloh asked.

"No." I handed it to her. At least he'd gotten the door open. "Houdini's a little enthusiastic," I said, trying to be flip about it as the lock-plate screws loosened one by one.

That wasn't good.

"He's breaking the door," Pirate warned.

"I can see," I said, nudging him out of the way.

"That's not our door," Pirate said, refusing to let it go.

"Halt," I told the spell as screws pinged down onto the concrete at my feet. "Heel."

"You are not going to get a treat if you don't behave," Pirate warned, in his best imitation of me.

I realized with a rising sense of alarm that none of it worked. How did you get a Lock Eater to lay off? Grandma hadn't warned me about this.

Dimitri watched, shoulders stiff. "He'd better not take apart the whole hotel," he warned, in the grossest exaggeration ever.

At least I hoped so.

The lock plate fell off and still, the spell was nowhere to be seen. Then I saw the door hinges begin to loosen. Maybe Houdini would stop with the door.

Maybe not.

I mean, if the thing started disassembling everything, surely the witches would step up and stop it. If they were here. And truly, I'd followed the recipe exactly.

The problem was, we were left looking at the hole where the doorknob used to be.

"Come on," I said, shoving the door open before it fell completely off its hinges. Houdini wasn't on the other side of the door, or anywhere I could see him.

In the meantime, we'd entered the third-rate hotel room decorated in contemporary biker witch. Silver thumbtacks bit into smoke-stained, formerly white walls, supporting long swaths of dental floss that crisscrossed the room like party lights. The floss sagged with squares of colored cloth, like do-rags, only in some of the wildest colors I'd ever seen. And they smelled funny, like gunpowder and peppermint.

Thwack.

The front door had fallen out onto the porch. Lovely.

"Houdini?" I called.

"There," Shiloh said. We watched as a screw unwound itself from the front window and pinged onto the sill.

Dimitri—because he valued his life—didn't say a word.

Covering my head, I ducked under the jangle of sorcery. "Let's find the witches."

At least Shiloh was willing to let it drop. "I can't believe this is where the all-powerful Red Skulls live," she said, pausing in front of an old cabinet-model television, stacked with grocery bags full of dried herbs.

Yeah, well, right now, I didn't know where they were.

"There's a back door," Dimitri said, opening it for Pirate.

My dog dashed out into a courtyard. "Heyyyy!"

A jumbled collection of voices carried inside. They sounded scratchy, like women who'd inhaled way too much road dust over the years.

"Thank the Lord," Dimitri muttered under his breath. Okay, he was allowed that. Frankly, I felt the same way.

"Come on," I said to Shiloh, who inspected the deerskin cape tossed over an old chair. "Hopefully you won't have to wear that," I added, when she couldn't seem to let it go.

I coaxed her through the doorway and into Red Skull heaven.

It should have been a courtyard, a normal open-air part of a motor lodge with a modest pool and maybe a vending machine. But nothing was ever so straightforward with Grandma and the gang. No. They'd made this place their own.

It was Route 66 meets Harley babes meets Witchcraft 101.

I noticed the pool first. They'd turned it into a perfect conduit for water magic. Homemade clay chalices lined the edges, filled with coral-colored sea salt. No doubt they'd scattered sacred salt over the water as well. A fountain made of colorful pots full of stones and crystals stood at the center. Water streamed down the rocks and onto fragrant water lilies and vines.

The water glistened, clear and vibrant. This was a sacred pond.

Surrounded by lounge chairs.

Pots of lilac, sage, and hibiscus dotted the concrete expanse and I saw that the witches had begun digging up one side of the courtyard to expose the earth underneath.

A massive wall of ivy rose up from the back. The tangled vines stretched all the way to the sides of the U-shaped building, guaranteeing total privacy from the neighborhood. Smaller pots of herbs formed rambling walkways, and tables loaded with jars of all sizes crowded the vending machine area. I'd never seen anything like it.

"Look up," Dimitri said.

I cast my eyes toward the heavens and saw a gorgeous pink-and-orange sunrise.

This was an ideal place for the witches to gather. And even though a part of me protested the destruction of somebody else's run-down motor inn, the other part was so happy they'd found a place to love and to tend.

The hotel owner would never have to worry about vacancies or protection as long as the Red Skulls were here.

Several dozen witches gathered in small groups, murmuring incantations as they tied the colorful do-rags on each other's heads. Others selected herbs from pots. They were getting ready for something.

But it was Grandma who had me rooted to the spot. She stood up from where she'd been sorting what appeared to be some kind of teeth into colorful glass jars. "Stay right there," she ordered.

She wore her usual black leather pants and a *Kiss My Asphalt* T-shirt, but I noticed something different about her—a power in her demeanor, an elevation in how she walked and moved.

She'd even braided her long gray hair. As she drew close, I could see she'd woven some kind of pink and silver thread into her braids as well, making a sparkly, vibrant, altered version of my grandmother that I wasn't sure what to do with.

"Is that tinsel?" I asked, when she stopped in front of me.

She frowned as she absently reached over to scratch the sagging tattoo of a phoenix on her arm. "You got a demon rising up in Beverly Hills and you want to talk to me about my hairdo?"

"What do you have planned?" Dimitri asked, quite boldly in my opinion. He'd never been invited to any of the witches' ceremonies before.

At least Grandma respected that. She gave him a curt nod. "High communion with the universe."

His brow furrowed. "Which means?"

Grandma frowned. "Secret and scary shit."

"What were you doing last night?" I asked. The burn marks on the concrete made it clear they'd had some ceremonies here recently. I hoped we didn't have more to worry about than the Earl of Hell.

The grin Grandma gave us had an exuberant, slightly maniacal edge. "We've grown more powerful. It's amazing what rooting yourself in one spot, focusing your power, can do."

"It's a fantastic space," I said, glancing out at the courtyard.

"We're going to use it," she said solemnly. "We need to look deep, go beyond, so we can give you the tools you need to kill this demon once and for all." Grandma turned to Dimitri. "Sorry to say, it's coven only."

"I wouldn't expect anything less," my husband replied, without a trace of irony. I had to admit he'd always been one to support me, even if he didn't understand witchcraft.

"Good man," she murmured, before turning to eyeball me. "What I don't get is the she-demon."

I glanced back to Shiloh and Pirate, walking along the ivy wall. "Half demon," I said, waving them over. "She has information on the second coming of the Earl of Hell."

"Damn it," Grandma said, as if I'd just told her somebody dinged her Harley.

"She's married to a demon slayer," Dimitri explained, waving her over.

Grandma shook her head, as if it were old news. "I know who she is."

"He might be in trouble," I added.

Grandma stared at Shiloh, as if in doing so, she could see *into* her. I'd been on the receiving end of that look before. It was intimidating as hell and it didn't help Shiloh relax in the slightest as she approached us.

"Hi." The half demon gave a small, uncomfortable wave.

Grandma shoved a hand at her. "Gertie. Head of the Red Skulls."

Shiloh took her hand. "Shiloh McBride. I'm married to Damien."

"Who is missing," Grandma said bluntly.

Shiloh paled.

"Grandma," I urged. She was as subtle as a sledgehammer.

"What?" Grandma said, "We're going to help," she added, as if the petite blonde wasn't shaking half out of her gourd. She clapped Shiloh on the shoulder. "You relax. We don't bite." Her mouth split into a wide grin. "Much."

Shiloh steadied her shoulders. "I'm ready to do what it takes."

"Atta girl." Grandma nodded. "Okay. Let's do this." She rubbed her hands together. "Dimitri, we'll need you to wait outside with Pirate."

"Right." He gave me a hard kiss. "Stay out of trouble." He scooped up the dog and walked backward, heading for the door, when he called to Grandma, "There's also a spell loose—"

"This one?" Grandma asked, pulling Houdini out of her pocket. "Or that one?" she asked, pointing to a jar by the pool, where my Mind Wiper pressed flat against the glass. "We'll talk about it later," she said, even as Houdini curled in her palm like a contented cat. She slipped him into her pocket. "Right now, we got shit to do."

Chapter Fifteen

Grandma clapped one hand on my shoulder and the other on Shiloh's as she steered us toward the sacred pond. "Tell us about your link to the demon," she said to my new friend.

As if that weren't direct enough, Shiloh almost tripped when Frieda and a curly-haired senior citizen witch named Ant Eater burst into the courtyard hauling a metal cart, its contents cloaked with a purple cloth.

Grandma nudged me with an elbow. "Secret side door," she said proudly.

Frieda gave me a wave. Ant Eater didn't bother. She wasn't the type.

Meanwhile, Shiloh cleared her throat. "Our clan wanted the Earl to come." Her gaze lingered on Ant Eater, as if wondering exactly whom she'd gotten mixed up with. "Our seer linked into his power in order to learn more. It was forbidden, but she wanted to know the signs."

"Good," Grandma said, stopping to look Shiloh in the eye. "I assume the demons in your coven shared power with you, even though you're a half breed?"

If the question embarrassed Shiloh, she didn't let on. "Yes," she said simply.

Grandma nodded. "So that means you have access to the link."

Shiloh's gaze traveled back to the covered tarp. "More now than ever, since I'm the only one left."

I nodded. I'd killed the rest of Shiloh's coven in Las Vegas. "We'll also try to see where Damien is," I told her, eyeing the way the rest of the witches were giving my new friend a wide berth. "Hopefully give you some peace of mind." I had no doubt she could do this. Shiloh was strong enough. "Just follow the Red Skulls' lead and we'll do just fine."

Grandma planted her hands on her hips, amused. "Well thanks, Lizzie. Now I really hope it doesn't blow up in our faces."

Shiloh looked a little startled. "How dangerous is this?"

"Very," Grandma said, studying me. "Not saying I won't move forward. I'm just surprised Lizzie is so gung ho." She looked me up and down. "You never used to be this bold."

A cool breeze blew in from the north. "Maybe." I rested my hands on my hips. We were in a precarious position here. Sometimes that meant stepping outside myself, taking a risk. "I've learned there's more to this world than me and what I want."

Grandma barked out a laugh. "I can't argue with that." Just as quickly, she lost her humor. "Still, linking into demon energy is a damn good way to fuck this up."

The wind blew in harder, tangling in my hair. "Or save us."

The witches moved in teams now, clearing chairs and colorful pots away from the sacred pond. Frieda and two others brought in large slabs of redwood. They were preparing for the ceremony. Yes, it was dangerous, but we had to work with the cards we were dealt.

Besides, there were good things that had come out of this demon connection. Grandma had to know that. I motioned for her to take a short walk with me. It's not like we could go far. "Listen," I said, "I might not have pressed so hard, gotten back there, and found my dad if it hadn't been for Shiloh's warning. I might not have learned my dad is in league with the Earl of Hell." It hurt to even say it, but there it was.

She gritted her jaw. "You're in its path now. It knows you're here."

"Only if my dad betrayed me."

Grandma gave me a sideways look. Yeah. Of course my dad would betray me.

Frieda and her compatriots began to assemble a wood structure in front of the pond. They bolted the solid pieces together into a beautiful, rough-hewn altar. They'd burned an elaborate pentacle into the center. I watched as Leggy Lucy, the new head of ceremonies, placed four iron candleholders at points representing the north, south, east and west.

"I'd like to go into the Cave of Visions," I told her, trying not to cringe as I said it. The Cave of Visions was a place apart that could be created only by the Red Skulls and their magic. It was dangerous and dark, an alternate reality where the veil thinned and the darkness could reach through.

Sometimes, it was the only way to see what truly threatened us, and in this case—see how to defeat it.

I braced myself, ready to argue if I had to. I'd been taken by a demon once while in the cave. A different time, Grandma had been sucked down to hell. But we did it because we couldn't have banished the darkness any other way.

"No," Grandma said.

Ha. No. Not going to accept that answer. "You and I both know it's the logical thing to do, even if it is risky. I've never seen you back away from danger before."

Grandma barked out a laugh. "It's not that." She glanced over at Frieda, who stood behind the altar, placing thick red candles in each of the holders. "Truth be told, we've moved beyond the Cave of Visions." She squared her shoulders, as if the idea still didn't quite fit. "Once the sun has crested, we'll begin the Seer's Ceremony. We can draw on the power of the entire coven." She gritted her teeth. "Trust me. It'll be even more intense."

Yeek. "And now I'm bringing a demon link into it." The Cave of Visions scared me enough. This, from what Grandma described, was on an entirely different level. I tried to tamp down the niggling of warning in my gut and go with the facts. "We don't have a choice."

"I like your style," said a witch in a wheelchair. Sidecar Bob had his long gray hair tied back in a ponytail and a birdcage on his lap as he dodged past us. "Three yellow warblers," he said, handing it to Frieda, who placed them on the altar. "They're drawn to magic," Bob said to Shiloh, as if that would assure her. "Wild animals have a strength all their own. They're the most powerful creatures to take into a ceremony like this." He caught Grandma's eye as he headed back. "I doubled the wards."

"Double them again," Grandma told him. She softened when Bob shot her a disbelieving look. "Try," she muttered. "We have no idea what's going to happen."

Bob turned to the she-demon, who was busy chewing on one of her nails. "Want to help me pick some sage?" he asked.

Shiloh looked relieved. "Yes. Thanks. I—" She searched for an explanation, a way to fit in.

Bob grinned. "Come on, then."

When they were out of earshot, I turned back to Grandma. "You said you have more power and that's a good thing."

She nodded. "It is. We just have to figure out how to harness it."

Forgive me, but that was an important detail. "You've never tried this new version before, have you?"

She swore under her breath. "We never had a reason. Besides, it's not like you're doing it by the book, either."

I looked out over the witches as they finished tying their headscarves. Several were now lying prone on the ground, meditating.

"Shiloh can hold her own." I hoped. "She's stronger than she looks." Her desire to please tended to tie her in knots. It made her awkward at times, but that didn't mean people should underestimate her.

"You like her," Grandma said. I could tell that surprised her.

"Yes." She had a good heart. And she'd been willing to put herself out there, to give what she could in the name of love and friendship. How could I not respect that?

Frieda tapped Grandma on the shoulder. "It's time."

I left Grandma and headed over to where Shiloh heaped large handfuls of sage onto Bob's lap. "Now," I said.

"You'll do great," he said to her. "You'll see."

For a second, I thought she'd hug him. "It's what I hear," she said, waving good-bye.

I'd have to thank Bob later. He'd been the first one to give me a welcome when I joined the witches. I'd considered it a small thing, really. But seeing it again, I realized it wasn't. A minor kindness could make all the difference.

It hadn't been that long since I'd been an outsider. I still felt like it from time to time.

Shiloh lingered close. "I didn't mean to listen in on you back there."

I gave her the hairy eye.

She gripped my arm. "Okay, maybe I did," she said quickly. "But it was freaky. I could see the sky darkening behind you."

"What?" I asked, before she pointed. Roiling thunderclouds had formed to the south.

"Not only that, but the air is shifting," she hissed. She was right. It had grown heavier. I don't think she blinked the entire time I was talking to her. "This is freaking me out. Where are Pirate and Dimitri?"

"Gone," I told her.

She looked as if she'd give anything to join them, no matter where they were.

The Red Skulls didn't form a circle, as I'd seen them do in other ceremonies. This time, they scattered in what would have felt like a random pattern, if only the witches hadn't been so precise.

Then it hit me. They were forming a human pentagram, surrounding the water.

Everyone had a place, a role to play. Including Shiloh and me.

"We can do this," I said. I hoped. "But the ceremony is going to require both of us to focus our strength." I took her hands. Squeezed them. "Together." I leveled a steady gaze at her. "A demon is using mortals. We need to know his weaknesses, tap into his power source." Shiloh was our perfect portal. "When the veil is lifted, we can also look for Damien." I didn't want to say it, but she knew: if a demon had him, it was likely the others knew about it as well.

"I'll try my best," she said. It came out as more of a question.

"You're not doing it alone," I assured her. "We only need you to help us focus our energy on the darkness."

It hurt her, I could tell. "I'm not dark anymore," she said quietly.

"You can be." We both knew it. "Please," I added. "Just once more."

She looked me in the eye and I caught the fiery red tint to her pupils. "Okay."

"Right." I kept my shoulders back and my voice steady as I led Shiloh to the altar. "Just…not yet."

We passed by Frieda, who shook her head. "We're using a demon in order to find a demon. You know how messed up that is?"

I kept going. "Half demon, and I appreciate Shiloh for trying to help us."

Her skin began to tingle where I touched her, as if it were electrically charged. "I have a stake in this too," she shot back over her shoulder to Frieda.

We pushed forward, directly toward Creely, the engineering witch. A lock of Kool-Aid-red hair fell over one eye. She didn't seem to notice. "The worst part is, the half demon knows where we are, where we worship."

Shiloh drew back, like a cobra ready to strike. "If you didn't trust me, why'd you let me in?"

"I didn't." Creely drew a small bottle of powder out of her bra.

I blocked her with my hand. "Don't screw with us, Creely."

She lifted her chin. "Us?"

I grabbed the bottle. Creely twisted my arm, trying to wrestle it back.

"Stop," Grandma commanded.

We both let go and the bottle smashed onto the pavement. A whoosh of green powder surged up into the night. I didn't even want to know what that was.

"Get back into line," Grandma ordered Creely. She frowned at all three of us. "You two," she said, pointing at Shiloh and me, "we need you up on the altar."

The sky had grown even darker to the south. A strong wind whipped through the courtyard, chilling me. It stopped directly behind the motel. Whatever it was, the wards held it back. For now.

"Get on it, Bob," Grandma said, ascending the altar, motioning for us to follow.

"Righto." He clattered toward the mounting storm, running over Creely's foot on the way.

"Son of a bitch!" The engineering witch yelped as Bob's chuckle floated in the early morning air.

We needed this done. For better or worse. My mouth went dry as we ascended one step, two, until we stood behind Grandma. She braced her hands on the altar in front of her and raised her voice to address the witches. "Don't look behind you. Don't give it power. Yes, this scares the pee out of me too. Especially against a demon as powerful as the Earl of Hell. We hadn't planned on bringing a demon along, either. Still, follow my lead and we'll survive this."

Shiloh gripped my hand tighter. "You promise?"

Grandma turned, gave her a hard look. "I can never do that."

Chapter Sixteen

The sky grew darker by the second. Thunderclouds rolled in from the south. Winds tore at us from the north.

Grandma raised her voice. "Seal the circle."

A hush fell over the coven. The witches parted for Frieda, who walked slowly, deliberately, to the altar, her arms aloft, carrying the skull of a goat.

Shiloh cringed. It was kind of ugly—mostly bone with half its teeth missing and a patch of dried skin stretched over part of the top and flapping near the right eye socket.

I leaned close and whispered against her hair. "My Great-Aunt Evie used it in her ceremonies. It'll help us focus our strength."

She shivered. "And you call us creepy."

Okay, that was fair.

Hades. It was getting dark quick. Something knew we were coming.

I squeezed Shiloh's hand. She squeezed back.

The witches closed their eyes and I felt the magic build. The air grew heavier. It prickled against my skin as they began a low, rhythmic chant. I couldn't make out the words, but it sounded ancient. Powerful.

The witches' voices lowered as the air grew warmer. The only sound now came from their chanting and the bubbling of the fountain at the center of the pool.

The birds gripped nervously at their perches and flapped their wings in the cage on the altar, as if they desperately wished to fly away. It was too late for them, and for us. The thick red altar candles cast tall shadows that grew closer and closer.

Sacrifice.

The word stuck in my mind.

It was the only thing that would make a difference against the darkness we faced.

Grandma bowed her head. "We, the witches of the Red Skull, are bound to the magic that has sustained our line for more than twelve hundred years. In it, we find warmth, light, and eternal goodness. Without it, we perish."

She paused as the clouds began to roll over us, blocking out the sun. "As we gather on this sunrise, this new beginning, we ask for the power to see beyond what is visible, to reach beyond the veil, to touch the evil that threatens us."

My hand felt clammy. Yes, I was ready to draw closer to the Earl of Hell. It was the only way to see what was truly happening. But having it stated plainly made me nervous all the same. Now I'd involved the witches. And Shiloh.

Still, how many more innocents would suffer if we *didn't* get answers?

A yellow bird raised up in a panic, tried to take flight, its wings beating against the others. The others bumped against him, wings flapping, erupting into a frantic flurry of shrieks.

Shiloh stiffened. "What are the birds for?" she whispered.

"To cheat the demon." Hopefully. They'd made me use guppies from Walmart in the past. "They're enchanted to be kind of like those canaries they used to take down into mines. An evil spirit tries to take you, it gets the bird instead."

At least that was how it had worked before. And we'd needed every damned one of them.

Tall flames erupted from the blood red candles.

Goose bumps raced up my arms as the air temperature plunged. The water in the sacred pool began to bubble, as if it were a pot set to boil.

Shiloh gripped my hand tighter. Her skin glowed orange.

I nudged her. "You okay?"

"Peachy," she said through clenched teeth.

The scent of sulfur tinged the air and I could feel the ominous, cloying touch of evil. Or maybe that was just my new friend.

The courtyard was dark as midnight. *Breathe.* Sweat chilled on my skin.

The witches' chanting grew louder, their faces lit by the climbing flames of the candles.

"Hold steady," Grandma called out. "We ask to see," she shouted. "We ask to know."

Water roiled in the sacred pool. It spit large, fat drops. They stung like hot bacon grease. "We ask to *see* the Earl of Hell!"

It was insane.

An invitation to damnation.

We were doing the right thing. I had to trust. Had to believe in the power of the witches or I would have been tempted to flee the cursed ceremony and never come back. The birds beat against the cage, desperate to take flight. There were two of them now, one dead, its lifeless yellow wings tangled in the wires of the cage.

The Red Skulls spoke in a rhythmic language I'd never heard, their words washing over me as I focused on the orange and blue flames of the candles. They danced on blackened wicks, like beacons in the darkness.

My blood turned cold as an image slowly took form over the sacred pool. Hellfire and damnation. I really wasn't looking forward to seeing the Earl. Or anything else that in a perfect world would be dwelling far down in the depths of hell.

My breath came in spurts, each exhale a cloud in the rapidly freezing air as the image took shape.

He appeared as a man. Beautiful, ethereal, with curling blond hair and a face like an angel's. His lips were generous, his cheekbones sculpted, marred only by a hairline scar that trailed from his left eye.

He tilted his head and turned to me, coy. Waiting.

His blue eyes caught mine and I felt it down to my core. Just as quickly, his presence faded away.

"Shit. He slipped the noose." Grandma threw up her arms and I could almost see the power arcing between them. Her breath came hard. Her voice was tight. "Get him, Lizzie. Shiloh! Everybody—we need a connection!"

I focused on the Earl with all my strength, his churning darkness and his deceptive light. I willed him into existence here, right now. I urged the universe to keep a part of him on this plane.

But he was strong, slippery. I could hear his laughter as I lost my grip on him and he disappeared into the mist.

"I got something," Shiloh groaned. Her eyes were closed, her skin glowing. Energy radiated from her like cold flame.

She shook violently. I gripped her hand, tried to lend her my own strength, my focus. My heart slammed in my throat.

Two birds lay at the bottom of the cage. Dead.

An image flickered. A woman in red.

Cripes. It was the dead succubi seer.

"Pull her in," Grandma ordered.

I closed my eyes and willed it to be so. I focused on the power of the succubi, the intent of the she-demons.

To make the Earl of Hell's intentions known.

I forced my mind to calm, my breathing to grow even. I wound my mind through the space like swimming through cold, dark water. I opened myself to Shiloh's dark side, her power. The glow of her orange hand against mine. I used it to make us both stronger.

The woman appeared hazy before us. She was bald. A beautiful gold scarf settled over her shoulders. Her fingers glittered with jewels. Her eyes blazed red with the power of the underworld. The Earl of Hell swirled in a mist behind her, beyond our reach. But not far from hers.

"*He speaks*," she said, her voice echoing over time and dimensions.

The seer closed her eyes, savoring his presence.

"*I will come when the fallen angel builds my church.*"

A smile stole over her lips.

"*I will come with the energy of six hundred sixty-six souls.*"

She stared directly at me.

"*I will come through the wall of death.*"

A dark portal swirled behind her. Every demon slayer instinct I had recognized it instantly. Screamed for me to leap headlong at it. It was a direct gateway to the underworld.

That was the one that the Earl was using to funnel his power. That was his instrument, his *wall of death*.

"Show us more," I ordered.

Shiloh gritted her teeth, pushed until her skin glowed bright.

The portal churned darker, larger, and I saw what surrounded it: a dungeon, cages, and, yes, above it— my dad's church.

Enchanted locks guarded the entrances to the catacombs. Their purple energy lit up the night. Powerful wards crisscrossed the space like the latest laser security system. The demon had built a flipping fortress under the old movie theater.

It had appeared so harmless from the street. But below, its power was all-consuming.

"How many souls does he have?" I demanded.

The seer grinned and placed a finger over her lips.

The Earl swirled behind her, angry now.

"It is safe," she assured us. "No one can enter without the blessing of the Earl or the angel."

My dad was no angel.

Then it hit me. Why had she told us that? It seemed like too much. Holy hell. The truth of it seized in my gut. "She's keeping us here."

"Where's my husband?" Shiloh pushed. "Where's Damien?"

The seer laughed.

We had to get out of there.

Now.

My mind hurtled back to the Seer's Ceremony. A violent wind buffeted the courtyard, spraying stinging water and dirt. All three birds lay dead.

Grandma reached for us in a blind panic. An unseen force held her back. She lingered just beyond the veil. She yelled. I couldn't hear her above the winds.

Shiloh's eyes blazed red as she communed with the succubus.

"Pull out!" I ordered.

A hole opened up where the seer had been. It sucked at us. I heard the dead succubus laughing.

It was a trap.

We'd gotten too close.

Shiloh didn't see it. Grandma and the witches were too far away.

I grabbed for my friend. We'd needed Shiloh, had to have her in order to connect with the succubus who knew the truth. But the presence of even a half demon, the power, had thrown us into a tailspin.

The candles fell. The altar crumbled. My aunt's goat head was dragged into the mist. I struggled against the power of the succubus, against the Earl of Hell, as Shiloh let out a piercing scream.

Time slowed. The air around us felt like soup.

We had to move, had to escape, or the gaping black hole would suck us down. But we had nowhere to run. Shiloh refused to move and I realized with a start that she was holding it back—or trying to.

The opening grew with every second I stared in horror. I tried to step back, to the side, but my body wouldn't move that way. We could only move forward, into the abyss. It had us trapped.

Unless...

"Go!" I pulled her with me, forced her to follow as I hurled us both forward, under the gaping, swirling chasm and into the roiling waters of the sacred pond.

The water stung like acid. It ate at my skin. Shiloh thrashed against me in the water as I forced her to stay under, to endure. It was the only way to escape the storm above and frankly I'd rather boil alive than be sucked into the darkness. Or worse, the clutches of the Earl.

My lungs burned, my body stung. I closed my eyes tight. Forced myself to stay under.

I thought of little Pirate. Dimitri. They'd gotten out. They'd survive this, even if I didn't.

Icy talons ripped at my hair, tearing it, trying to take me. I swam for the bottom, forcing Shiloh with me.

Another body plunged into the pit with us, then another. They hit the water like depth charges. I couldn't see anything. I only knew I was surrounded.

But I had nowhere to go.

An unknown force gripped me under the arms and dragged me to the surface. I reached for my switch stars before my hand was shoved away, yanked up and out of the water. My face broke the surface and I took a long pull of frigid air, the water burning my mouth and tongue.

My captor struggled to subdue me. "Stop fighting, Lizzie!" More arms wrangled me. "For fuck's sake!"

I opened my eyes, choking, my throat burning, my lungs dry. Through the sting of the water, I saw Ant Eater. She had my hands. Grandma had my back. They were sopping wet and scared as hell. I forced the words out between gasps for air. "Where's Shiloh?"

"She's out," Grandma said.

"Taken?" I shook off Ant Eater's grasp and whipped around to see Frieda and Bob hauling her from the pool. Thank God. "What the hell happened?" I tried to ask. It came out as a choking garble. I looked up, fighting the stinging water as I wiped my eyes.

The demon's vortex had vanished. In its place hung a sky thick with clouds.

Ant Eater still felt the need to hold me up. I shook out of her grasp.

"It tried to take you," she said. "You jumped into the sacred pool and burned the evil off." She snorted, looking like a drowned rat. "It was the scariest fucking light show I've ever seen."

Grandma shoved up against the side of the pool and dragged herself out, her shirt and leather pants streaming with water. She sat on the edge, as winded as I was. "Your friend Shiloh here saved you."

Shiloh stood at the edge of the pool, wrapped in a towel, looking like Daryl Hannah in that mermaid movie. Was it too much to ask that she look as bedraggled as I felt?

Ant Eater pulled herself out of the water as well. "Shiloh closed the vortex."

"Then you tried to drown her," Grandma added.

"I did not." The water no longer burned. In fact, it felt cool against my irritated skin. I thought we were escaping.

I studied my arms. There were no marks from the burning, only pink, irritated skin. It looked as if I'd loofahed too much.

Shiloh clutched the towel around her closer. "I had to cut off the power. So I did," she said, as if she couldn't quite believe she'd done it.

Frieda, who had used the stairs to get out of the pool, made her way behind the she-demon. "You're stronger than you look." Shiloh watched her, wary. Good call, because Frieda hadn't finished yet. "You're also good."

It made me glad the witches realized that. Well, except for Grandma. She'd known all along. I let Grandma stand up before I hauled myself out of the water. Nobody offered me a towel, but frankly, I didn't care. The cold helped me focus.

"Clean up," Grandma ordered the witches. "We'll figure out what to do next."

It still amazed me how cavalier these women could be about a demon attack. Then again, when I'd first met them, they had been on the run from a demon for thirty years.

Shiloh and I, along with Ant Eater and Frieda joined Grandma near the remains of the ruined altar. We stood in a small circle as the witches began cleanup work around us.

I touched Shiloh's arm. "Any word on your husband?"

She took a deep breath, let it out. "Just a big black hole."

"I'm sure he's okay," I told her. I mean, if he wasn't, she'd have seen that, right?

"I don't think he is," Shiloh said, with the certainty of a wife.

I hoped to God she was wrong.

Grandma scratched her head, the tinsel in her hair sopping, but unspoiled. "So what have we learned?"

Other than how fucked up things were? "The Earl of Hell knows about me," I said. Or at least he hadn't been surprised to see me.

"We knew that," she answered. She crossed her arms over her chest. "Now it seems they're aiming for six hundred sixty-six souls. At least they haven't gotten there yet."

"Yet," Shiloh repeated. "Six hundred sixty-six isn't a lot."

Frieda's eyes bugged. "It isn't?"

"Not in LA," Shiloh said, drawing off the towel and tossing it over her shoulder. "Trust me."

I leaned in closer. "Okay, well if they're drawing the power through that dark portal in the church basement, we need to shut that down."

"Well yeah," Ant Eater said. "You saw it, though. It's locked tight."

Frieda nodded. "We already tried to sneak in. Didn't work. You heard what the seer said. You have to be *let* in."

Oh, sure. No problem. My throat still stung from the water and I cleared it. "Let's keep this in the realm of possibility." Truly. "There's no way the Earl of Hell is going to let any one of us in. Even Shiloh."

"Agreed," Grandma said. "But your dad will let you in."

She might as well have doused me with a bucket of stinging water.

No, he wouldn't.

Okay, maybe he said he would, but it was a ridiculous thought. "I can't join with my dad. I already told him to go to hell." Not literally, of course. I didn't want to encourage the man. But, "He knows I'm not on his side."

Grandma shook her head, as if she'd already come to a decision. A nutso one. "You have to convince him otherwise," she said, pointing a finger at me. "You have to go back to him and say you've changed your mind."

Oh yeah. Right. "He'll never buy it."

"Then make him believe," Ant Eater urged. Great. Her, too. "Gertie's right. You have to convince him you'll work with him. It's the only way."

This was crazy. "The demon knows I'm here."

"Exactly," Shiloh said. "He's growing more powerful by the day. You saw it."

Of course I did, but—

"Once you're in, you can get us past your dad," Grandma said.

"Oh hell," I said.

Ant Eater nodded. "Exactly."

"I'm a terrible actor," I told them. "There's no way he's going to think I suddenly changed my mind."

"Then you'd better be real convincing," Grandma warned. "It's the only way, Lizzie. We need to stop this."

We did and we would. Even if my dad was the last person on Earth I wanted to see.

CHAPTER SEVENTEEN

I retreated to the rear of the courtyard and faced the wall of ivy as I dialed my dad's cell number. All the while, I kept trying to think how I could possibly convince him I'd work with him, that I'd want to draw closer to him and the Earl of Hell.

I shivered and told myself it was the result of standing around once again wearing wet leather. This demon slayer business had never been easy on the wardrobe.

I chewed on my lip as the phone rang once, twice. I wasn't sure I even wanted him to answer. Things were much better when I'd cut him out of my life.

My dad was dangerous. He didn't think like a sane, logical person.

I toyed with the ivy on the wall.

When I'd saved him the last time, any reasonable person would have taken that second chance at life and run. But Dad had gone back to the demon and doubled down. He was like a bad gambler, one who didn't want to quit and couldn't believe he'd lose in the end.

He answered on the fifth ring. "Who...? Who ish this?" He sounded drunk, or high.

I glanced behind me, as if I could possibly escape this, and saw Frieda lingering close, placing a pot of sage less than a yard away, as if she absolutely had to be within earshot.

I gave her a sharp look. "Get lost."

"Real nice," my dad said, shaking off the cobwebs. "You wake me up before ten in the morning and you insult me." His voice still dragged, but at least he wasn't under the influence. Who knew he wasn't a morning person? Not me.

"I wasn't talking to you," I said, wiping at my phone. My ear sweated against the glass and we'd barely started the conversation.

Frieda wrinkled her brow. "That didn't sound too friendly," she whispered, scooting the pot to follow me when I moved away from her.

Like I needed the peanut gallery right now. I walked away, toward the vending machine, using full strides now, moving faster than she could inch that pot.

Frankly, it surprised me that Dad wasn't out of bed yet. After my run-in with the Earl, I would have thought they'd be in contact, coming up with a plan to zap me.

I ran a hand through my hair. "I'd like to talk," I said to my father. "I don't like how we left things yesterday."

"Is that so?" he asked, his voice sounding far away. He was noncommittal, overly casual. I heard the bedsprings creak as he sat up.

I dug my boot into the dirt near a cluster of lavender.

Maybe Dad wasn't as tight with the Earl as he'd claimed. It wouldn't be unusual for the man to exaggerate. Or flat-out lie.

This entire thing made me nervous. I had no idea what to say next.

Less than twenty-four hours ago, I'd told him to get lost, that I'd never be on his side. Now I had to do a complete flip-flop. I didn't know how I'd convince him I'd changed my mind. Yes, Dad was a reckless jerk, but he wasn't an idiot.

I could almost hear the indecision on the other end of the line, the mistrust.

Ant Eater wheeled the purple-draped cart out of the ceremonial area at about zero miles an hour. If she hadn't been careful, she'd have grazed my back. I ignored her.

At last, my dad spoke. "What do you want, Lizzie?" His tone was cold, calculated.

I watched the breeze play over the wall of ivy and I tried to play it cool. Relaxed. "I'd like to come by the church. Can you meet me there?"

He let out a low laugh that I didn't like at all "Let's make this more social." I heard ice hit a glass, the sound of a drink being poured. He'd better not be *drinking* drinking. Then again, I supposed it wasn't my problem. "Meet me at the Lynx at noon," he said, taking an audible sip.

"What's that?" I asked, hoping it was on Google Maps.

"Just be there," he said before hanging up.

I double-checked my cell phone, making sure the line had indeed been severed.

Fine. I'd take what I could get.

At least he'd hung up before either of us could change our minds.

I turned around and was startled to find Grandma and Frieda standing directly behind me. "Geez, people."

Grandma wore her rhinestone-studded readers. "The Lynx Club?" She asked, lowering her glasses. "On Sunset Boulevard?"

"You know it?" I asked. Hell, for all I knew, she'd partied there. Grandma and the gang got out more than I did, and there was a ton of nightclubs on the Strip.

I planted my hands on my hips. I just hoped this one opened at noon. Then again, I'd be willing to bet Dad knew his watering holes.

On one hand, I was glad he'd agreed to see me so soon. On the other, I really wished he'd have let me into his church. He probably didn't want me anywhere near the evil vortex that we now knew was located in the basement. I had to figure out a way to get down there and destroy it.

"Want me to lend you an outfit?" Frieda asked, glancing down at my soaked leather.

I wasn't sure how to respond to that. In the past, she'd lent me pants that zipped up on the sides and over the crotch, as well as a neon-orange top full of badly designed holes (I'd worn it with a sports bra), and a black barely there thong with "My Vibrator Has Two Wheels" embroidered on it (I went commando instead).

"What? Is this place so stuck-up you can't drip on the floors?" I asked, a little desperate and, well, it was kind of funny. Right?

Grandma didn't get the humor. "Don't fuck around, Lizzie."

"Yeah, yeah." I knew. For the good of mankind and all.

I just wished Frieda hadn't been so happy as she ushered me off to her room. Long nails caressed my back as she gently led me toward the motel. "Come on, Cinderella."

"I hate to break it to you, but where I'm going is a lot more twisted than any meet-a-guy-and-marry-him ball."

She simply laughed.

Shiloh was helping Ant Eater and a few of the other witches clean up planter pots that had turned over in the ceremony. She gave me an envying look as we passed. "Can I maybe get some dry clothes, too?"

I was about to say no when Frieda of all people gave pause. "What the hell?" she said. "You did good enough today." She gave the blonde she-demon a mock once-over. "I've got a corset I grew out of a couple years ago. I'll bet it'd look darlin' on you."

Well, yay for open minds. Although I was forced to point out as we followed her to her room, "You never gave me a corset."

"You look better in animal prints," Frieda said. "I don't have any corsets like that"— she considered the dilemma—"although maybe we could make one for you."

"You know what? Don't worry about it," I said. I did fine on my own.

Frieda opened the door to a hotel room with an earlobe-shaped rune on the door.

"What one is that?" Shiloh asked.

"Made it up myself," Frieda said, pushing inside. "It means vibrancy."

That was one word for it. Another word was *disaster*. It looked like a tornado hit her room. There were clothes on the bed, draped over the television. Plastic costume jewelry necklaces over loaded every doorknob. Motorcycle boots and flirty platform wedges in all colors lined the walls. Some of the shoes came very close to fitting my definition of hoochy-mamma stripper heels.

"Those are so exotic!" Shiloh said, rushing over to a pair of clear plastic heels with at least a two-inch lift to the underside of them. Add the five-inch heels and we were entering break-your-neck territory. She held them as if they were the most gorgeous things on earth. They had orange straps and fake goldfish in the heels. At least I hoped the fish were plastic. They almost appeared to be swimming.

Frieda lit up. "You want to borrow them?"

"Yes," Shiloh gushed, as if the answer were obvious.

She was a better woman than me.

"I don't think I need shoes," I said, squishing around in my soaked boots.

"Good," Frieda said, making her way toward the closet. She glanced at me over her shoulder. "Because I don't have any fancy shoes that go with the skirt you're wearing."

"Can I choose?" I asked, heading her off at the pass. It's not as though I'd find anything super appealing among the zebra prints and red sequined halter tops, but it was worth a shot.

Frieda slid open the mirror door and stepped aside. "Pickings are low," she said to Shiloh and me. "You can't have anything hanging around the room because the spells on those are still curing."

Shiloh took a step back. "You spell your clothes?"

"I'm on a manhunt, sweetie," Frieda said, "as in the kind that gets you laid." Her red plastic dangly earrings swung as she talked. "Now I'm not saying a nice spell is the only way to get that done," she clarified, serious as a heart attack, "but it sure can't hurt."

Not her, maybe, but "I don't want to attract men," I told her.

"I'll help you find a man," Shiloh said to Frieda, without missing a beat.

"No, you won't," I said quickly. Frieda didn't know what she was asking for.

"What?" The she-demon raised her brows in response. "I'm good at it." She gave a small huff. "Besides, it helps me keep my mind off things."

Focus on what you can control. I turned back to Frieda. "So you're saying the clothes in the closet aren't spelled yet."

"I didn't have time before the ceremony this morning." She drew out a white leather skirt shorter than my forearm with a zipper right up the entire front. "This is still cute, though," she said, holding it up.

Sweet Jesus. "I don't think you need a spell to get laid in that skirt." You just needed a pulse.

Shiloh clapped her hands together. "I love it," she gushed.

"Why?" I asked. That was another thing: "You don't dress like this." Shiloh's personal style was more Lilly Pulitzer than Layla the Stripper.

Shiloh took the skirt from Frieda and held it to her waist. "I love to dress sexy. I just tame it down as part of my 'good girl' campaign." She grinned at Frieda. "Now I have an excuse! At least for today. Your clothes are so beautiful."

I took the skirt from Shiloh because the only other thing in the closet was a red latex dress that looked like it belonged to a dominatrix. "This one's mine," I said, heading for the bathroom.

"I'll find the matching top," Frieda called after me.

I could hardly wait.

If I'd been in a smaller bathroom, I couldn't recall. I tossed the skirt over the edge of the tub because the tiny counter was scattered with makeup, hair sprays, and what looked to be homemade skin remedies in recycled Vaseline jars. I picked up a container marked "Eyelash Bling" before hastily putting it down. I liked my eyelashes just fine.

It took some doing, but I managed to peel the wet leather pants from my legs. It felt good to get them off. Them and my soaked bustier. I dried off with a towel and grabbed for the white leather skirt before I could think about it too much. That's when I realized it was more of a skort, or at least it had a panel at the bottom, so I wouldn't be showing my hoo-ha to the entire interstate as I rode my bike. Yay for that.

The two halves zipped up and I studied my bottom half in the mirror. I was flashing a lot of leg, but at least I was presentable. Mostly.

Pretend it's shorts.

Frieda knocked on the door. "Lizzie." She inched it open. "Here." Her hand thrust inside, holding a white leather top. At least that's what it was supposed to be.

I took it, turning it over in my hands. "Do you have anything that's bigger?" And less like a tank top?

"Nothing dry," Frieda responded from the other side.

Lordy.

I tried on the top, which also had a front zipper.

"Brace yourself," I mumbled as I dared to look at my new outfit in the mirror.

It was official. I didn't need goldfish shoes to look like a stripper.

Frieda rapped at the door. "I don't mean to hurry you, but your grandma says you better get on the road if you want to make it to the Lynx Club on time. Parking's a bitch."

I groaned. And then there was the issue of persuading my father to work with me once I got there. Maybe this outfit would convince my dad that I truly had lost my mind.

Frieda whistled as I left the bathroom.

"Do you have any biker shorts I can wear under this?" I asked. Even with the little crotch guard underneath, I felt exposed.

Frieda broke into a proud grin. "Don't you look pretty?" She turned me around. "You'll do just fine."

I didn't have time to argue it. "Thanks," I said, buckling my demon slayer utility belt.

On the way out, I passed Shiloh, who stood modeling the red latex dress in the closet door mirror. Her boobs were pushed up to within an inch of her life and her hem was even shorter than mine. Frieda was right. I had the conservative outfit.

Heaven help us.

"Good luck," Shiloh said, stopping me to give me a big hug. "I know you'll do great."

She didn't say it, but I already knew the rest: they were all counting on me.

✝✝✝

I ignored the feeling of way too much wind at my back—and my front—as I rode north toward Sunset Boulevard. It was dangerous to have so much skin exposed on a bike, but then again, it was also a little insane to chase down a demon.

I punched my bike and cursed at the late-morning traffic. I hadn't consulted my Google Maps application as to the exact location of my meeting place with Dad. I wanted to get the lay of the land first, see if I could spot anything unusual.

I opened my demon slayer senses and purposely pushed a little farther west in order to scope out my dad's church on the way up.

Darkness hit while I was still blocks away. It poured down the streets like water.

Cripes. I paused at a boulevard stop a few seconds longer than usual. There were people out, walking dogs, shopping. They shouldn't be here. Energy like this could tear little pieces out of regular mortals, making them tired, sick, *less*.

I didn't know how it had gotten this much worse in only a day. It seemed impossible, but maybe they'd fixed the tomb, or had another installed quickly. They had to have done *something*. If I could get in there, I could figure it out.

The Earl was gaining power fast.

The dark forces hit me like needles on my skin. They threw me off balance, muddled my head.

I braced myself and pushed forward. The worst part was, I wanted more.

I took a deep breath, then another. I couldn't afford to get distracted right now. Or worse, to succumb.

Easy does it. One step at a time. The turnoff for the church came up and I gunned straight past it. I didn't know if I could handle getting too close.

And as I fled the place, the *knowing*, an unwelcome realization settled over me: if the Earl gained too much power, I wouldn't be able to stop him.

I sped up, weaving in and out of traffic, running because I had no other options at that moment. The darkest shadows gave way to the light with every mile I put between the church and me, but they were still present, lurking between storefronts, oozing from the storm drains.

It's a wonder the regular people who lived and worked here didn't sense it.

Maybe they did. The traffic was awful, with people honking at each other and driving like maniacs. I couldn't decide if it was demonic influence or just a typical day in Los Angeles.

At last, I made it to Sunset and North Sierra Drive, on the west end of the block. The energy felt more muted here, which I took as a good sign. Sunset Boulevard was crazy enough.

I made a left and eased down the street, observing everything from the squat bars and restaurants to the low-level entities that seemed to cling just out of reach. I passed the dull black painted facade of the Viper Room, and the Roxy.

It was a wonder the Red Skulls hadn't holed up here. Then again, expensive real estate wasn't their style, even if it tried to look run-down. I kept driving until I spotted the Lynx Club, down by the Chateau Marmont.

I'd expected leather, leopard prints, and a dark facade. But knock me sideways; it looked like a nice place. Bamboo fencing barricaded the outdoor seating area, mimicking a jungle setting. Colorful palms decorated the patio, and well-dressed diners ate on tables laid with china and real linen napkins.

Leave it to my dad to try to throw me off again.

Parking was a bitch and I ended up leaving the bike in a twenty-dollar lot almost a block from the restaurant. Ridiculous.

I tried not to think of the picture I made walking out of the alley in my hoochie outfit. It wasn't as if I could change now. The restaurant didn't have a side entrance, so I strolled through the fancy patio and into the restaurant.

I bypassed the gawking hostess, glad to see my dad for once as he waved to me from a table by a rustic-looking fireplace with a portrait of a stalking leopard over it.

"Nice digs," I said, sliding in across from him.

The lunch crowd was out in full force and I didn't see a single empty chair. He must come here often to get a table at the last minute.

He took me in, from my knee-high black leather boots, to the rest of what I wasn't wearing. "Determined to rebel, aren't you?"

If that's what he thought, then sure. I might as well keep him guessing. "Sometimes I'm impulsive."

Like when I decided to eat all of the ice cream in the container instead of just a little. Sometimes, you had to live it up.

He handed me the drink menu. "Would you like a cocktail?"

At least we were coming up on noon. "No, thanks," I said, placing it on the table. Truth be told, I would like another hangover cure, but this wasn't the time to get nostalgic for my husband. I had work to do.

I had no clue how to convince Dad I was on his side. I had absolutely no reason to do it and I wasn't that good of an actor.

I heard the roar of motorcycles outside and we both looked out the large front window to see the biker witches do a slow pass. I saw Grandma, Ant Eater, Frieda, and Shiloh in her Miata convertible, with Pirate hanging his head out the window.

Subtle, they were not.

I gave a shrug. "They don't approve of our meeting," I told my dad.

He eyed me before downing a third of his cocktail in one gulp. "Your Grandma's never approved of me."

That was a minefield. I stepped in it anyway. "How did you meet my mom?"

Grandma didn't like talking about it and the only time I'd met my mom, she'd tried to drug and kidnap me. Not the best bonding moment. As long as I had my dad here, I wanted to know.

He played with his glass, making the ice rattle. "She found me," he said simply. "She never wanted to be a demon slayer, you know."

"I'm familiar with the idea." It was why she'd foisted her powers off on me. Before abandoning me. I played with the water glass that had been in front of me when I sat down.

Every girl had some kind of issue with her mother. Too bad mine was such a doozy.

Dad went on, as if all of this were par for the course. "Your mom wanted to skirt the system. And she liked me. We decided to help each other."

That didn't sound too promising. It didn't matter. It shouldn't, but I had to know. "Did you love her?"

He shrugged. "She was beautiful," he said wistfully. "And she had power to burn. I figured she could give some to me. Right?" He took another gulp of his drink.

I didn't think the meeting would go well if I called my father an asshole, so I went for my water glass. I hoped the cold liquid would calm me down, but the only way that would happen is if I poured it over his head.

He didn't notice. Or maybe he didn't care.

"Anyhow," he continued, "all the power went to you, so there was no reason for me to stick around."

Gee. I could see where I'd gotten my practical side. Paired with his narcissism, it was quite disarming. "Do you still want it?" I asked. "The power, that is."

He moved his glass in circles on the table while he considered the question. "I'm not going to slay my own daughter for it, if that's what you're asking." He glanced up at me. "Even if I were the type, your power wouldn't go to me."

Of course not. The Earl would keep it for himself.

I studied him, from his pointed features to the sharp tilt of his shoulders. "Were you ever an angelic angel?" I really wanted to know.

He gave a quick shrug. "Why are we even talking about this?" He raised his empty drink and rattled the ice cubes. "Waitress?" he called to a server placing down salads several tables away. "Can I get another one of these?"

"I just want to know more about you," I told him. It was the God's honest truth. I may never have this opportunity again.

He looked as if he had just tasted something bad. "Of all the… See? This is why I didn't have kids."

I kept my face neutral. "You have a kid," I said slowly. "I'm right here."

"Naturally." He waved me off. "Bad choice of words. Do you want a salad?" He motioned for the waitress. "Two salads!"

His behavior was exceedingly odd, even for LA. That's when I noticed his hands were shaking. He was nervous. He fingered his collar, as if it were choking him. "I'm glad you're here," he said, with enough directness that I at least wanted to believe him. "I'm glad your mother's not," he added, shrugging. "I'm not good at these kinds of things."

Clearly.

But as long as we were making random, uncomfortable revelations. "I have angel powers," I told him.

If he'd had a drink, he would have spit it out. "You're only half angel."

"I'm aware." What I didn't know is if I was unusual. It seemed like I was.

He leaned forward, ignoring the waitress as she slipped another drink in front of him.

She smiled at me. "Would you like anything?"

"The water and the salad are fine," I told her. Normally, I'd feel cheated if I didn't have more, but as things stood, I doubted I'd be able to choke much down.

When she'd gone, Dad leaned in close. "Tell me about your powers."

Like I'd give him or the Earl that advantage. "I can focus on goodness and shove away darkness," I said. The Earl already knew that.

Dad shook his head. "I can't even do that anymore." He hesitated before he asked, "Can you shoot bursts of power?"

Yes, but I wasn't telling him that.

"I'll have to try it," I said.

He studied me, as if he could decipher my added powers just by looking at me. "You're good at relating to people. It's easy for you to get them to like you."

Ha. "No, I'm not." I was pretty awkward, in fact.

He didn't buy it. "You had Mimi snowed." He leaned back, sipping at his drink. "Angel powers are good for helping you commune with the power of the universe. Everything you do has that added kick." He set his drink between us. "Even I still have that."

"For the good of mankind?" I asked, just to be a jerk. I couldn't help it. It ticked me off that he been born with the powers of the universe and he'd squandered them.

The waitress returned and placed Caesar salads in front of us. "Enjoy," she said.

I didn't respond. I was too caught up in my dad.

"There's no 'good of mankind,'" he said, ignoring how close our server was. "None of it matters. Angels are a race, just like any other. We can use our powers however we see fit." He leaned closer, but didn't bother to lower his voice. "Take the werewolves. They have supernatural speed and strength. They can use it for whatever they want. You don't take a wolf and say, this one is a 'fallen wolf' just because it uses its power to serve its own interests."

He speared his salad, as if he'd won the argument.

I looked to the table next to us. The two women had started to stare. "Movie treatment," I told them.

They nodded and relaxed.

Geez Louise.

I had to make my move. I forked a crouton, smashing it to bits, as I tried to act as if I were just asking a conversational question. I buried it under a pile of lettuce. "So if I help you and gain a little power from the Earl, that doesn't mean I'm bad." I shoved a fork full of lettuce into my mouth, not even tasting it.

Dad, on the other hand, was suddenly hard to read. "Of course it doesn't mean anything bad. It means you're smart."

Right. I took an extra big bite of salad, trying to think of what I needed to say next. I had to make it clear I was willing to work with him. I had to do a complete one-eighty from yesterday and make it believable. I needed a solid reason, a way to twist the truth just enough for him to believe it.

I swallowed the lump of lettuce and felt it travel like a rock down my throat. "We did a biker witch ceremony this morning."

"I knew it!" His fork clattered on his plate. "I could feel the power on you the minute you sat down."

Holy Hades. He was elated. Vindicated. I couldn't have predicted that.

I pushed forward. "I saw the Earl. He was captivating."

Dad was antsy now. "Did he reach out to you? Were you paying attention?"

"Yes," I said quickly. "And I felt different afterward. I liked it," I lied. "He's beautiful."

A grin split Dad's features. "He's special. Magnetic."

I went all-in. "You said he was only taking the bad energy out of people's lives." I glanced out at the street as the biker witches rumbled past again. "I admit, I felt better after seeing him. That's why Grandma and the girls are worried." I looked to the street again, as if they were going to barge right into the restaurant and haul me away. I focused on Dad once more, locked eyes with him, and sold it for all it was worth. "They're afraid I'll team up with you."

He forced his grin away as much as he could and steepled his fingers between us. "Let me ask you one simple question." He asked it as if he were truly concerned for my personal welfare and salvation. "What has your side ever given you?"

I had to pull back or I'd make it too easy. I leaned away, frowned. "I'm not sure what you mean."

He pressed forward. "Demon slaying," he said, as if it were a profession like teaching or fixing cars. "What has it ever earned you?"

Self-respect. Focus. Friends. Love. The knowledge that I was doing the right thing. I'd saved souls. Vanquished demons. Saved the world. I was one of the good guys.

I nodded slowly. "I see your point. "But"—and here was the kicker—"what can the Earl give me?"

Dad seemed impressed by my display of greed. "He can give you wealth, respect. Look at me. I'm a pastor now. I have control over my own life. And others." He grabbed for his drink. "Want me to show you?"

Yes and no.

But the most important question was, "How?"

Dad rapped his knuckles on the table. "We'll do a power meld. Right here, right now."

I glanced around jungle-themed restaurant, at the other diners.

"Here?"

He grinned at me.

"What's the catch?" I asked.

"None," he said, acting like Mr. Innocent. "I'm your father."

He should have known better than to make that argument.

"You've already said you don't trust me." And I sure as hell didn't trust him.

"Right," he said, tamping down his enthusiasm. "This way, you can see some of the benefits of working with me, and I know you're not going to do anything foolish."

Like slaying his boss.

"I see your point," I said.

There was no bullshit now, no lines. "It's the only way I can let you back in the church," he said, "or work with you at all."

So there we had it: out on the table.

I didn't even know the implications of binding part of myself to my dad. I assumed I was stronger than him, but I didn't know that for a fact. It scared me.

And then there were the issues with Earl. Dad was tied in with his power.

It was a risk. A frightening one. But what were the risks if I didn't do it?

The Earl would keep growing stronger and I'd be locked out, unable to do anything about it.

If I gave a little, something manageable, something enough for Dad to trust me, I could make this work. I could get on the inside of their operation.

If I dared.

"Well?" my dad asked, as if the answer were simple.

If I did it, I'd be like a double agent. I'd have my people on the outside and I'd work from the inside. It wouldn't be fun, or easy. But we'd decided this morning—it was something I had to do.

He raised his brows, waiting.

I should have known Dad would want more than a conversation, a pledge of loyalty. He wanted proof.

Sacrifice yourself. It was one of the Three Truths of the Demon Slayers. Not my favorite one, to be honest.

I scrubbed a hand over my chin. "What's involved?" I had to make sure I did it right, that I didn't give too much away or bind myself too intricately to my dad and the Earl.

Close enough to make friends, not so close he'd steal my power or make it impossible for me to escape.

If their ceremony were anything like the Red Skulls', I'd have to deal with candlelit rituals and maybe a goat head or two. The Earl even had the one that my Great-Aunt Evie had passed down to me. It had flown out of our grip at the Seer's Ceremony this morning. I thought I'd never see it again. Now I wasn't so sure.

"It's nothing big," Dad said, as the waitress stopped by to refill our water glasses. I let her take my salad as well. I wasn't hungry anymore. Dad let her take his plate too, and when she left, he leaned across the table, hands clasped. "You'll find this path is much easier than the one you chose before."

I felt my heartbeat speed up at his words, and saw the gleam of pure evil in his eyes.

He took one final sip of his drink. "All you have to do is ask for it."

Chapter Eighteen

I should have known. Wasn't darkness always the easier road to travel? It was hard to seek goodness, truth, light, and all too simple to throw it away.

A trickle of fear ran down my neck.

The dark path was slippery as well.

But I wouldn't go far. I could rein this in. I'd been touched by serious evil before and had survived. I steeled myself, as if by sheer will alone I would make it okay. Part of my job included this dance with the devil. Of course this devil happened to be my father, but I couldn't help that. I could only try to use it to my advantage.

I'd never get this chance again.

"Lizzie?" He leaned forward, his slick black hair catching the light, his pointed nose lowered as he closed even more of the distance between us. "This is what you came for, isn't it?"

Yes.

But I hadn't planned to go this deep.

"This is a commitment," I told him. One I wasn't sure I could take back.

But every minute I wavered, each second I took to decide, made me suspect in his eyes. I could see it in him as plain as I could feel the indecision swirling through me.

Time to make the choice.

I could walk away, thereby ensuring nothing would change. In doing so, I would protect myself and my view on how things *should* be done. I'd be whole, pure, and completely unable to help as I watched others succumb to the Earl and his church. Or I could take a risk, open myself up, and save those poor souls who would have no one else to stand up for them. I'd have to give something of myself to make things right.

But wasn't that true of anything worthwhile?

I had to believe it was worth the risk. I had to.

"Let's do it," I said, before I changed my mind.

My dad broke out into a big grin. His winning smile.

Dimitri would have puppies when I told him.

Don't think about it.

That was also part of the sacrifice. He'd come around. He understood my job, my calling. And he loved me without question.

"Are you ready?" Dad asked, reaching out to me.

"Yes," I said, joining my hands with his. That alone made my stomach turn.

I cleared my mind of second thoughts. They wouldn't help. It was done.

Dad's eyes shone with an emotion I couldn't name. It didn't matter. It could have been excitement, greed, or dark religious fervor for all I cared. I let go of that and focused on the task at hand. I wasn't doing this for him. I was doing it for the good of mankind.

His grip was solid, chilly. "Ask," he said, rubbing his thumb along the top of my hand, the way he would if he were comforting a child.

I swallowed.

Keep it together. I needed to bind only enough of myself to my father that he'd trust me, and so that I could influence what went on in his church.

I closed my eyes and called out to the power roiling inside me. It responded immediately. I teased out the essence of who I was, the white-hot strength of my demon slayer side. I held it up, ready, as I focused once again on the world outside me. I looked my father straight in the eyes and spoke. "I ask," I said clearly, with no hesitation, no doubt. "I ask to meld a part of myself with you." The moment the words left me, I felt a deep pull, like an unbelievingly powerful wrenching on the door of my soul.

I'd never felt anything like it before.

I could do this.

I blew out a breath and forced myself to relax while I opened the door inside my soul barely a crack. Just enough to see what lingered on the other side. I reached out with my true self and felt the seeping frigid pull of my father's power—and no doubt, the Earl of Hell's as well.

And while I expected needles of pain, an icy blast, I only felt an invigorating presence. It cleared my head and made me sit taller.

It was hard to understand, even harder to explain. But I felt like I stood under a waterfall on a hot day, letting the cool, refreshing water wash over me.

There was none of the darkness or fear. No icy coldness of hell somehow marking me. "I don't understand," I said to my father.

"There's more," he said, as if he were giving me an exciting gift.

"No doubt." Of course I knew better than to think that was the sum of it. I pulled back. "I think we've done enough."

Less was more in this case. I could always go back for seconds. As it stood, I felt great. It wasn't a dramatic shift, nothing that a good hair day and the perfect outfit couldn't conjure up in me, but still, I could see the appeal.

Even better, I was in control. In fact, I felt more confident, stronger than I had going into this. If this panned out, Dad might actually be able to help me.

"You're radiant," he said, as excited as I felt. Dad seemed to glow with an inner fire as well. "You like it?"

As if he didn't know the answer. I shouldn't. I really shouldn't. But... "Give me a little more."

This time, the force at the door pulled harder than before. I let it swing open an inch. Frigid air rushed in like a fall breeze after the blistering heat of summer. Amazing. I soaked it in, letting it wash over me. It felt good. Really good. I felt powerful.

Ever since the fenris showed up on my beach, I'd been operating under a steady thrum of fear. I'd felt a lack of control and the pain that comes from not knowing. Now I could see the answers so much clearer.

I could recognize things for what they were. Yes, we had a crisis, but I certainly had the power and the experience to face the Earl. I'd gotten what I could from the witches and now from my father. And if I could make it through the Earl's defenses...

I couldn't help but smile. It was time to strike.

Dad squeezed my hands. "Why are you smiling?"

I'd almost forgotten he was there.

"I think you need more," he said, half teasing, leaving it out there for me to grasp.

I slipped my hands from his. "I'm good."

The power exchange was complete. He'd marked me and he'd entered my realm as well. He'd seeped into my consciousness. I could feel him now, as I would a good friend. Or a father. A real father.

"Is it always this way?" I asked. Asking seemed too simple for what had just happened to me.

He held open his hands, palms out. "It's beautiful, isn't it?"

"I don't know what it is." My body sang with it.

Maybe I'd needed a touch of darkness in order to see the light.

I sat back and enjoyed the subtle energy of the restaurant. When I'd walked in here, I'd felt *less*, just because of my unfortunate white skirt and barely there top. It was the story of my life. I'd always felt slightly awkward. Even with friends sometimes. Like I didn't fit in. Either I didn't know what to say, or I wasn't sure what to do in a social situation. I was never the one who had the answers. And now?

None of it mattered. I was fine the way I was. I was perfect.

The waitress left us our bill and I slid it over to Dad. He'd asked me here. He could pay.

I wasn't naive. I knew Dad had tried to corrupt me. But I could only think that it had backfired on him in the worst possible way.

If I could control this, use this, I could not only make a difference for the people of Dad's messed-up church, I could be a different kind of slayer. A better one. With more confidence, more trust in my sixth sense, I might be able to anticipate attacks before they happened or even prevent tragedies like the one we were facing. I wouldn't be as afraid. I'd have the answers. I'd be so much more powerful.

It warmed me to think about it and a rightness settled in my chest that I'd never felt before.

And all I'd had to do was ask.

Meanwhile, Dad placed cash for both of us in the black bill folder.

I was eager to test this further. "So you need me to take care of some things at the church." I wanted to see if I could get past the wards in the basement. After that, we'd play it by ear.

Dad pushed his chair back and stood. "I've created a monster."

"Now's as good a time as any," I said, joining him. "I've proven myself to you. You might as well get me up to speed and start using me. You said you needed me."

He shook his head, amused. "I do. But you sucked a little more from me than I'd planned," he said as we walked out.

"No kidding?" I hadn't noticed. Fear pricked the back of my neck. There was no way I'd reached too far beyond the door. Had I?

I would have noticed. My prior experience with dark forces involved icy blasts and debilitating power. This was nice.

Dad used his hand on a chair back as we wove in between empty tables. It appeared we'd outlasted the lunch crowd. "You caught me in the middle of a renovation. Seeing as you blasted the tomb yesterday."

"Sorry about that," I said, not really meaning it.

He just laughed. "I was actually kind of proud of you." He shook his head. "I know. It's dumb." He continued on. "We're installing a new tomb upstairs tonight, so it's not like anything new will be coming through. You can come by tomorrow morning and I'll show you what we have so far."

Because whatever beasties he wanted me to tackle could wait. That was so *Dad*.

On the other hand, logic said he wasn't being completely honest with me. The tomb installation was a big deal. And the Earls powers had been growing even after I'd destroyed the Tomb of Kebechet.

Whatever he had planned for tonight would no doubt enhance the Earl's influence.

Dad gave me a hug outside the restaurant and I let him. It didn't mean anything. He pulled back and studied me. Did he wonder if he'd gone too far? Given me too much?

Well, it was too late now.

"Come by the church at nine o'clock sharp," he said, his hands on my shoulders. "I'll be waiting for you."

I broke away. "I'll see you then."

Maybe.

After all, I had a lot to do in the meantime.

Excitement ripped through me as I went to retrieve my bike. Those stares I was getting? Some came from women who judged me for flashing a little skin. But the ones from the men? Try lust, desire. Amazing. I'd never seen it before.

Maybe dark angels really did have more fun. I laughed out loud, stifled it as best I could.

I wasn't dark. Just... touched.

I walked through an alley, to a lot wedged between two of the taller buildings. My bike was parked between two Aston Martins. You had to love Hollywood. I rolled it out, careful not to so much as breathe on either of the cars that cost more than my house.

A presence approached from the west: a solid wall of witchcraft. I had about two seconds' warning before the witches blazed into the tiny parking lot.

Jesus Christ on a Christmas tree.

They came two abreast. That's all that could fit down the narrow side street. They poured into the lot like hot sand through a sieve.

I shut off my engine because—let's face it—I wasn't going anywhere. I got off my bike and walked over to an old rock median that was really just a glorified speed bump. I'd barely yanked my helmet off before Shiloh ran up, boobs ready to pop out of her red latex dress.

"Goodness, Lizzie, what did you do?" she asked. "I can't believe you'd touch the darkness."

"I can't believe you can run in those," I said, pointing to her goldfish stripper heels.

She grasped my arm with both hands as I hung my helmet over my handlebars. "I felt you go down. What happened?"

I yanked my arm back. "I took a little of my dad's power to show he can trust me."

She dropped her hands. "But he can't trust you."

"Fuck." I glanced out toward the Strip, hoping he wasn't witnessing this. "That's the point."

But her eyes were wide, her cheeks flushed. "You're in with them now."

Chapter Nineteen

Because I cussed. I cursed sometimes. Okay, rarely. Used to be never.

I shook her off. She acted like a child, speaking her truth without understanding what was truly happening.

Grandma strode up. "What's going on?"

Ant Eater and Frieda barked orders to the witches behind her.

I'd tell her what. "I had this thing going down with my dad." I was in control. I had him where I wanted him. "You driving past twelve times didn't help." At best, it was embarrassing. At the very worst, it could have kept my dad from trusting me.

Grandma held up her hands, as if I were the one out of line. "Hey. Sorry, hotshot. We were just keeping an eye on you."

Ah, yes. The stalker method. "I got it."

How could I get anything done with Harleys blasting up all around me?

Oh, and here came the talking dog. "Hey Lizzie!" Pirate leaped for my leg, missed, and planted a wet nose on my shin. He shook it off without missing a beat. "Did you see us with the top down?" His eyes danced and his entire body shook with excitement. "I have got to get a ride like that!"

"Yes," I agreed. "When they start selling convertibles to dogs, we'll be the first in line."

He lit up at that. "Promise?" he asked, completely missing my sarcasm.

I had to give him points for enthusiasm. "Sure," I answered. Why not? "Now excuse me. I'm busy." I turned back to Grandma. "You've got to rein it in. I'm not sure what you're doing anyway. There's nothing demonic in this parking lot."

She studied me, her tinsel highlights sparkling in the midday sun. "What are you smoking? This place is *off*. You want a repeat of this morning?"

"Of course not," I began.

She took a step back, completely unaware that I might have been the cause. "Spread out," she ordered the witches, "this is as good a place as any to get the bead on the bad guys."

"I call the sunny spot by the car!" Pirate hollered.

"For the love of Pete," I said as the witches began to work at an alarming rate. "If there was something to worry about, I'd know."

"Did you get in good with your dad?" Grandma asked.

"No thanks to you," I told her. "You know, sometimes it would be nice to be able to go someplace without the full armada behind me."

"Yeah, right," she said, as if I'd suggested going in naked. "Just remember: you called us."

And now I regretted it.

The witches clustered in groups. Every few seconds, a swirly blue anti-demonic spell zipped into the air. They usually smelled sweet, like cherries. Only these must have been a different recipe because they gave off the odor of Limburger cheese.

A particularly zingy spell thwacked me in the leg, stinging like a dragonfly. "Ow." I brushed it away and crushed it under my boot.

I glanced back at the assembly of witches. Creely stood, arms crossed, giving launch orders to Ant Eater. Shiloh was halfway down the alley, escaping a small swarm of spells. Poor thing.

Cripes. Frieda sat on the hood of an Aston Martin.

"So there's no way to get back into the church," Grandma stated, no doubt ready to plan an invasion.

Another anti-demonic spell zipped past me, buzzing my left ear. "I didn't say that." Two more spells spiraled south. I knew exactly where they were headed. Sue me if I wanted to go with them. "He's letting me in tomorrow at nine."

She watched me for a long second. "Impressive. How'd you talk him into it?"

"Never mind," I told her, "just let me handle things tomorrow."

She let out a snort. "No way, chica. We're with you to the end. You can sneak us in the side door."

Yes, because the Red Skulls were so good at sneaking.

Frankly, I didn't know whether to involve them or not. "We'll talk about it tomorrow." Despite my better sense, I added, "at dawn." That would make them happy.

A spell nipped at my ankle. I shook it off.

Part of me wished the biker witches understood the concept of sleeping in. Or at least staying in bed until the sun came up. But the only way that happened on their end was if they'd been making friends with Jack Daniel's the night before. I certainly didn't want any hungover witches on my team.

"Okay, then." Grandma clapped me on the back, just about knocking the wind out of me. "Good plan."

Exactly. "So can you all just...go?" It sounded harsh, and they had helped me out tremendously this morning, so I softened it a little. "I'll call you if I need you. But right now, I'd like a second to think."

Frieda slid down off the car. "Seems to me like it was just getting interesting."

"Not when you know how to hot-wire one of these babies," Creely said, easing out of the yellow Porsche convertible three cars down.

Oh, help me Rhonda. Yes, they had to leave. Now.

Grandma took a look around. "Yeah, you know the spells aren't hanging around here anyway." She shot a glance at me. "Let's go, ladies," she said, addressing the Red Skulls. "Pack it up and move out. We may still have time to prepare for Flea Fest."

Lord, I hoped their motel didn't have fleas. I was wearing one of Frieda's outfits. "How did you get bugs?" I hoped Bob didn't have them. I watched Pirate hop into his sidecar and settle into his lap as he tried to buckle his seat belt under fifteen pounds of dog.

Grandma rolled her eyes. "Flea Fest is a craft fair, genius. We sell enchanted soaps, body lotions, and marital aids."

I didn't even want to know. "You're not supposed to enchant people against their will." One day, they'd understand that.

She gave a sly grin, watching her coven as they took to their bikes and began pulling out of the lot. "It's okay to give a little help now and then."

I could never get over how quickly they could get assembled and on those bikes. I guess thirty years of running from a demon could do that to you.

"You coming?" Grandma asked, holding back.

I shook my head. "I just need a second to think."

She winked. "See you on the flip side."

"Thanks for this morning," I called.

She kept walking toward her bike, not bothering to turn around as she raised her hand in a casual wave.

I turned my back on them and let out a sigh as the Red Skulls rumbled away. I looked up to the blue sky, to the clouds gathering in the south.

What I'd done with my dad, what had happened, it couldn't be too bad, could it? I didn't feel different.

I let the tension ease out of me as the last roars of the Harleys faded into the distance. I closed my eyes and breathed in the hot desert air, tinged with exhaust fumes. It was all good.

Until the bike noise started up again.

This time, I heard the roar of a single engine, flying full-tilt down the alley.

I opened my eyes.

Dimitri.

He didn't even bother to pull in the right way. He drove straight across the median next to me, his tires spitting rocks and dead grass. He barely missed the luxury cars and cut his engine with his front tire a foot away from my leg. I could feel the heat radiating from the machine.

"Are you insane?" I asked, as he shut down his bike.

He yanked off his helmet, focused on one person: me. "What's wrong?" he demanded.

"You're looking at it right here," I told him, referring to craziness that was my life. It was like being followed by the circus. "If I ever have to go undercover, I'm in deep shit." I couldn't even make it out of a parking lot without a two-act stage play.

Dimitri got off his bike, and as yummy as he looked doing it, I wished I could stuff him back on.

His black hair curled with sweat and he had a dark look in his eye. "Walk with me," he said, wrapping a leather-clad arm around my shoulder.

"Where?" I asked. We were in a parking lot.

He led me a short distance away toward a grassy spot that had a little shade.

"Level with me," he said. "I know something's up." His grip was strong. "I felt something inside you shift. It scared the hell out of me."

I sighed. I didn't know what to say.

Dimitri lowered his head to look at me. The sun shone directly overhead, and shadows from the tall buildings on either side of us cast hollows under his cheekbones. His eyes had gone piercing green, like they did when his adrenaline was pumping. "I know you, whether you like it or not."

Not.

"What you felt is nothing." Okay, that was a lie. It was *something*. But nothing he needed to think about. "It was a blip. A means to an end." His eyes crinkled at the corners. He wasn't buying it. I ran a hand down his arm in an effort to calm him. He was drawn tight, his muscles as hard as granite. "My dad needed to trust me, and so I let him in."

"How?" he demanded, his voice clipped.

If I told him the truth, he'd have puppies. An entire litter. Dozens. I'd be buried in dogs.

I wound my fingers in his. "I followed the Three Truths of the Demon Slayer." Lessons he'd taught me. "Look to the outside. Accept the universe. Sacrifice yourself." I really hated that last one. But this time, it wasn't so bad.

He wasn't convinced. He squeezed my hand, his grip strong and steady. "What you did," he said slowly, "it didn't feel right."

There was a time when he wouldn't have known better. He would have been reacting on instinct and not concrete experience. But I'd tied myself to him when I married him. Our powers had melded. He could tell when I was off. And it was biting me in the ass at the moment. I went on the offensive with the only bit of solid fact I had. "I think I know more about being a demon slayer than you do." He couldn't argue that.

He tilted his head, as if he could see it by looking at me.

I ran a hand down his arm, reached up, and gave him a peck on the cheek. He eased up under my touch. "I think I just need some time alone. To think." He understood how crazy things had been lately.

His expression softened and I knew I'd won. "Let's get you home," he said, wrapping an arm around me.

About that... I extricated myself from his grip. "Give me an hour or two. I want to take a walk." I needed to chill out, to try to figure out what I just did.

He hesitated, his need to respect my independence warring with his desire to keep me safe at all costs. "You're just going to walk," he said, both as a question and a statement.

"Maybe buy a new outfit." I felt like a hooker. "I'm going to leave my bike here for the moment," I said. "I mean, I paid twenty bucks." As far as I was concerned, I'd have to leave it there for a week to earn my money back.

"And you won't do anything crazy," he said.

I gave a slight shrug. "I don't know. I might skip."

He looked slightly horrified at that.

"Relax, babe." I reached out and squeezed his hand. "I need ten minutes. A half hour, tops. I'll see you at home."

Reluctantly, he let me go.

✝✝✝

Walking felt...great. In all honesty, I hadn't had a moment to think, to *be*, since that fenris showed up on our beach. I half expected Dimitri to follow me, but he let me have my space.

I passed a clothing shop featuring ripped jeans and rocker T-shirts. I almost stopped. I'd told Dimitri the truth. I could use a new outfit. Then again, I liked the looks I was getting in this one. I kept walking, past the clothing shop and a store full of knockoff movie memorabilia. I paused outside the dull black exterior of the Viper Room (good-bye River Phoenix), and resisted the urge to stop and get a henna tattoo. With every step, I felt the tension begin to ease out of me.

The sun felt a little warm, but the sky was blue and the air refreshing. I might save my sanity yet.

I headed south on Alta Drive and walked down into a more residential area. Palm trees stood guard outside squat retro apartment complexes and immaculately kept 1950s- era homes.

It was quaint, fun, and…interesting the farther south I walked. Shadows beckoned, slinking between the cracks of the sidewalks and under doorways as I approached. It was almost as if they were teasing me.

I smiled as I picked up my pace. At Santa Monica Boulevard, the residential street opened onto a more businesslike avenue.

That's when I admitted to myself that I was drawing closer to my dad's church. Hadn't I known it all along?

There was no harm in it. Not truly. I mean yes, I hadn't exactly planned it, but now that I'd headed in that direction, I might as well see if anything had changed there. After all, the witches let all those anti-demon spells loose. No telling what trouble they would cause. I didn't want anything to disrupt the meeting with my father in the morning.

The presence grew stronger the farther south I traveled. Only this time, it called to me.

I gave a slight pause before continuing on my way. It must be linked to that taste I'd had of my dad's powers. If this was what it felt like to him, no wonder he was proud.

The biker witches would never approve.

But truly, as a demon slayer, I owed it to myself and to the Red Skulls to see what might have changed at the Salvation of the Hills.

I broke into a jog, anxious to see what I would find. I sensed the growing presence, the strong, rich power. I darted across the street toward Saint Lucia, ignoring the honking of horns and the squealing of tires. Pedestrians had the right of way. Probably.

It's not like anyone hit me.

I turned one final corner and hurried toward the gleaming art deco theater turned worship center. Hades, it was gorgeous.

A group of men in a black pickup truck started honking and catcalling. I thought it was for me, until I saw them gesturing at Shiloh. She stood in the park just across the street, and made quite a sight in her skintight red dress and crazy stripper heels.

Shiloh didn't even notice the men. She stood, arms dangling at her sides, every bit of her attention focused on the power emanating from the church.

Tell me about it, babe.

I crossed the street, even though it almost killed me to do it. As I drew up next to her I almost moaned. The call of the church zinged up my arms and swirled up my spine, a fabulous, delicious blast of power. Oh yes, she'd found a sweet spot.

"What'cha doing?" I asked, knowing full well.

She jumped at the sound of my voice. "Nothing!" She bit at her plump lower lip, guilty as hell. There was no need. I totally got it now. "I'm not absorbing the energy of the portals if that's what you're thinking," she said quickly.

I smiled and gave her a nudge. "This is a good spot."

A furrow formed between her brows. "Oh, God." She turned her gaze back to the church, as if that would change things. "I was right about you."

"I'm fine," I assured her. "Just...enhanced."

"You're trouble is what you are," she lectured, before losing the battle and breathing the power deep into her lungs. "Oh, baby." She closed her eyes. "I had to stop by. Just for a little bit. It was so close and I did my part this morning." She let out a small sigh. "I deserve a little pick-me-up."

"Absolutely," I told her. The church looked deserted. Maybe Dad had told the truth when he said he'd shut it down for that tomb installation.

I could feel Shiloh watching me now. "We should go," she said breathlessly. She didn't say the rest, but I understood clearly enough.

Before we do anything stupid.

Too late. "I think we should sneak in," I told her.

"That's crazy," she snapped, but not fast enough. I heard the hesitation, saw the lingering interest in her expression.

"Is it?" I winked at her.

The power beckoned to us. It *wanted* us to come.

Shiloh's fingers closed around my arm. "We need to leave," she said, panic tinting her voice. "Right now. I'll even let you drive my Miata. I'll teach you how to knit."

I held steady. She didn't really want that. "My dad has a portal in there." I could practically feel the hum of it. "It's the one we saw in the vision this morning. A dark vortex. He's pulling energy down through purgatory and into hell. It's almost like he's building an escape tunnel. I want to see where it leads. We can discover exactly how strong the Earl of Hell really is."

After all, I was a planner, and this would definitely help me in my meeting tomorrow.

Her mouth worked, but no sound came out. She cleared her throat, steeled her resolve. "We don't have to go anywhere," she said. "Right? Because I don't think I could actually go in it without…"

"No. We'll stay here." I just wanted to get close. Hopefully I could now that I'd drawn in part of my dad's power. "We'll get a read on it. Enjoy it a little."

We needed a break. Besides, this was the perfect opportunity to see what was truly happening with the Earl.

Truth be told, I was set to go without her.

If Shiloh was shocked, she didn't show it. "I could be a big help," she said, her voice barely above a whisper.

"You've felt it all before," I told her.

She was the only one I knew who might be as adept as I was at reading this situation.

"Okay. I'm in," she said. She really was a friend.

Hand in hand, we crossed the street. As we did, I saw Dimitri turn the corner on his Harley. He had his bike in low gear, riding slowly, clearly searching for me.

He just couldn't leave it alone.

Well, if he was going to deceive me, I didn't feel so bad about doing it to him.

"Hurry," I said, slipping inside the gold front doors with Shiloh.

CHAPTER TWENTY

The lobby was deserted. Thank Hades.

Yes, it was mean to keep Dimitri in the dark, but he'd go all caveman if he knew what we were about to do. The last thing I needed was to get dragged out by my hair.

If I could find the dark vortex on my own, if I could see for myself where the Earl was drawing his power, then hopefully we'd be able to figure out how to defeat him.

Or at least end this debacle and save the people in this church.

"Quickly," I said, urging Shiloh deeper into the lobby as Dimitri drove slowly past.

Yes, my husband was the good guy. He'd named himself my protector from day one, but that didn't mean he could help us with this.

I paused, breathless, waiting to see if Dimitri stopped.

He didn't.

I rested a hand on my switch stars and I moved farther back. So far, the Earl had been the only demon I couldn't slay. Shockingly enough, my weapons didn't work on him.

I'd have to find another way.

Shiloh paused in the shadows, just past the statue of Ammut. She fidgeted with the neckline of her obscenely low-cut dress. "Did he see us?"

I passed her, moving deeper into the dark. "I don't think so."

He'd made it his life's work to shelter me from the evil that pursued us, and usually he let me go do what needed to be done, but he wouldn't understand this.

"I don't think Damien would approve, either," Shiloh whispered, following me.

I paused as I rounded the corner. "Who?"

She winced as she said it. "My husband."

Right. I turned back to the task at hand. I knew she worried about him. I ran a hand along the wall in order to keep my bearings. "Have you heard from him yet?"

"No."

"It's going to be okay," I promised.

I'd make it okay if I had to go to hell and back. Which considering my history was a very real possibility. Still, I didn't want to think about that right now.

One thing at a time. I wasn't even sure if we could get close to the vortex. It depended on how well my melding with my dad had gone. My boots echoed off the marble floors. The quicker we got downstairs the better.

"It's this way," Shiloh said, hurrying for the darkened hallway to the left.

Now that she mentioned it, I could feel the dark churning under that part of the church. I had to settle down.

"There should be a basement entrance," I whispered, my voice sounding unnaturally loud in the deserted space. "There," I said, pointing to a wood door about ten feet from us.

With my dad's powers in the mix, I should be able to get past the locks and those wards that stopped Dimitri and Frieda last time.

Call it supernatural camouflage.

Or temporary insanity.

Shiloh perked up. "Wow. It tastes good," she said, as if she were about to indulge in a super sized bowl of Häagen-Dazs.

I wished it could be that way for me. "Why do succubi get to have all the fun?" I asked, only half teasing.

It really wasn't fair.

Shiloh pressed her lips together as if she had a delectable secret. "Fun is kinda in the job description." She ran a hand absently down her skintight latex dress. "Hades, I miss it sometimes."

Shiloh reached for the door first. She turned the knob eagerly and I pushed the door open the rest of the way. A steep staircase, as old as the theater itself, led straight down.

I pulled a cord overhead and lit up a series of bare white bulbs that cast watery light down into the abyss.

Perfect.

"Me first," I said, edging around her. The antique tile under my feet was slick. It didn't slow me down in the least.

I wasn't the accidental demon slayer anymore. I'd proven myself more times than I could count.

I'd defeated the mad-scientist demon who'd kept the Red Skulls on the run for thirty years. I'd torched every last succubus in Las Vegas (save Shiloh). And now I was on the ultimate dark power rush in order to shut down what could turn into the second coming of the Earl of Hell.

Boy, I loved my job.

The air cooled the lower I got. Nice. It felt familiar, as if I'd been here before. Of course I hadn't, but it occurred to me that I was drawing off my dad.

Fan-fricking-tastic.

A small landing at the bottom of the stairs led to a twisting corridor.

Shiloh was right on my ass. "There it is," she said over my shoulder as we came to a heavy iron door. There was a smaller, most likely decorative door in front of it, done in an iron-bars-and-metal-studs motif. Cute. Kind of like a medieval castle door.

Power zinged over my arm as I pulled the first door open. It must have been what burned Frieda.

I ran my finger down one of the metal studs. The wards were comfortably chilly, but they didn't hurt.

Shiloh rubbed up against the next door and gave a small giggle.

"Oh, to live like a succubus," I said to no one in particular.

I could feel the powerful vortex pulsing on the other side.

It felt amazing to be so close. I planted my hands on my hips and soaked it in. This was my reward. I'd changed, evolved. I had enough of my dad's power to get past his wards. He was such a manipulator. Such a jerk. And now I'd turned it around on him.

"We'll make it." At least to the dark vortex. If I could get a sense of how it worked, hopefully I could at least cut off my dad's power source. That would give me some breathing room to try to free the people he was draining.

It had an outside throw-bolt. Very medieval dungeon. "Stand aside," I told Shiloh. And when she was out of the way, I popped it open easily. "Thanks, Dad."

The door creaked outward and she poked her head closer. "It smells terrific."

"Rub it in." It smelled like a zoo to me.

Ornate bronze torches lined the stone walls on either side. "Boy, Dad really goes for this medieval theme."

Shiloh was right behind me. "Egyptian," she corrected.

She was right. The cups of the bronze torches resembled lotus flowers.

The hallway was narrow, the torches sizzling near my cheek. The door closed behind us with a boom.

I looked back and saw only darkness and shadows.

A low, rumbling growl echoed from up ahead.

Shiloh gasped, but I smiled. I knew what that was. "I heard it the last time I was here." When I'd first encountered Mimi and her measuring rocks.

"It sounds scary," Shiloh said, her voice echoing off the walls.

"It's tied up," I assured her, picking up the pace.

Metal rubbed against metal as she withdrew a torch from its holder. "Why do you say that?"

Logic. "If it were loose, it would have attacked us by now."

Shiloh didn't appear too comforted. But she didn't have time to dwell on it.

The hallway opened up on the wickedest dungeon I'd ever seen. It was as if we'd stepped back in time and entered the maze under the Roman Colosseum.

We stepped into a rather large central room with barred prison cells on all sides. An immense cobra was coiled in the one directly across from us. It was as big around as a storm drain, five times as long as a man.

Its purple scales shone in the dim torchlight. I stepped into the cavern and it flared out its hood and gave a bone-curdling hiss. Its curved white fangs could pierce straight through me and still have room to spare.

"Have you ever seen anything like it?" I asked.

"Yes," Shiloh said on a croak. "My old boss kept one as a pet. The thing fed on anybody who pissed the boss off."

Good thing Shiloh's husband, Damien, had taken care of that demon. "Where does it come from?"

"Lower Setesh Wastelands," she said on a whisper, as if that would make her invisible behind me. "I don't want to look at it anymore."

Well, I hated to break it to her, but all of the creatures were staring at us.

A pair of imps slunk from the shadows in the cell next to the cobra. Purple eyes glowed from under dark, furry brows. They had weasel-like faces and the bodies of thick, hastily constructed people. Dark hair clung to their bent frames. That cage not only had bars, but also a thin copper mesh to keep them from slipping through.

Good thinking.

The imps' congested breathing grew more and more excited as they drew closer, weaving in and out in an attempt to confuse their prey: us.

"What are they doing?" Shiloh asked, breathless.

"Hunting," I said quietly.

I kept a hand on my switch stars, just in case.

Tiny goblin-like creatures occupied the cages on both sides of us. They separated them by color. Gray and black on the right, brownish-tan and white ones on the left. They scampered about on their hind legs, letting out low grunts.

"Poor things," Shiloh clucked.

"What are those?" I asked, wrinkling my nose as a brown one scaled the bars and tried to squirm through the top.

"You know," Shiloh said, drawing closer to me. "Bakhtaks."

Their eyes were tiny specks, set back under large brows. "I think I would have remembered."

Shiloh gave me the look that said she knew better. "Ever wake up in the middle of the night and you have this weight on your chest? And you can't move or breathe?" She lowered her chin. "Those are Bakhtaks. They feed off your dreams." She studied them from a distance. "They're not the most pleasant creatures, but they certainly shouldn't be caged."

"Let's go," I said, before she decided to let any of them loose.

Two passages led out of the prison block, one on the left and the other to the right. I was unsure which to follow, and not really sure I even cared, as long as we got out now.

A low growl sounded deep down the left side passage.

"That's our ticket," I said, stepping over the manacles and chains littering the center of the room.

Shiloh ran her hand over a holder full of sticks with very sharp, pointy ends. "I'm not so sure about this."

"You can still go back," I told her. The door was just down the hall. "I won't think less of you."

She hesitated, her fear written plainly on her face. "No," she said, steeling herself. "You're my friend and I'm going to see you through this."

"I'm glad," I said, grabbing a torch and heading off toward whatever had been growling. Shiloh knew more about enchanted creatures than I did. Plus, I could use the company. While I was fairly certain that the vortex I'd seen in my vision was down here, under the church, I doubted my dad would keep it in plain sight.

I slowed my steps as the floor underneath me angled downward. I braced a hand against the wall and kept going.

"Lizzie…" Shiloh said, as it slanted even more.

I'll bet she was regretting those stripper heels now.

The air was growing cooler. Dark power prickled at my skin.

Shiloh cleared her throat. "This isn't part of the old theater," she said, her voice wavering.

I ran a hand against the wall. The stone was wet, oozing. "None of it is," not since we'd passed through the warded door. "This place has been conjured up by the Earl. No one else would build a basement in California."

"Well, that's comforting," Shiloh said drily.

The torches were spread wider now. Shadows lingered between each glimmer of light. In truth, it was scary as hell, but I wasn't going to tell her that.

"He can't see us," I assured her. "Or he'd have stopped us by now." No doubt he could open those cages with a thought.

My foot snagged on a bar and I glanced down before taking a hasty step back. Below was a prison cell full of creatures I didn't even know existed.

Snorting horned creatures butted up against uneven lumps that could have been rocks except that they were black and scaly. A thorned spike shot out of one of the scaly lumps, poking a horned troublemaker in the ass. It skittered sideways and straight under a giant gray lizard with two heads. "What do you call that?"

Shiloh held her nose. "I don't know, but they all need baths." She gave me a sympathetic look. "I'll bet this was what your dad was going to have you clear out."

"Unless he was sending me after the snake." So far, there hadn't been a favor big enough for him *not* to ask.

Shiloh sighed. "At least Babydoll didn't get stuck in there."

No, she'd come home with me.

"Let's keep moving," I said. We'd help the creatures, but it was too dangerous to attempt it now.

I walked over the bars on the balls of my feet, careful that my heels didn't get caught. I didn't know if any of the lumps or horned things could jump.

As I feared, our journey caused a small riot below. The mini-rhinos, as it turned out, were quite springy. Fat gray tongues reached up to lick at anything they could. Luckily just our shoes, but eww.

I was relieved when we'd finished crossing the cell. Mostly. The wards felt even stronger on the other side. Cool power pressed heavily on us as we continued down the sloping passageway. It was almost too much. I was going to get a headache if this kept up.

Unease prickled at the back of my neck.

"Do you think we're getting closer?" Shiloh asked, hovering close.

"Yes." The creatures had come from Dad's attempts to pull power from the dark vortex. He'd admitted as much to me.

It also stood to reason the nearer we drew, the heavier the security.

The passage opened up into a circular room. It was pitch black, save for an immense lamp in the shape of a full moon. It stood on three bronze legs, and the rounded alabaster holder in the center burned with an unearthly red fire.

A low growl rumbled from the far corner. A pair of blood red eyes watched us.

I drew back.

Holy hellfire.

I didn't see any cage bars blocking this one.

Shiloh placed a hand on my shoulder, her nails digging in hard as a jackal the size of a car stalked out from the shadows.

It bared its teeth, snarling.

It's not as if we could run back from where we came. The passage was too narrow. The underground prison would trip us up. If this creature wasn't on us before we'd even make it that far.

I drew a switch star.

If it leaped, I'd have one shot before it was on me.

And if I killed it, I just had to hope the Earl wouldn't be right on my ass.

Because I still hadn't figured out how to kill him.

"Stay calm," I said to Shiloh and myself. "Let's not be the aggressors." I didn't see any way that would work out.

The jackal moved like the predator it was, lithe and smooth. I took in its sinewy muscles. The gold hoops piercing its ears. The skin of a leopard draped over its shoulders, the lifeless head hanging between its powerful shoulders. I'd never encountered anything like it.

I watched it draw up on its hind legs in a move that looked almost…human.

"Maybe it doesn't want to eat us," Shiloh whispered.

"Yet," I told her.

I kept moving, step by careful step. Shiloh followed as we attempted to skirt the creature.

Her shoulder knocked into mine. "It's the god Anubis," she said, breathless.

"No, it's not." I had bought her line about the Bakhtaks, but the Egyptian god of death? That was just plain crazy.

Although I'd grant her, any ancient person seeing this thing would never forget it.

It watched us, stalked us. It let out a low-throated growl that sent chills up my arms. I'd been hearing the jackal.

My chest felt tight. It was impossible to take a deep breath, even though I wanted to heave with exertion. We were halfway past it and it hadn't attacked.

Maybe it didn't have us where it wanted us yet.

"Did you know," Shiloh began, her voice shaking, in the most inappropriate round of trivia I'd ever had the misfortune to witness, "Anubis selects worthy souls and takes them to Osiris."

I didn't bother answering. It took everything I had to keep focused on the beast. I wasn't about to take folklore as fact. There was a reason ancient people made up stories. The truth was too fucking terrifying.

And if we were really following this Egyptian theme, maybe we wouldn't mention the fact that I destroyed the Tomb of Kebechet. Kebechet being Anubis's daughter. No doubt she was a treat.

But it didn't matter. We just needed to find my dad's vortex. Once we got past the beast.

It took a step toward us and we both froze.

Cripes. This was it. I hated to switch star it. Creepy or not, it was a living being. Besides, its death it might alert my dad, or worse, the Earl.

I cleared my throat, willing my voice to come out strong. "What do you want?" I asked it. It was worth a shot.

It lowered its head and let out a blood-racing growl that echoed off the walls of the small chamber.

Right.

The creature watched me without blinking. Its body coiled down, its head pushed forward, ready to strike.

The crackling intensified. Beyond the creature, deep in the shadows, I could feel the pulsing of the dark vortex.

"That's it," I said, my throat tight. "That's where the Earl is drawing his power."

It called to me with its icy pull. We must be directly under the part of the church that housed the tomb. I'd be willing to bet Dad was drawing the darkness straight down, through the vortex and straight to the Earl's base of operations.

We were so close. Almost there.

Maybe the beast would let us pass if we didn't actually touch the vortex. I sure as Hades wasn't about to get caught up in it. I just needed to draw close enough to try to see if I could shut it down, or at least get a bead on how it worked.

I couldn't imagine how anything made it through. I'd sealed the Earl into hell. I'd locked him away. He couldn't open this up on his own.

Of course, he had had the help of my dad.

Good thing I did, too.

"Can you tell where it goes?" Shiloh asked.

I glanced at her. "No." I almost didn't hear her over the pull of the portal beyond. "I'm not sure I even care right now." I just wanted to shut it down. "How does it taste?"

She let out a breath, as if she'd been holding it. "Stale."

I hadn't expected that.

We needed time to figure this out, preferably without something hunting us. But I didn't see how that was going to happen.

The jackal had moved in behind us, blocking our exit.

An icy chill settled against my back. "The vortex should taste deliciously evil or something, right?"

"It's strange," she said.

"Fuck," I said, as the jackal bared its fangs and attacked.

Chapter Twenty-One

We had nowhere else to go. Shiloh grabbed my arm as we tumbled backward into the vortex. It was like falling off a cliff in the dark. Nothing behind us, no solid ground to grab. My stomach hollowed from the sheer drop and I tried to grab something—anything—from the endless black void.

Freezing wind whipped through my hair, tangling it in my face and mouth. I lost Shiloh, my palm suddenly cold from the stolen warmth of her grip. She was with me one second and gone the next.

Shiloh! I hollered for her. No sound came out, and that terrified me as much as tumbling down a deep endless pit to a bone-shattering fall at the end.

Shiloh! I screamed until my throat burned.

But there was only silence.

I don't know how far I fell, or for how long.

My shoulder struck first, hitting hard as I slammed sideways into something solid and cold. I grabbed for it, intending to hold on for all I was worth.

A sudden white-hot light stung my eyes, blinding me as I went for my weapons. *Shoot,* my mind screamed.

But where?

I rolled onto my back, gasping for breath. My lungs burned. I had no air. I slammed my switch star into the soft, giving surface next to me and foul dirt spewed up.

I spit it away from my lips and tasted metal. I had to be dead. Dying, at least. Usually I fought harder. What in Hades was wrong with me?

A horrible prickling sensation wound over my skin. It settled into the deepest, darkest parts of me like a parasite and I knew I had to get out of there.

I curled into a ball. Stop, drop, and roll.

And then I really was rolling, downhill.

Cripes.

I used my arms to try to stop myself, battering my wrists. I sliced my hand on the switch star in the dirt and felt the rush of pain. I cradled it against my body and felt it slippery with blood. I rolled several more times until I came to rest on my stomach. I reached out, winding my fingers through scratchy grass. I felt it against my cheek.

Muu-bork.

Something pointy and alive shoved up against the back of my head.

Muu-bork.

At least the invasive prickling sensation had ceased.

I blinked against the light and opened my eyes to see a twirly black horn aimed at my face.

Muu-bork.

I batted it away and sat up two seconds before an overgrown who-knows-what whacked me again. It had a beak instead of teeth, so that was a plus. But Hades, the thing was ugly. It looked like a mix between a goat and a parrot and was covered in shaggy silver-and-white tendrils of fur. It had floppy ears, huge black eyes and a horn like a unicorn.

At least it didn't want to eat me.

"Get away," I said, batting the horn as it tried to poke me again. I looked at my right hand—my throwing hand—and saw a long, bloody slice through the groove by my thumb.

Fan-fricking-tastic. If I were at home, I'd be driving to the ER for stitches.

Here? My eyes felt like sandpaper and my nose wouldn't stop running. I rubbed at it with my good hand and tried to think of what to do next. I was sitting in a depressingly barren field. Sparse gray grass clung to sandy soil. I'd rolled down a slight incline and sat among a flock of grazing horned creatures, like the one that was now sniffing my leg.

Phew, it smelled like the gorilla cage at the zoo.

Shiloh was nowhere in sight.

My knees felt weak and my legs tingled as I drew them up under me and stood. Black clouds billowed over gray skies. There were no birds, no trees, no real plants anywhere, save for the scrubby brush. Aside from the annoying goatlike thing sniffing my ankle, it was eerily quiet.

My stomach drew tight. I knew where I was. Purgatory.

The land was mostly flat and I could see for miles—nothing but barren wasteland.

Hot and dry air, tinged with sulfur, made me want to sneeze. Now that I looked closer, I could see the yellow substance clinging to rocks and errant blades of grass.

Lovely.

Nothing like a romp in the purgatory countryside. I'd been down to this realm only once with my dad. It had been a nightmare, but at least we'd explored a city. There was no telling what lurked in the rural stretch between Earth and hell.

A hissing sound erupted from the incline near me. I backed off fast. The creatures did the same, grunting and chirping as needles of energy pierced the air.

I drew a switch star with my left hand, ready to at least try to defend myself.

Shiloh came crashing down on the ground near the spot where I'd landed. Her fingers clutched at the barren soil and she let out a groan.

Thank God she hadn't hit the switch star I still hadn't bothered to pick up. What was wrong with me? I gave a mental curse and rushed for her.

"Don't move," I ordered, too late. She'd turned on her side and had begun rolling down the rise away from me. She missed the star. Thank heaven. I stopped before I reached the top of the rise. I wasn't about to cross over the vortex.

Instead, I went around, dodging curious horned busybodies.

"Are you okay?" I asked, drawing my star out of the dirt and re-sheathing it before I knelt next to her and helped her sit.

The black vortex that had dumped us here had to go both ways. Otherwise, how had I seen these crazy goat creatures in the dungeon under the church? This was probably how my dad was sucking up unsuspecting wildlife. And then going the other way, the vortex stole the energy from the souls my dad captured for the Earl.

It was all so…wrong.

It was a wonder we'd survived it. I had no idea how we were going to destroy it and go home.

Shiloh pushed her hair out of her face, cringing. "Oh my God, I got in so much trouble the last time I was down here."

"Are you sad to know that's the least of our problems?" The last time I'd gotten sucked down here, the Earl was trying to lure me to my death. And now? Oh wait…

"Why are you shaking your head?" Shiloh asked, as I reached a hand down to help her up.

"Nothing," I told her. "I'm surprised they let a half demon like you into purgatory." This wasn't exactly the party palace.

She struggled to her feet, wobbling a little on her goldfish stripper heels. "What part of fun sneaking around don't you get?"

A lot, apparently.

I planted my hands on my hips and looked out over the wastelands. "Well, obviously I suck at this because I'm here instead of in Dad's church." At this rate, I'd never figure out how to stop him.

Shiloh eyed the top of the rise. "At least we know where he's drawing his energy."

We'd traveled *through* his gateway to ruin. It was a wonder we'd made it out alive. I walked toward the top of the rise, ignoring the harsh needling of the dark power. What I saw stopped me dead in my tracks.

My throat tightened. "Shiloh," I uttered.

She drew up next to me and gasped.

The absolute top of the rise formed a crease as long as a man. Nothing grew there. Not even a wisp of a blade of grass. Instead, it was covered in sandy dirt. A vein of white rock pierced the ground running straight down.

I pointed to it. "There's our line in the sand."

Shiloh let out a groan. "I hate being right."

I wasn't so sure I agreed with her. Yes, this sucked, but in my line of work, I'd take all the warnings I could get. The seer had predicted the fenris, the Egyptian symbology, and the line in the sand. I turned to her. Her skin was flushed, her eyes wide. "What's next?"

She touched her fingers to the long column of her throat, her voice hitching. "The demon rises."

"That's not going to happen," I told her. I wouldn't allow it.

"But, Lizzie—"

I stepped away from her, ignoring the magnetic push of the energy. It was shoving at me hard. The vortex must work like a one-way street. No doubt it could reverse directions, but right now, it was in sucking mode. I pushed my way through and reached for it.

"You're bleeding," Shiloh said, as if that mattered.

I touched the line in the sand. It was ice cold. I felt the pure chill of it a second before demonic energy singed my fingertips. "Ow!" I yanked my hand back and studied my reddened fingers. "The Earl's down there." I wet my burned fingers with my mouth. Yes, it was gross, but it hurt.

Now that I'd physically touched the line in the sand, I could feel the thrum of the energy traveling through the vortex.

Not a one-way street at all. The Earl was taking in massive amounts of soul energy with every pulse. He must have permanent ties to those poor people on Earth. And he was growing stronger by the second.

Shiloh pulled a handkerchief from in between her boobs and handed it to me. I didn't even want to know why she carried that. I accepted it and began wrapping it around my injured hand. "I'd bet anything this is where I locked him down before." Only some of the energy was escaping. I finished tightening my bandage, and ran my finger a hairbreadth over the white rock line, testing it, until I came across an area where the beat of it changed. I didn't know what to make of that until I spotted something. "There." A cold metal scarab was wedged in next to it, almost under it.

Shiloh hovered behind me. "I've never seen anything like it."

Me, neither. Still, "I'd bet anything this is my dad's relic." Dad seemed to have an affinity with insects.

And the scarab was the symbol of rebirth. Hades, I didn't want the Earl to have his second coming. I glanced up at her. "Dad's sending power through this relic."

"Straight to the Earl," Shiloh finished.

I continued my exploration of the line, hoping to find something more. "We've got to seal this off." We needed to cut the ties to those souls Dad had captured for the Earl. As long as they were linked to this relic and feeding their power into hell, they'd never be free.

And the Earl would rise again.

Shiloh reached out a trembling hand and touched the relic. She jerked as she made contact. Her eyes went red and her nostrils flared. I didn't like it. "Are you okay?" I asked.

She appeared as if she were in some kind of a trance.

Even her voice had changed. It was rusty and deep when she spoke. "He has enough power now."

How could she know that? "What do you see?"

Her fingers pressed down on it, flattening against the scarab. "The exchange is complete," she said, her voice deepening. "He's locked and ready."

My own heart thundered in my chest. "Impossible," I said, praying I was right. "If he could, he'd attack."

Her eyes watered; her breath came in pants. "He just needs one more piece."

"What?" I demanded. We'd steal it from him, rob him, lock him down for good.

She stared at me. "He needs you."

The truth of it slammed into me. I understood exactly what my dad had wanted from me.

I stumbled backward down the hill, cursing my arrogance, my blind belief that I knew what was best. My dad had played me.

Sure, he'd had a chore for me to do. He didn't need me to handle creatures.

No, I was the final piece of his power puzzle. He'd melded his powers with mine not so that he could trust me, but so that he could open me up and drain me alive. As soon as they reinstalled the tomb, he was probably going to put me in it.

Well, I'd screwed up his plan, taken things into my own hands. I'd gone through the vortex and came out on the other side—whole. Yes, I might have a touch of his power inside me, but I still had free will.

And I was going to stop him.

Shiloh was still touching the relic, with her eyes closed. Like she enjoyed it.

"Back off!" I ordered, breaking her away.

She hissed at me, her eyes red, her hair a mess of tangles. I cupped her cheeks in my hands, fought her back. "This isn't you." She shoved against me, slamming her eyes closed as she did. "You're better than this, Shiloh."

She was my friend. She helped me.

And heaven knows, I needed her now.

"Stay with me now," I ordered. "I can't do this without you."

She nodded, her face a mottled mess. "I'm here," she said, shaking me off. She coughed violently, fighting for more than just breath. When she opened her eyes, they were going from red back to blue.

"Good," I said, hoping I was right.

She nodded, hand still at her mouth, as she cleared her throat. "I hate to admit it, but it's actually getting easier."

I helped her balance, so she didn't tip over. "We have to stop using you like this," I said as she straightened.

She didn't respond to that, most likely because she knew she might have to step up again. It may not be right or fair, but we both understood what needed to happen here. "How do you plug the gap?" she asked, brushing the hair away from her face.

"I don't know." I'd never done it before. The closest I'd come was sealing demons in. It required a massive influx of power. Now that Dad had rigged the seal with his relic, any added energy might backfire on me and open the gates. I wasn't about to take the chance. "It was a little too convenient that the jackal backed us into the portal." For all I knew, they might want me down here, adding energy to the line in the sand. "We need to find my mentor, Rachmort." He'd know how to approach this.

Rachmort was one of the most powerful necromancers in this or any other dimension. He specialized in dealing with black magic and demons. Which was why he lived and worked in purgatory.

"Oh, him," Shiloh said, without much enthusiasm. "He slew my half-sister."

"I'm sorry," I told her.

She shook it off.

Maybe I wasn't sorry. Her half sister had probably tried to kill me in Las Vegas.

I sighed. We had bigger problems. "I usually call Rachmort. Not that it's going to work here." I had good cell phone reception, but even my stellar plan didn't cover purgatory. "Are we near a city?"

Shiloh glanced toward a blip on the horizon. "The only city." She chewed at her lip. "Lizzie, I'm not kidding you about what I saw. The soul lines were complete. He has his energy. We need to get you out of here."

"You want to tell me how?" We were at the bottom of the well. I couldn't just pick up my marbles and go home. "Anyway, you know I can't leave. I'm the only one who can do this."

She wrapped her arms protectively over her chest. "If you screw up, you could free the Earl of Hell."

"Thanks for the vote of confidence," I told her. I wasn't discounting her warning, though. I'd be smart about this.

She pressed her lips together for a moment before nodding. "Okay. Let's head for the city."

"I knew you'd see it my way," I said as we began walking.

Shiloh rolled her eyes.

A pack of wild fenrises darted out in front of us, running and barking. "Do you know where to find our necromancer?" she asked.

"Not exactly," I told her. But I knew a good place to start.

Chapter Twenty-Two

Shiloh pointed to a gray lump on the horizon. "Town is this way."

I squinted to see, but there wasn't much to it. "How do you know?"

She shrugged, running a hand through her disheveled hair, drawing it into sexy, messy waves. Her voice went breathy. "I can smell the sin."

Oh Lordy.

I simply had to bring a sex demon into an underworld Sodom and Gomorrah.

We started walking. "Maybe I should have brought your knitting," I said. I couldn't resist.

She snorted.

I pressed on. "I thought souls were here to serve penance." My boots crunched on the rocky soil. "Maybe earn their way to a better place."

She shot me a sideways glance. "Some folks never learn."

Touché.

We pressed forward. I had to admit, I liked having Shiloh around for this. I wasn't sure exactly how or when, but she'd grown on me.

Sure, she had her faults. Everyone did. And, yes, I wished her eyes didn't glow red sometimes. But she'd proved herself to be a good friend. A solid ally. I knew from cold, hard experience both were hard to come by, at least in anything other than biker witch or griffin form.

As we neared town, I could start to make out some of the buildings. "Look," I said, pointing out a pack of wild fenrises. There were at least a half dozen of them. They were large, like Babydoll, with gray-and-black coats. The pack munched on a garden of dull gray plants near the rear of a building.

"They should be eating devil's grass," she scolded, "from the barren plains behind us." She sighed, as if that were our biggest problem. "Oh well. Let them have a treat. We'll just hope someone's not too upset about their cauliflower crop."

And my mom thought she had trouble with rabbits in her garden.

"Okay, let's keep our guard up," I said, as we entered an alley between the stubby building and the taller one.

"Just a sec." Shiloh paused near the fenrises in the yard. I kept walking.

Cities in purgatory were like supernatural slums, at least the parts I'd seen.

Overflowing trash cans crammed the alley. I could smell the rot, the almost palpable sense of despair. The black clouds hovered thicker over the city, as if the suffering itself drew them, bearing down on the inhabitants even more, in a depressing circle of almost-life.

"You know where we're going?" Shiloh asked, drawing closer to me.

"I hope." I'd been to Rae Rae's pawn shop only once before, but I had to believe it was still there. And that we could find it.

The alley opened up on a city street swirling with debris. Directly ahead of us, a gang of grayish-skinned men shoved at one another.

A particularly menacing one with black swastikas on his cheeks drew a gun. "You want a taste of me, motherfucker?"

Three more of the men pulled out weapons.

"Fuck you!" His rival lifted a gun and shot the man in the gut.

The bullet passed straight through, lodging in the cracking grey stone building to our right.

I stopped dead. It didn't faze the skinhead or the gang member or whatever the hell he was, but it could have killed me or Shiloh.

She gripped my arm and pulled me forward. "Come on. Act casual."

Easier said than done.

The thug's attention had turned to us. His face broke into a leer, stretching his tattoos and making his face look even more ghoulish. "Look who wants to have some fun."

A fat sweaty guy behind him eyed Shiloh's outfit. "I'll get you out of that dress."

Lordy. My friend wore red in the land of gray tones. We were a walking target.

Sweat flushed my skin as I reached for my switch stars. I didn't know if I could kill them all. Or if I should. They hadn't gone after us directly. Yet.

"Stop," Shiloh said, her breath hot against my ear. "Let me handle this."

She pushed away from me, her skin taking on a faint gold shimmer. Her eyes glowed pink. Her skin flushed. I watched an unnatural calm settle over the men as a delicate scarlet-toned bubble encapsulated Shiloh and me. Warmth and energy washed over my skin and right down to my bones. It made me feel relaxed. Sexy.

Not that I was going to do anything about it.

I couldn't say the same for Shiloh. She curled a hand over her hip, thrust out her chest, and gave a decimating come-hither smile. The woman positively radiated sex. She licked her lips, eyeing the large thug with the swastikas on his cheeks. "One at a time or all of you together?" she purred.

The guy puffed up, obviously into it. "Fuck these assholes. You want me."

A man like that should have attacked already. It was in his nature. But he held back.

All of them did.

Shiloh's skin glowed and I realized with a start that she was drawing power from him. That couldn't be safe. But seeing as it was the only thing keeping us out of a fight, I let it go. She had a handle on it.

I hoped.

She'd obviously done this before.

The she-demon drew a finger over her skintight red latex dress, somehow managing to make the bust even more revealing. Hells bells. If she didn't watch it, one of her boobs was going to pop out.

"Thing is," she drawled, "I work for Frisco."

The gang members flinched as a group and I made a mental note to avoid this Frisco.

Shiloh strolled over to the shooter. He'd dropped his hands to his sides, unsure for the first time.

I followed her, staying closer than I wanted because—let's face it—I wasn't about to leave her power circle.

She arched her back and pressed her breasts toward his chest, drawing him into her glistening bubble of power. "I like it rough." She traced a finger down his chest. "And I like *you*."

Her power flared red as she drew more and more from him. His shoulders and spine relaxed, as if she'd already given him the workout she promised.

Shiloh paused, rubbing her glossed lips together. She had him mesmerized. She tilted her head and her hair fell away, exposing a long white expanse of skin. "How about you meet me at Frisco's establishment in an hour. I'll treat you real special."

"Fuck yeah," he chuckled, still off his game, still not touching her.

She turned and gave me a wink. "Come on. I think I'll need to warm up for this one." She puckered her lips at him and I tried not to gag.

She took one step away, then two. I kept up with her. I stayed in the bubble, even though it made me uncomfortable as hell. I wasn't one for sneaking around, *seducing.*

I leaned close to her. I appreciated her getting us out of there, but, "Don't include me in your sex talk," I hissed.

"Don't look back," she said, not even looking at me. "Don't show weakness."

"I'm not weak," I muttered. Had she seen me fight? I desperately wanted to see what was behind us. "I'm just not a sex demon."

"Tell me about it," she said, as she linked her arm with mine. "Today, I gotta tell you, I'm really enjoying it."

Sin and damnation. If we had to be on a street full of brothels, I supposed I should be glad one of us could appreciate it.

Nothing had followed us. Yet. I glanced over my shoulder. Narrow gray buildings crowded the streets, with signs that said Donner's, Mac's, Odessa, and Famous Fire.

"I'll give them one thing," I murmured. "They're discreet."

"If you've been here long enough, you know," Shiloh said.

Lovely. I glanced around. "Why are these on the edge of town?" It seemed like the underworld would celebrate debauchery. "Or are these the really kinky ones?"

"Crazier than anything you can imagine," Shiloh said, nodding to a man out in front of Frisco's. Holy Hades. She really did know Frisco. "I don't miss it," she said quickly. "Much," she added.

She used to feed on lust. Maybe it was exciting, but it couldn't make her truly happy. "You have a better life now," I told her, just in case she needed a reminder.

She glanced at me. "That's why I keep walking."

We drew plenty of stares, but the bubble held and no one approached us as we walked deeper into the red-light district. Most of the buildings were plain, with handwritten cardboard signs out front. Nothing made them stand out, other than the various crowds of shifty-looking men outside. There were a few women, mostly wearing few to no clothes. Everything in shades of black and white.

"Still whorehouses," she said, as if anticipating my question.

We headed deeper into the city until Shiloh started pointing out as many bars as she did bordellos. It was an improvement.

"I don't get it," I told her. "When I was here before, the people acted as if they were already dead. They just shuffled down the street." I shook my head. "We're in trouble if the Earl has somehow altered the energy of purgatory itself."

"It's not that," Shiloh said. "There's a Dead Section. This way." We made a hard right down a street that looked more like an alley. Tall buildings cast shadows over the narrow corridor and I swore I could sense movement in the corners.

"This is even creepier than the live section," I told her.

Shiloh's power shimmered around us. "I think so. But from what you're saying, I'll bet your friend is this way."

"There were a lot of fast food places and the people moved like drones."

"That's the Dead Section," she said, as the alleyway grew darker. "There are different districts down here," Shiloh explained, "neighborhoods if you will." She glanced up at the buzzards circling overhead. "Although you're going to have to help me with this one, because I've never been out of the section we just left."

Okay. "I can do that." At least we were headed in the right direction. Frankly I preferred the less active trapped souls. We were conspicuously alone in the narrow passage, with no one ahead of us or behind. We sped up our pace. "How are you doing in those heels?" I asked. Mine were starting to pinch.

Shiloh tossed her hair back, managing to look like a model in a shampoo ad. "I get off on heels."

I brought my gaze back to the long road ahead. "Of course you do."

The passage opened up into the place where the inhabitants' eyes had deadened and their spirits caved. I was actually glad to see it, which I knew was wrong on about ten different levels.

But we had a job to do. We had to find Rachmort so he could help us sever the links to the hundreds of church members who were tied to the Earl. The demon was drawing energy from them because my dad had broken the seal, opened up a crack if you will. We'd close it and free those people for good.

Shiloh's bubble weakened the farther we drew from the brothels, until it shimmered away completely. "That's all I can do," she said, slightly worried.

It would have to be enough. "Stick close," I told her.

I had worries of my own. About our security, yes, that was a given. But I'd also come to the sickening realization that I felt more comfortable here than I should. My body felt stronger. My heels didn't hurt anymore. In fact...I glanced down at my hand and saw smooth, healed skin.

Yikes.

Shiloh noticed as well. "I've been where you're going and it's not pretty."

I knew that. What to do about it was another matter. "At least I'm recovering." Look at the bright side, right? With more strength, I'd have a better chance to seal away the Earl for good.

That's what I told myself, anyway.

Shiloh wasn't swayed. "It's going to tempt you with things you want."

Like hope, healing, and a chance to save people. "I'm aware," I told her. I didn't know if I had a choice. Or if it was entirely bad, as long as I could control it.

I sidestepped to avoid a lost soul. Here, the people with grayish skin wandered up and down the confining streets, with no apparent rush or direction. We passed several shuttered businesses, a few open ones.

Fast food seemed to be the most popular, just like the last time I was here. I know when I had a bad day, I needed Taco Bell, but this was ridiculous.

There was no energy here, no life.

I thought I might almost prefer the naked violence of the kinky whorehouse area, and then I remembered the live bullets flying.

Here, nobody even looked you in the eye. A trashcan had toppled on its side, spilling empty cups and fast food wrappers.

Nobody seemed to care. These people were like empty shells. They bumped against streetlights, unused parking meters, and even one another with barely a nod of recognition.

"Why are they like this?" I asked.

Shiloh gave a slight shiver. "When you have nothing else to trade down here, you trade part of your soul." A glassy-eyed woman stumbled toward us. She wore a business suit with a large bow tied at the neck. Her glasses were skewed on her face and her eyes were blank. Shiloh stepped sideways to avoid the woman. "Trade too much and you end up like her."

I felt sorry for her. Did she get credit for time served? "How does she get saved?"

Shiloh's shoulder nudged me as she moved aside for the woman. "She doesn't."

I refused to believe that. Or maybe I just didn't want it to be true.

"At least it's better than hell," Shiloh said.

I wasn't sure if it was.

I could see why my mentor, Rachmort, had chosen to spend his life reaching out to the trapped souls here. I wondered if he worked with them like this, or if he saved them before they got this bad.

We passed a guy with a Toasty Almonds cart. Only the nuts had no smell. Probably no color or taste, either.

"Look," I said, pointing down the street toward a small, sad park. An expanse of gray grass featured black benches and a dry gray stone fountain with an immense gargoyle in the middle. I remembered that garden from when my dad and I ventured down here.

"Rae Rae's is close. This way" I led us across the street and then down to the next block to a drab storefront. And sue me, I let out a sigh of relief when I saw the spray-painted sign over the door. *Rae Rae's Re-Usables.*

Shiloh looked it up and down. "This is a dump."

"A good one," I told her. Rachmort trusted him. My dad had as well, but that was neither here nor there. I only hoped Rae Rae himself was working. I didn't know anybody else down here and didn't think Shiloh's friend would take too kindly to helping us find a necromancer. "Come on." I opened the creaky, dirty door and stepped inside a small shop.

The only light came from an array of stubby white candles and a busted-out part of the roof, currently covered in makeshift glass and duct tape.

A freakishly tall man stood behind a glass counter. If we were still in LA, I would have mistaken him for a professional athlete. He had the kind of wide-shouldered, lean-muscled physique that made you stop and take a second look. He also had the largest hands I'd ever seen. Today, he'd painted his nails silver and decorated them with white polka dots. He'd shaved all the hair from his body and wore a rust-and-brown-chevron dress.

All put together, Rae Rae looked like a black Vin Diesel in drag.

And sue me if I envied his slim hips.

I shook my head. I had to think of him as a *her.* Anybody who referred to Rae Rae as a guy got kicked out of the pawn shop.

Rae Rae didn't even glance up as the bell over my head jingled. Instead, she lowered her chin and glared at the handsome man in front of her.

"I don't care if you have all the king's gold and half his men back at your place in New Orleans. You got to have some cash now if you want that crystal."

The man's wide shoulders bunched as he slammed a hand down onto the counter. "Damn it. You know I'm good for it." He wore a long leather duster jacket and cowboy boots. The ornate bronze clockwork ring on his right hand advertised his status as a necromancer. His shoulders strained as he worked hard to collect himself. "At least let me use credit."

Rae Rae drew up to her full height. "Excuse me. Does this look like a fucking savings and loan? Is my name Charity?"

"This is important," her customer ground out. "Life and death."

Rae Rae clucked. "And this is me getting bored." She curled a hand and placed it on her hip. "If you weren't so cute, I'd have kicked you out by now."

The necromancer ran a frustrated hand through his spiky brown hair. "I could turn you into a spider."

Rae Rae batted her lashes. "Oh, snap! But you won't. You're too goody-two-shoes."

"Damn it."

"Ohh…talk dirty to me."

She was just baiting him now.

We watched from the narrow foyer. Shiloh leaned in close behind me. "The guy in the black coat is hot."

"He is," I murmured, not quite believing I'd said it.

What was wrong with me? I loved Dimitri. I shouldn't be staring at Rae Rae's customer. Even if he was all sinew and muscle.

Stop it.

He looked as if he was about my age, with that badass edge you get only from being on the front lines.

"I received a sign," he was saying to Rae Rae. "It said to come in today. I'd be given the crystal today."

The pawn broker shrugged. "Sorry, beautiful. Your signs are off."

That got him going. "My predictions are never wrong."

She rolled her eyes. "You believe this know-it-all?" she asked, turning to us by the door. When she saw who I was, her face lit up. "Lizzie Brown," she exclaimed. Of course she would be excited to see me. The last time I came here, I'd had lavender hair and Rae Rae had given me a super short cut, in the name of profit. Color was like currency down here. This time, Shiloh stepped out from behind me and Rae Rae about went into a faint. "Queen Mother on a boat." She spread her arms and strutted over to greet us. "What do you have?"

The man at the counter turned, his blue eyes blazing hot. "Oh, God. It is you."

I looked behind me to Shiloh, but then I realized he was talking to me. "Do I know you?" I think I would have remembered.

He crossed his arms over his chest. Great. I guess he was pissed at me now. Or maybe he was grouchy because of what he was. My mentor Rachmort's attitude was abnormally positive, for one who dealt with the dead. But this necromancer definitely needed to get out more.

I stepped back as Rae Rae brushed past me and headed straight to Shiloh. She ran her manicured fingers over Shiloh's shoulders and skimmed over her red latex dress. "Oh you are mine, babygirl. All mine."

The drag queen could try to be a little subtle. Or not. "We're looking for Rachmort," I told her.

Rae Rae didn't answer. She was too wrapped up in my friend's wardrobe. "I could pair you with silk stockings, love. Maybe add a broach."

Shiloh tilted her head at me, a bit put out. "You set me up, didn't you?"

"Relax." Maybe Rae Rae would point us to our necromancer without Shiloh trading her dress.

Nah. Shiloh was losing the dress.

"Where's Rachmort?" I asked again.

Rae Rae drew back. "Oh, don't tease me," she crooned. "I don't know that. What else do you want?"

"Him and only him," I told her.

Rae Rae gave a pout. "Then I would lie to you if Rachmort wouldn't kick my ass later." She sighed. "He doesn't check in with the likes of me, sweetness. And I haven't seen him in a month." She gave me a level look. "Now let's focus on what's important. What else can I get for you?"

The hottie behind her stared daggers at her back. "Give me my crystal."

"Sashay in here with a skintight dress and we'll talk," she said to him, not even bothering to turn around.

We had to get beyond commerce here. Souls were at stake. "Listen to me very carefully," I said to Rae Rae. "I locked a demon away, but he has a dark vortex open and he's drawing power from Earth." The shop owner looked bored, but I pushed on. "It could be very, very bad unless a necromancer like Rachmort shows me how to close this thing."

The man at the counter joined us, his arms crossed over his chest. "Rachmort's in the Setesh Wastelands. He should be back soon enough."

Rae Rae groaned. "Oh, now come on. I could have charged for that information." She planted her hands on her hips and glared at the man. "This is why you're poor."

I ignored the queen. "How soon do you expect him?"

The man thought for a moment. "I don't know." He shook off the question. "It doesn't matter. Rachmort wouldn't help you anyway. It's dangerous and stupid to go near a demon vortex."

"Well, aren't you a ray of sunshine?" I still didn't know how he knew me. But it seemed late introductions were in order. I held out a hand. "Lizzie Kallinikos."

He took it. "Evan Carpenter," he said. He had a solid, sure grip. "You're Rachmort's mentee," he said stiffly. "He told me about you."

"So then you know how powerful she is," Shiloh said.

He glanced at her. "Rachmort told me Lizzie fell out of a tree."

Great. "That was during training," I clarified. It had been hard for me to grasp the whole concept of levitation. "I've come a long way. I'm much more skilled now."

He looked me up and down, as if he didn't quite believe it. "I'll bet."

"Will *you* help us shut down the dark vortex?" I asked. He was a necromancer. That's all we needed. And if Rachmort knew him well enough to tell stories about me, I figured I could at least let him take a look.

"Absolutely not," he shot back, not even thinking about it.

He had to understand. "We'll pay you."

His eyes narrowed. "I can't get involved with you. It's too dangerous."

"What's a little danger?" Shiloh asked, winking at him.

He didn't go for it. His eyes were cold, hard. "If I help you, something bad will happen." The man was a block of ice. "I shouldn't be anywhere near you."

This was ridiculous. I glanced at Rae Rae. "Is he good?"

The queen crossed her arms over her chest. "One of the best. But he's a cheap-ass and a pain in the butt."

Yeah, well, we needed to stop a demon. I couldn't afford to care about everybody's feelings. "All we have to do is seal the fissure," I told him. "It'll take ten minutes, tops."

Carpenter drew up to his full height. "It doesn't work that way. You can't just walk in here and expect me to jump in and join your little stunt."

"Because none of us do what we don't feel like doing," I shot back.

Did he think I chose to get pulled into this hellhole? Did he think I wanted to mess with demon powers?

But he was already running off at the mouth again. "This is why I don't take on students," he said over me. "You have no idea what the science of necromancy involves. Ten minutes my ass. Fissures are complicated." He cursed under his breath. "And don't get me started on if an outside force is holding it open. The only thing that could make that more difficult is if a relic like a phoenix or a scarab were somehow involved. And if we did manage to seal it, you'd just go about your merry way without ever thinking about the seven hundred ways the project could have gone wrong."

Exactly. "You do know your stuff," I told him. Then to Rae Rae, I added, "even if he is a pain in the ass."

Shiloh nudged me. "That's not how you get him to work with us."

No, but I knew another way. The man wanted this crystal thing and we could get it for him. I turned to my friend. "Take off your dress."

Lucky for me, sex demons aren't shy. "This had better work," she said, clearly more bothered by the loss of the dress than by stripping naked in a pawn shop.

"What the hell are you doing?" Carpenter demanded. He darted his gaze to the ceiling as she slid out of her bodice.

Rae Rae, on the other hand, looked at the dress with pure lust. "Tell me it's a size six."

"I'm thinking this is enough to buy Carpenter's toy," I said. I wasn't going to take no for an answer on this.

"You can't take my crystal," the necromancer roared, still staring at the ceiling.

Oy vey. The man was a prude.

"The shoes, too," Rae Rae purred, "and it's a deal."

"I'm not taking your rock," I said to the necromancer, "I'm buying it." He looked like he'd just swallowed a bug. "And if you want it, you can have it... After you help us."

Carpenter cursed under his breath.

Hey, it made sense. We needed a necromancer. He needed his crystal. I was betting the necromancer wasn't allowed to steal the thing, or he would have already.

I turned to Rae Rae. "You think you can get Shiloh something else to wear?"

The pawn broker touched a fingertip to her chin. "You got any matching underwear?" she asked.

"Sorry," Shiloh said, bending over to slip out of the dress.

"Not even a thong?" Rae Rae pressed.

"Absolutely not," she said, straightening, buck naked as she kicked the dress at Rae Rae.

The pawn broker merely grinned. "Damn girl, I like your style." She reached for the dress, handling it like a holy relic as she cradled it over her arm. "Give me a minute."

"I sure hope she's getting you something," I said to Shiloh as Rae Rae ducked behind the counter and went behind a dingy curtain that led to the back room.

Shiloh shrugged. "Carpenter's more worried about it than me," she said, pointing to our necromancer. His broad shoulders were tense. He swallowed hard, a lump traveling down his thick neck. The man couldn't take his eyes off the ceiling.

"What are you? A virgin?" she asked.

The muscles in his neck corded with tension. "That's none of your business," he gritted out.

Shiloh looked at me. "Virgin," she concluded.

"Hey," I said, trying to make him feel better. "This is a good thing. You wouldn't have gotten your crystal any other way."

"I shouldn't be doing this," he muttered, refusing to look at the bright side. "I shouldn't even consider it. Why does everything have to be so difficult?"

Why indeed?

Rae Rae came back wearing Shiloh's dress. It was a wonder the drag queen could breathe. The latex stretched over her hips and muscled thighs. It was a size or three too small and I swear it was about ready to split at the chest, even if Rae Rae didn't have boobs. "Gorgeous," I said.

The pawn broker batted her lashes, every bit the lady. For now, anyway. "Thank you." She tossed a white sack at Shiloh. "Here you go, sweetie."

"Ugh." The she-demon held it up. It appeared as if the pawn broker had cut head and armholes into an old sack.

"It's better than nothing," I said, as Shiloh reluctantly tugged it over her head.

"Now for the merchandise," Rae Rae crooned, stepping behind the counter.

Carpenter was still staring at the ceiling. "You can look now," I told him as we joined the pawn broker.

Rae Rae hitched up a hairy, muscled leg and slipped a key out of her garter belt.

"Jesus—" the necromancer muttered.

Okay, maybe he looked too soon. "Sorry," I told him.

Rae Rae opened up the dingy glass case and pulled out the plain black crystal. It was the size of my palm and I could feel the power as I reached for it.

"Stop," she said, opening a drawer behind her and pulling out a green velvet bag emblazoned with runes. She eased the stone inside without touching it. "Now you can have it."

Carpenter practically drooled as I slipped it into my demon slayer utility belt.

"At least now we know he can lust," Shiloh said, earning a scowl from him.

"Thanks, Rae Rae," I said, as the broker walked us to the door.

"One more thing," she said, drawing closer to me. "I gotta tell you. Woman to woman." She stared me down. "You smell like you've been cozying up to a demon."

"Right," I said, hoping Carpenter didn't hear. "It's nothing. I took on some of my dad's power to get me down here."

Rae Rae straightened, her nose wrinkling. She didn't counter me directly, but I heard the words she spoke to herself as we departed. "Something's not right with that man."

Chapter Twenty-Three

Yes, I had daddy issues, but I wasn't going to discuss them with Rae Rae the pawnbroker. She'd made out like a bandit. No wonder she enjoyed seeing me.

At least we'd gotten what we came for, in a manner of speaking. I glanced at the necromancer, walking a step ahead of me.

Our new companion was tense, stoic, and he didn't even hold open the door as we left the shop and set out onto the streets of purgatory.

"So your name is Evan," I began, hoping to strike up some sort of conversation with the man who was about to help me lock down one of the most powerful demons I'd ever known.

He barely spared me a glance. "Call me Carpenter."

I shared a what-the-frig look with Shiloh and she shrugged. At least Carpenter ignored her, too.

"He reminds me of a client I had once," she said, tugging at her sack of a dress.

"Oh yeah?" I asked, feeling sorry for her. The material looked rough. It had to be uncomfortable. "What happened?"

Maybe he'd cooperated, done his job, and then left her alone.

"He was a disaster," she said, lips quirking ever so slightly. "I married him."

We traced our way back toward the narrow alley that led to the brothel district and out to the barren wastelands beyond.

We still hadn't heard from Shiloh's husband, wherever he may be.

Shiloh caught up with Carpenter, or at least she tried. He always managed to stay one step ahead. "So you've been down here awhile?" she asked, clearly fishing.

He wove among the gray, shattered inhabitants as if he'd been doing it all his life. "Long enough."

We passed closed shops with rusted locks. Sirens blared in the distance.

Shiloh pressed forward. Small, but tenacious. "Do you know my husband, Damien McBride? He's a demon slayer." She dodged a shard of glass on the sidewalk. Poor girl had given up her shoes and gotten a ratty pair of flip-flops in exchange. "I haven't heard from him." She didn't quite manage to keep the worry out of her voice.

That got the necromancer's attention. He slowed. "So you're the half demon married to the slayer." He said it as a statement rather than a question, as if he already knew.

"He asked and I said yes," she told him. She didn't push back or get defensive. That had to be hard. I admired her poise. Information was more important than pride at this point.

He shook his head, whether at the idea of their marriage or at the situation, I had no idea. "I haven't seen Damien since I ran into him and Rachmort a week and a half ago." He watched Shiloh with a certain amount of mistrust. "They were keeping a low profile. It seems a demon had managed to break through a seal and set up a dark vortex."

"You knew?" I demanded. "Why didn't you say so back in the shop?"

He looked at me like I'd sprouted two heads. "In front of Rae Rae? Not a chance." He turned to Shiloh. "I have every reason to believe your husband is safe. I just don't know where he is."

She visibly relaxed at that.

"I always tell the truth," he added.

Like I believed that.

We reached the narrow passageway between districts and Carpenter entered first.

"Tell me how I know you," I said.

"Rachmort talks about you," he said, keeping his eyes forward as he walked, "and he showed me every damned one of your wedding pictures."

"That's sweet," Shiloh chirped.

He shot her a glare. "He made me sit through all two hundred and forty-seven of them before he'd give me a formula I needed. Did you really have to put your dog in a bow tie?"

It occurred to me that he wasn't a man who came upon things easily. Perhaps it had something to do with his sunny disposition. "Look," I said, "what have you got against me, anyway?" It would be nice to be on good terms with another necromancer besides Rachmort.

Evan stopped cold. "I know certain things," he said cryptically. "Like you're on the brink of a disaster and any outside influence can set it off."

"Meaning you?" I asked.

"Meaning anything." He frowned.

I understood his trepidation. "Yes, the dark vortex is scary." We all knew that. "But if we don't shut it down, we'll face a lot worse."

He clenched his jaw. "There's more to it than that." He turned away from me and began walking again. "I wish I knew what."

Things were always more complicated than they seemed. He had to let it stop bugging him or he was going to drive himself nuts. "Once you help me with this…" He'd see. I'd seal in the Earl. "Then you can go along your merry way and you never have to speak to me again."

"If only I were that lucky," he said to himself.

Yeah. We both knew I'd track him down again if I needed him.

Still, Carpenter had me interested in learning more. He was reading some kind of signs. Although somehow I didn't think he'd be eager to discuss the inner workings of his gifts with me. "You think you're so smart," I said, more amused than anything.

He turned around and stopped so abruptly that I nearly ran into his chest. "I know I am." He drew back. "I just wish I knew about you two."

He turned and started walking again. Shiloh rolled her eyes as he departed. "Is it possible to kick his ass and accept his help at the same time?"

"We'll let him help us," I said, loud enough for him to hear. But I couldn't help but murmur, "Then maybe later, we'll kick his ass."

The red-light district had grown livelier now that it was later on in the day. Red vapor poured from open windows and the clubs blared music. And while Shiloh and I both received a few catcalls, nobody bothered Carpenter. That in itself told me something.

We made it back out to the field by early evening and it creeped me out that I could see the line in the sand from several miles away. Silver light streaked from it, glittering in the cool desert air. It reached straight out from the plain, pale wasteland, reaching toward the Earth above.

"It appears exactly as I saw it." Carpenter spoke for the first time since we'd entered the desert. "But it feels stronger."

I didn't have any basis for comparison. To me, it looked and felt the same as it had this afternoon, complete with a handful of one-horned grunting friends wandering around nearby. I dodged one of them as I kept up with our necromancer. "We were sucked down here by that dark vortex."

"Impossible," he said, slowing as we drew nearer.

Maybe he wasn't as smart as he thought. "The dark vortex goes both ways," I reminded him.

"Not for demon slayers," he said simply.

I didn't like the sound of that. But I couldn't determine if he had special knowledge, or if he was just a close-minded jerk. "So how do you operate?" I asked, breaking down and asking. I needed to know if I should take him seriously or not. "What kind of signs do you get?"

He seemed reluctant to answer. "Visions," he said, as if the word itself were repulsive.

Rachmort had never mentioned anything like that to me and he was a necromancer.

"So what visions did you get about this place?" I asked. I could use all the warning I could get.

"That's none of your concern." Carpenter pulled a pair of black gloves out of his pocket and pulled them on, as if the conversation were over. He shot Shiloh a disdainful look. "You," he said to her, "step back, but don't go too far. I need you out of the way."

The guy really needed to take it easy. "You don't have many friends, do you?" I asked, as Shiloh did what he'd ordered.

He tested the fingertips of his gloves. "I can't afford close ties."

Well, didn't we luck out on that one? "Fine. We'll do the job and that's it." I couldn't force a partnership, and frankly, I didn't want to be around him any more than I had to.

Carpenter approached the line in the sand as he would a beast about to strike. He crouched down on his heels in front of it, running fingers along the top of the rise near the place where the crystal protruded from the rock. His touch hovered over the scarab relic embedded in the center.

He held his hand out. "Give me the black crystal."

Nice try. "Do you need it for this job?"

He sighed and sat back on his haunches. "No."

"Then do your job first," I told him.

He focused on the relic again. "Forgive me if I'd like to have payment before I start messing with this seal."

He ran his hands over the barrier I'd created, testing it.

I'd secured it well. Except for the part where the Earl had gotten around it.

We just needed to eliminate my dad's relic and make the barrier whole again.

"Just be sure to do what I tell you to do," Carpenter murmured, focused on the seal in front of him. "We only get one shot." He studied the relic, as if it were about to jump up and bite him. "As soon as we start messing with it, the Earl will know we're here."

"You do realize I'm on your side," I said.

He leaned close. "Listen, sugar," he said, betraying a slight Southern accent, "no one's on my side." He reached into his pocket and drew out a brown leather bag. "Stick close," he added as he sprinkled a fine powder in a circle all around us and the rise in the desert. Somehow, he managed to avoid our horned friends, and by the time he finished, I saw that they had wandered away.

I doubted it was coincidence. Carpenter had sealed us in.

"How do you remove the relic?" I asked him.

He shook his head. "We don't. At least not without a dozen more necromancers and probably more slayers than exist. But we can lock him away. In truth, you're going to bury the Earl again. This time, for good. He won't be able to get another relic past this one. I'm going to help." He drew a small red fragment out of his pocket. Upon closer inspection, it appeared to be a painted fragment of a skull. "I'm going to place this on the relic in order to draw and center our powers." He held it up between his fingers. "Once this goes on, the Earl knows we're here. You apply a barrier, the same as you did to lock the Earl away. I'll enhance your powers and concentrate them so he can't break through again."

"Got it," I said, just a touch worried. If it were Rachmort, I'd have asked for advice. With this guy? It was harder. But I didn't want to screw up. "Listen," I began, not too crazy about explaining it. "I've never sealed a demon down without having my back against the wall." Every single time, I'd been under duress, nearly out of my mind. "I don't know exactly *how* I've done it before. Only that it happened."

"Then draw on that," he said, as if it were easy. "Get in the same place. Find your power, and do it."

"God, I wish Rachmort were here," I said to myself.

"You and me both," he answered. "Come on. The sun is setting. I'd much rather do this when I can see." He stood over the relic, holding the skull fragment. "You ready?"

"Give me a minute," I said, bracing myself. I concentrated. I called on the power churning deep inside of me. *Focus.* I felt it in my bones, flowing through my veins. It was a part of me, a living, breathing force of nature.

"You ready?" he repeated.

"Stop it," I snapped. He of all people should know I couldn't rush this. I concentrated again, this time going even deeper inside myself. I found the spark of my power and drew it out. I played with it, teased it. I toyed with my energy until it swirled inside me, hot and ready.

I felt my face heat, the tender skin of my neck and chest flush. I lifted my hands as energy flowed down my arms and into my fingertips.

"Damn," Carpenter uttered, impressed for the first time.

Oh sure. Now I got him going. When I was too focused to enjoy it.

This was my chance to lock away the Earl once and for all. Never again would his power seep out, corrupt, destroy innocent people. He'd be buried in the depths of hell where he belonged, unable to torment suggestible souls, like my father. One less devil. One less temptation. One less evil in this world.

I raised my hands, locked and loaded. I nodded to the necromancer and he placed the skull fragment on top of the relic.

It blazed red and I immediately attacked it with a blast of power.

Carpenter cursed and joined me. Roiling blue waves shot from his fingers, twining with my white-hot power. It kicked back on me and I ignored it, doubling my efforts. Pushing against the dark vortex, tearing at it, destroying it.

Instead, it grew.

Fuck.

The power blew back on me, tearing at my hair, stinging my skin, practically blinding me.

I shoved harder. Willed everything inside of me against the relic, into the rapidly forming hole around it. Cracks splintered the ground near my feet.

It was wrong. So wrong.

This couldn't be happening. My power should seal it, not tear it apart.

I struggled to see, the brightness singeing my eyes and making me tear up. The force was mine. The aid was Carpenter's. None of it felt tainted or wrong or...

Carpenter hollered something. I couldn't tell what. He gritted his teeth, his muscles straining as he fought.

My seal splintered and began breaking apart. The ground opened up in front of me.

Holy hell.

I yanked back. Carpenter tumbled forward, straight for the abyss.

He dodged sideways, barely missing it. The demon's power poured from the breach, icy cold. It stole my breath.

I doubled over. Shiloh gripped my back, keeping me upright.

Carpenter glared at me. The winds whipped at his hair, stole my breath.

"Why didn't you tell me?" he demanded over the blaze of demon energy. The entire top of the rise tumbled into the abyss. "You're one of the six hundred sixty-six!"

Shock slammed into me. *Impossible.*

Only it wasn't. I was compromised with my dad's power.

It had felt good. Right.

I didn't know.

Carpenter stared at me, disaster written plainly on his face. "You can't close the gate," he said, eyes wide. "You open it!"

I stood frozen. Shocked. My dad did this. Or maybe it had been the Earl all along. I'd taken my dad's power. Or had it been the Earl's? I'd compromised myself in the worst possible way. And now I'd set loose the one demon I had never been able to kill.

A demon that had corrupted me.

Carpenter glared at me as if I'd planned it, as if I'd known. "You tricked me," he roared, letting loose a blaze of blue energy at me instead of the breach.

It smacked me in the jaw, bit like a thousand mosquitos. I tossed it off.

I didn't have time for his idiot games. "How do we stop this?" I demanded. I racked my brain for a solution, any shred of an idea I could cling to, something that would stop this.

"What about your vision?" Shiloh demanded.

A large chunk of ground opened up right behind him. He stared at us, eyes blazing, hair wild. "It was a nightmare."

We fell.

Blackness seized us as we tumbled down into the abyss. Frigid winds tore at me as I struggled to gain a foothold, toehold, anything to keep from tumbling farther.

I landed hard on a cold white platform in the icy depths of hell. The chill tore at my bones and soaked into my skin. Walls of ice rose up on all sides, separated by a fissure that fell down into depths I didn't even want to contemplate. Carpenter lay near the edge, unmoving. I didn't know how we were going to get out now, much less if we fell farther.

"Damien!" Shiloh said, rushing to kneel beside a figure chained to the floor.

I slid as I hurried over on the slick ice to join her. But before I could make it, I found Rachmort spread out on the ice in chains. His vest was torn open and his white shirt underneath lay in tatters. His white beard thrust out, shaggy and unkempt, and he had panic in his eyes.

My heart thumped as I caught a glimpse of hands, faces buried in the ice under my feet, below our friends, reaching for them.

"Get out," Rachmort ordered, his face red, his lips blue with cold. "Get out now!"

The demon chuckled low behind me. "All right. I'll leave. Now that the demon slayer has given me a way."

I turned. The Earl stood directly behind me. He had the scaled body of a lizard and face of an angel. Silver-and-white wings sprouted from his leathery back. He smiled, showing sharp bloody teeth.

"I didn't know," I said to Rachmort, and myself, and anyone else who would listen.

I hadn't meant for any of this to happen. I'd taken a risk, drawn myself close to the demon in order to defeat him. I'd been willing to sacrifice myself. I was ready to put my soul on the line so I could to do what was right.

Instead, I'd opened up the world for a demon.

The Earl's wild golden hair fell across one eye. Parts of his face had rotted away. He didn't even attempt a glamour.

"She's tied to me." He gave me an intimate, smoky look like that of a lover. "Permanently."

"No. I never agreed to that." I stared at him in horror. Only I had opened myself up willingly. I just hadn't realized what I let through. He'd seeped into my consciousness.

And he'd controlled my powers just now. No one else had ever done that.

The Earl continued on, as if we were discussing a trip to the ice cream shop. "Did you really think you could speak to your father…without me? He lives for me." The demon leered. "He loves me."

"This is sick," I said. "All of it." I had to get out of here. I had to find another way.

The demon's power washed over me, into me, tearing at me until I didn't even feel like myself anymore. "You have no idea how long I've been watching you, waiting for you." I felt him like a black sludge in my veins. "You are a challenge, sweet Lizzie. But I've got you this time. And I intend to use you, your body, your power." I felt him under my skin. "With you as my willing slave, I'll be able to destroy anything I want. There'll be no way to stop a demon and a demon slayer." I felt him in every heavy beat of my heart. "The world will know fear, Lizzie. You'll see."

I reached for my switch stars. I might not get another shot like this.

"You know those don't work on me," he chided.

I fired anyway. I slammed it into his disgusting scaly chest. The power of it streaked through me, burying in my own chest, hurtling me to the floor as wave after wave of pain washed over me, stealing my breath away. I couldn't think. I couldn't see beyond the pain.

My world went black as I passed out.

I came to consciousness with the Earl of Hell standing over me.

His chest glowed where I'd run him through, but his flesh had already knit back together. "Aren't you glad that didn't work?" he asked, as if it were a mere mistake and not a shot to kill.

He offered a hand to help me up.

I skittered away as fast as I could, and to my complete and utter relief, he didn't pursue me.

Although something told me it was only a matter of time.

"We're linked," he said, taking one leisurely step toward me, then another, as if it were the most natural thing in the world. "If you kill me, you kill yourself."

"No," I gritted out. I refused to believe it. There had to be another way.

He tsked. "Your loving husband would be crushed. Imagine Dimitri the widower. Couldn't happen to a nicer guy."

I glared at him, as if looks could kill. "I hate you."

"You might be hearing that from Dimitri soon," he mused. "I can't imagine he'd embrace your demon side."

I struggled to stand. "Fuck off."

He ran a hand through his thick blond curls. "Now don't go trying to sweet-talk me. Your dad is enough of a kiss-up."

I had to kill him. I had to end this. It was the only way to put a permanent stop to this power cycle and eliminate the Earl of Hell for good.

He tilted his chin down at me. "Face it, sweetheart. You're mine."

"Never." I'd fight. I'd win.

"Ah," he mused. "I do enjoy it when I get to prove things. Come along, then," he said, dragging me by the elbow, depositing me under the center of the ice shelf. I could feel the power of the dark vortex pulling at me, trying to draw us upward. "First order of business" — the Earl grinned at me, baring row after row of sharp teeth—"we'll show you just how much I control you."

Chapter Twenty-Four

It was like nothing I'd ever faced before. I forced myself to focus, to try to stand straight. "Why don't you just take my power and be done with it?" It was what he wanted. It was what every demon craved.

My power. My force.

Me.

His gaze bored into me. "I'm not going to take it from you," he sneered, amused at my utter horror. "At least not yet."

What the frig was he waiting for?

I drew a switch star, for all the good it did me. I sheathed it again. My weapons were useless. We were in the depths of hell. My mentor was a prisoner. The other slayer as well. A short distance away, Shiloh wept as she desperately tried to free her husband.

This asshole demon deserved to die.

The Earl drew so close I could almost touch him. I let him.

There was nothing else to do.

He hovered so close I could smell the sulfur on his breath. "I shall very much enjoy *corrupting* you." He said it like he was testing the word on his tongue, relishing the sound of it. "In fact..." He wrapped a hand around my back. He glanced over my shoulder and I followed his gaze to Rachmort, who watched in horror. Prickles raced down my spine at the points where the demon's talons dug in. "I'll give you some of my power."

"Oh, hell no." I was barely holding on as it was.

I struggled to break his grip. He leaned forward and his hot breath washed over me, straight into my mouth. It stung my tongue and tasted like rotten eggs.

My skin erupted and my spine collapsed as a blaze of energy jolted through me. It burned under my skin, squeezing my chest and stealing my breath as if I'd been tossed out of a high tower and plunged straight into the sea.

My body shuddered. My limbs were useless as the Earl nipped at my neck, ran a wet tongue over my collarbone. "Too much?" he asked, nuzzling my cheek. "I was hoping to make that fun."

He smelled like putrefaction and death. I tried to fall away and out of his grip, but he held me tight, his nails piercing my skin.

My throat was dry. My mouth refused to work. "You." I fought for each word. "Can't. Have. Me."

I gripped at his arms. His scales were rough. "Ah, Lizzie," he said, touching a fingertip to my forehead, running it down between my eyes like I was a pet or worse. "I already have you."

I stared into his soulless black eyes and realized he was right.

From the moment I'd taken that power from my father, I'd set myself on this path. Dad was a fallen angel. He'd surrendered himself. And now, I'd fallen too.

I hadn't even realized it was happening. And now? It may be too late to get away.

Panic seized me. I twisted my head, fought the spider's web. "Rachmort," I hollered. He'd tell me what to do.

But Rachmort lay unconscious on the ice. Or dead.

Please don't let him be dead.

"What did you do to him?" I choked out.

The Earl chuckled and ran a finger over my rib cage and shrugged. "That last blast of power did him in. The other slayer, too."

I fought to see. This time, the demon let me go. I struggled to keep my feet as I turned to see Damien's body, curled on the ice. Shiloh cried over him, trying desperately to revive her husband.

The Earl pressed close to my back. I shuddered as he caressed my shoulders. "They aren't as strong as you are." He ran his claws up and down my arms, piercing my skin, watching rivulets of blood stream down to my fingers. "Now you see why I wanted you so much."

This was sick. Wrong.

This demon wanted to bond with me completely. He'd already changed me on a fundamental level.

I didn't know how I'd get my old self back. Or how to resist falling even more.

My friends were trapped. The biker witches had no idea where we were. The demon had gotten inside of me. And now that the pain from the Earl's power transfer had cleared, I had an even bigger problem: I felt good.

I flexed my hands, felt the energy zip through my body. I was whole. Alert. And no doubt stronger than I'd ever been before.

I was also corrupted. Tainted in the worst possible way because I didn't feel sick or evil or even dangerous. I felt like me, only better.

He chuckled behind me. He knew.

"What happens next?" I whispered. I had to escape this. Somehow. I turned to face him. "What do you want?"

The Earl raised a brow, as if my attitude surprised him.

Good.

It's not like wailing or gnashing my teeth or a dozen screams of "no" would get me anywhere.

Fuck him. I was beyond all that bullshit.

He tilted his head to the side, studying me. "You've given me trouble," he said slowly. "A lot of trouble." He opened his arms wide, raised his voice. "You see this place?" The winds of hell tore at his hair. "You locked me on a fucking ice cliff."

I scoffed. "As if I could have put you in the Taj Mahal."

Malice glittered in his eyes as he advanced on me. "I owe you a lot of suffering for just that."

Oh, shit. I backed up one step, then two. I had my strength back, even if it came from him. I also had no weapons. No plan.

Then I saw Shiloh sneaking up behind him.

I wanted to cry I was so happy to see her alive and unhurt, but I couldn't let on. I kept my face neutral. Wary. And hopefully not too terrified.

Shiloh held a dagger in her hand. I didn't know where she'd gotten it or what she planned to do with it, but she sure as hell needed a few more seconds.

And a distraction.

I cleared my throat. "I'm sorry," I said to the Earl, desperately attempting to sound sincere, and not a though I was buying time.

The show of weakness only fueled his aggression. "You're not sorry," he sneered, flexing his claws, raising a hand to strike, "but you will be."

Shiloh drew closer. The Earl lashed out at the same time she did. Only he swept his arm backward instead of at me. He hit Shiloh square in the jaw. Then he turned and in one swift movement, flung her right off the ice cliff. Straight into hell.

Oh my God. "Shiloh!" I rushed for the edge.

I could barely see the outline of her as she fell, headfirst. Then I couldn't see her anymore. There was only an endless abyss.

She was gone.

And I may be joining her sooner rather than later. What a pair we'd make.

"Damn," the Earl said, joining me on the edge. "I was planning to have you kill her."

In one quick movement, I was behind him. I shoved him hard. I used all of my strength to deliver him into the depths of Hades.

But he didn't budge.

He just smiled. "That's exactly what I would have done." He gripped me tight around the waist. "This is going to be even more fun than I thought." His power washed over me. My strength swelled. My focus faltered.

The vortex swirled above us. He leaped straight for it, with me at his side and the shells of Rachmort, Carpenter, and Damien crumpled below us on the ice.

Even if they weren't dead, they couldn't do anything to stop him. Not now.

He drove straight upward in a blast of icy power. The winds of the vortex tore at me. I flung myself at them, used the winds to try to dislodge myself from the maniac demon. I'd rather fall into a wild current of power than spend one more second locked to the demon's side.

We rose up, straight into the next dimension.

The warm Earth air sent needles of pain up my arms as the Earl stepped out onto firm ground, with me at his side.

He leaned close, so that his fetid breath was a whisper against my ear. "Now you are going to kill everyone you love."

Chapter Twenty-Five

Screams greeted us as the Earl of Hell—with me at his side—walked the Earth once more.

To my utter horror, we appeared in the witches' sacred garden.

Grandma clutched a wooden altar, her hair streaming wild, shaken from her trance.

Had they been channeling me? Had they seen what happened?

The sacred pond was dry and broken. Frieda lay where she'd been flung—halfway across the courtyard. Ant Eater struggled to her feet among shards of broken pottery and torn plants. And Creely had built a trebuchet, an immense medieval-style slingshot on wheels.

"Lizzie," she hollered, as two more witches pulled back the firing mechanism. Her voice held panic and excitement. "I need something to load!"

We'd done it before. We'd locked the Earl of Hell away with a blast of angelic power. This time, now that I'd gotten under his armor, now that I'd melded my powers with his, a shot like that might just kill him.

But now it would kill me as well.

"Wait," I screamed to them. For what, I didn't know.

Witches scrambled to their feet, drawing spell jars.

"Kill them," the Earl ordered. "Now."

I couldn't do it. I wouldn't. But goddamn it, they wouldn't listen. They kept drawing weapons. I felt the power rise up inside me, the rage.

They were puny and insignificant and they actually thought they could defeat the Earl of Hell.

They deserved to die.

I lashed out a hand and struck Creely's trebuchet with a blast of angelic power. Wood splintered, ropes flew, and I laughed as I watched the startled witch fall over backward.

But I didn't kill her. Yet.

I shouldn't.

Yes, I had to kill her.

Grandma stood screaming at me. I couldn't hear her words. They didn't matter. She'd climbed on top of her altar, the crazy woman. The demon's power tore at her hair. It drove her backward and she still shrieked.

I hit her with my eyes and spun her right off her pedestal. I burned her with a red blaze of demon energy that sent a thrill straight down my spine. This was winning. This was glory.

This was power.

It had been available to me for my entire life and I never realized it. Like a blind fool, I hadn't indulged. I didn't know how it could really be.

Frieda crushed a jar that sent up a purple cloud over the entire courtyard. It flung me backward. The Earl landed next to me.

Broken glass and pottery sliced into my shoulders and back, but I didn't care. She'd attacked the nobility of hell.

She'd pay.

I leaped to my feet and almost bowed back down again when I realized I should have let him stand first. I waited. Deferred. His red eyes searched me as he stood. He wiped a trail of blood from the corner of his mouth. "By all means demon slayer," he said, the corner of his mouth turning up. "Proceed."

"Don't call me that." He was mocking me.

He'd see.

The witches cowered behind hasty barricades made from plant shelves and carts. It wouldn't save them. They fired spells at me now. The magic burst in sickening waves at my feet. But they didn't break me. I was both slayer and demon. I was invincible.

Then the dog of all creatures came running straight for me.

"Stop it! Stop it!" he hollered, dodging the witches who tried to catch him. "It's me, Lizzie." His stubby tail thrust out. His words mashed together as he tried to say them fast. He dodged broken glass and flaming pieces of the trebuchet. "I don't care if your eyes are red or if you got demon breath or you came out of hell. I love you!"

Blind trust and love shone in his eyes. He truly believed in me.

"Babydog!" I called, without even thinking. It was the thing to say, to feel, to do, when he came to me as he did at that moment.

But this was only an animal and I had a job to do.

I unleashed a killing blast of power straight at the dog.

It seized him around the middle. He gave a sharp cry and fell lifeless to the ground.

The pride of it washed over me. And the horror. And the elation.

At least I'd put him out of his misery.

In another world, I'd cry for what I'd just done. But I couldn't find it in myself to regret it. I wanted it.

Then something deeper pushed at me, stabbed at my throat and my eyes. My chest felt heavy and tears welled up, temporarily blinding me.

He'd been the smallest puppy at the pound, a runt with an attitude. His legs were so small he waddled when he walked, and he'd darted straight for me, tongue out, razor-sharp baby teeth ready to gnaw on my hand.

And when we got home, he used those teeth on my most comfortable pair of worn-in oxfords. The shoes were as long as he was, but he brought one to me to show me he'd conquered the beast.

Now that little spirit had met his last challenge. He'd trusted me with everything he had and I'd killed him.

What was wrong with me?

"Oh good," the Earl said next to me. "I was afraid I'd given you too much unmitigated evil. I do want you to suffer."

I glared at him, this monstrosity. The half man, half lizard who ruled in hell, who would bring his legions to conquer the Earth as soon as he'd wiped out the witches and anyone else who opposed him.

With me at his side, he was invincible.

No one should have that kind of power. I had to kill him. I had to end this now.

But I didn't want to.

A wave of spells exploded around us, blinding me for a moment. The fucking witches didn't know when to quit. I drew a switch star.

"Leave me alone!" I hollered, hurling it straight at the one in the wheelchair. He'd tried to retrieve the body of the dog. Useless sap.

Then I saw a man stride through the smoke. Dimitri.

He held his body rigid, his mouth set in a grim line as he walked through the front line of witches. He was shirtless, wearing only a pair of black trousers, but he didn't shift.

It was a very foolish move.

As a griffin, he might have given me a challenge.

As a man, he was worthless.

The Earl smiled. "Kill him."

The order was clear. I knew what to do. Still, I felt myself hesitate. "What happens then?" I asked, hardly recognizing my own voice.

The Earl crossed his arms over his chest. "We eliminate the witches and get what I want." He'd steal their power. He'd have what he needed to open up the gates for his six-hundred and sixty-six legions of demons.

Dimitri, the fool, walked straight for me, even though I had to kill him. Even though he had no power to stop it.

He was going to make me do it, just like the Earl. And I hated him for that.

He didn't hesitate. He refused to make this easy. "You're stronger than the demon," he said, like a warning.

Was I? I'd blasted Creely. I'd killed my dog.

Yes, I had immeasurable strength, but darkness flowed through my veins. I was the walking weapon for the Earl of Hell.

Love and concern flooded his expression. Behind it was fear.

Smart man.

No good could come out of this. I drew a switch star.

I took one step toward him, then another. My boots felt heavy. We'd end this together.

I itched to plant my switch star in his chest. To blast him to hell with demon power. He deserved it for this reckless pride, this insistence that I be something I wasn't.

I held out, just barely.

We met in no-man's-land. The witches' artillery had ceased, replaced by a choking blue smoke. It stung my eyes. It burned my throat. But it didn't stop me. Nothing could anymore.

My husband watched me, the pain clear in his eyes. Caustic smoke tore into my lungs. My body shook, my head swam. I needed to kill them all and be done with it.

We'd both faced death before. It was part of what made us so good at living. This was the man who battled werewolves and banshees with me, who had made love to me on an ancient altar, who tied me to a tree to keep me out of a particularly gruesome fight. Come to think of it, I'd never gotten him back for that one. Now I never would.

We'd never make love in the rain again, or go crazy trying to entertain my mother. We'd never have children. Never grow old together.

We'd been given more than I'd ever hoped for in my life, but it was over now. There was no winning this time.

Instead, I had to die. It was the only way to save him.

"Kill me," I told him.

His nostrils flared with shock. "You don't mean that," he said quickly. He reached for me, then thought the better of it and withdrew. "You're corrupted."

"You know it's worse than that," I said, glancing behind me. The Earl watched us. I didn't know how much time we had left. Dimitri had to see it. I certainly did. "It's the only way to kill the Earl and end the power cycle."

He had to destroy the demon. And me, too.

This time, Dimitri pulled me close. He wrapped me in his arms and I relished the heat of him. Hades, I felt so cold.

Tears swam in my eyes. I refused to return the embrace. It would hurt too much. We both knew what he had to do. My nose touched the base of his neck. I brought my lips up to his ear. "I don't want to hurt anyone else," I whispered. He had to understand. "Please. Do this for me. For us. Trust me. Save me. It's the only way."

The Earl hit me in the back with a blast of power. It drove into me. I clutched Dimitri's arms. For the first time, I tried to fight it. But it was no use. I felt myself grow stronger, bolder. I wanted to kill.

Dimitri hissed as my fingers tore into his skin. I was just like the demon.

The tears in the muscle excited me. I wanted to lick the rivulets of blood. They were mine. I'd marked him. Too bad I had to kill him.

He stared at me in horror. "Lizzie...your eyes."

Burning red, no doubt. "Do you see it now?" I dug my fingers harder into his skin. The Earl was playing with us, no doubt enjoying our pain. But he'd tire of it soon and the next blast of power would make me his slave. Dimitri had one last chance to end it all. I used my nails like claws, feeling his flesh give way under them, watching the tears spring up in his eyes. "Shiloh's in hell. Rachmort is dead. Pirate is dead. I came here to kill you all. Now you have to love me enough to kill me.

"Please," I said. It was now or never. "Love me enough to save me."

His shoulders shook and his breath was hollow. "I do."

I released him. Blood smeared my fingers as I slipped off his wedding ring and held it out to him. The Skye stones contained griffin power. They were enchanted to protect me.

The Earl chuckled behind me, delighted as I dropped the ring into Dimitri's outstretched palm. His fingers closed over it, clasping it tight.

"Now," he said tightly.

Dimitri stepped back and so did I, until I was once again side-by-side with the Earl.

"You forgot something," the demon said.

I looked into his soulless black eyes. "I'm ending this my way."

"It had better be good," he smirked.

"Don't interfere," I spat at the demon. "I've challenged the griffin to a duel."

The Earl tossed his head back and laughed, just as I hoped he would.

I would die while the devil laughed. But the demon would lose his weapon. He'd be robbed of me and my power. And maybe someday, someone else would have the power to defeat him for good.

One thing about my husband—once he committed, he was on board 100 percent. Dimitri stood facing us like a god of war. His shoulders shook. His eyes shone with moisture as he raised both hands and blasted me with a wave of griffin power.

It was like being on fire. Pain seared through my skin and stuck to my body. It boiled my insides. It melted my bones. My hair blazed. And I screamed.

Dimitri's Skye power, his love and his loyalty, had been all I'd ever craved. Now it decimated me on a cellular level. I felt the evil lift. It sizzled as it burned away, torching the rest of me at the same time.

The Earl's laughed turned to a scream. He fell to his knees next to me, on fire. His skin curled black. His hair was gone. His eyes blazed red.

No wonder I'd never been able to kill him before. He had angel power.

But that was no more.

The base, animal part of me struggled against Dimitri's power. I'd told him to kill me. I needed him to do it. But on a fundamental level, I wanted to live.

Sacrifice yourself.

I had to see this through. I used every bit of strength, every bit of love to push back enough to lift my arm. My entire being screamed in pain as I unhitched a switch star. In my last act on this Earth, I reared back and plunged it into the demon's chest.

Ice-cold fire exploded all around me.

I felt him dissolve. I felt his body turn to ash and scatter at my feet. I'd dropped to my knees. My vision faded and a sudden sense of peace washed over me. I didn't have to fight anymore. I couldn't feel my body anymore. I'd done what I set out to do. I'd killed the Earl of Hell.

Now I'd be dead soon, too.

CHAPTER TWENTY-SIX

I lay in Dimitri's arms. He clutched me tight, his face against my hair. His chest heaved. "Oh my God," he murmured. "I'm so sorry." My skin felt wet where it touched his.

I really did sacrifice it all. I was dying. In doing so, I'd broken the man I loved.

Light streamed down behind him, like heaven. Everything was so bright.

I couldn't move or breathe. I could feel my angelic half lustrous inside me. I was whole again. The light filled me. It wanted me to rise up.

Except I didn't want to leave him. Not now. Not like this.

Couldn't I at least kiss him one last time?

He pulled away and gazed down on me. I saw it all in that moment: the longing, the hurt. The love.

Could he see that I was here? I tried to reach for him, but couldn't.

I blinked my eyes.

Hope flared to life in him. "Lizzie?" he stammered, as if he couldn't quite believe what he'd seen.

He searched my face. He wanted me to do it again. I didn't know if I could. My body felt heavy, as if I might actually be a part of this world.

I blinked once more, and then coughed.

"Thank God!" He held me tightly, as if he were afraid I'd somehow slip away.

"Am I dead?" I asked against his shoulder. My voice sounded rough and strange, even to me. Maybe this was heaven. I might have killed him too. The shame of it washed over me. I'd tried so hard not to fight. "I'm sorry." I struggled to move, but my arms didn't cooperate.

He pulled back, laughed. Tried not to cry. "You didn't kill me," he said, blinking hard.

Look at that. I'd made a grown man cry. I tried to touch his tears and failed.

He'd released his full griffin arsenal on me, the power of his love and his loyalty. It had purged me of the evil.

He touched my face, cupped my cheek. "I watched the darkness leave you at that last moment, so I stopped. I thought I'd lost you."

He couldn't have possibly known whether or not I'd been fully exorcised. "I could have killed you."

"I know," he said simply.

I stared at him in amazement. The one thing the Earl never considered was Dimitri's love for me. The demon couldn't possibly understand the kind of bond I had with my husband.

"It was the only way," I said, still amazed I'd made it out of the battle alive. I'd corrupted myself. I'd had to atone for that choice with sacrifice. I just hadn't thought Dimitri would join me in it or that he'd find another way.

The Earl was gone. He was no longer a part of me.

I sat up slowly, with Dimitri's help. We were on the battlefield. Nearby, witches drew each other to their feet and waded through the wreckage.

Several feet away from me, a caustic burn mark scorched the ground. It was all that remained of the demon. At long last, I'd killed the Earl of Hell.

I was just about to remark on it when I heard a sharp, hoarse bark. "Hey." It melted into a series of tight, dry doggy chokes. "Anybody want to see if I'm alive?"

Oh my God. Dimitri helped me turn and I saw Pirate stumbling for me. His legs were stiff like a puppy's, his fur thrust out at strange angles. "Babydog!" I reached for him, folding his scratchy, warm little body into my arms. My throat constricted, along with my chest, and I felt my eyes go liquid again. "I thought you were dead."

"Aww, I'm tougher than that," he said, nuzzling his nose into my elbow.

I stroked his head, the silk of his ears. "How did you ever survive me?"

"He didn't." Carpenter stood over me. He had a wicked cut on his cheek and a series of bruises blossoming across his neck. "I revived him."

"How?" Carpenter should be in hell.

He stared me down. "I'm a necromancer," he said, as if that were any kind of an explanation.

He really was one of the most annoying people I'd ever met. But he'd saved one of the most precious things to me in this world. "Thank you," I said. "I can't imagine how I'll ever repay you."

His eyes lit up at that.

Rachmort walked next to him, trying to button his torn waistcoat. "I'm getting too old for this sort of thing." He gave me a once-over. "Nice work, Lizzie."

Dimitri helped me to my feet and I embraced Rachmort. Carpenter, I left alone. "How did you escape hell?" I asked my mentor, still surprised to see him.

Carpenter scoffed. "You think you're the only demon slayer?"

He glanced behind him and I followed his gaze. Damien and Shiloh were behind him, making out.

Dimitri snorted.

Carpenter rolled his eyes. "They need to get a room."

"We have plenty," Grandma said. She was limping a little, and she looked like hell, but from what I could tell, she was unhurt.

"How are the witches?" Dimitri asked.

Grandma shook her head, as if she couldn't quite believe it. "A few twisted ankles. Some cuts. A broken wheelchair. But everyone survived."

That was a first. I'd never been more grateful.

I leaned against Dimitri. My legs still didn't feel very solid.

"You okay?" he asked against my ear.

"I will be."

Maybe I didn't feel as powerful or secure as I did when I had demon power inside me, but I certainly didn't need that anymore. I could make it on my own.

Carpenter had begun to ease away from our little group. Social he was not. I'd let him go, but I had a question for him. "Why were you so into that black crystal? It didn't do jack when we needed it."

He froze mid-retreat. "I needed it for my mission, not yours," he said, as if the answer were obvious. He gave me a pointed look. "And now you owe me one."

"Right," I exchanged a glance with Dimitri. No doubt he'd be collecting soon.

"Look at this," Frieda said, coming up behind us. "I broke my heel."

I looked down at the outfit she'd lent me. The leather was torn, and no longer a pristine white. "I owe you a trip to the mall."

Frieda tried to give me a stern look and failed. She bust out into a grin. "Oh, babe. I need to teach you where to shop."

"I'll go!" Shiloh said, dragging Damien over to us. "I need to start dressing better," she vowed. "No more pastel nightmares." She ran a hand through her gloriously tousled hair. "I'm going sexy."

Damien's eyes followed her every move as if the mere thought of it turned him on.

Oh Lord.

"Thanks for getting everyone out of there," I said to her husband.

He forced himself to tear his eyes off his wife. "Glad to do it," he said, reaching a hand out to me. "It's nice to finally meet you."

We shook hands in a belated hello.

Dimitri gave the demon slayer a handshake as well. It seemed strange, given the circumstances, but who was I to fight a little normalcy?

"Shiloh tells me she's been working with both of you," Damien said. His tone suggested he was surprised. He shouldn't be. His wife had some amazing gifts.

I hadn't expected it, either, but there it was.

"She's one of a kind," I told him. "We'll have to have you guys over and we can tell you about it."

"They can also take home their new pet," Dimitri added.

Shiloh clasped her hands to her chest. "You'd let me keep Babydoll?!"

In a heartbeat. "We already have a dog," I told her.

"Damn straight," Pirate agreed, weaving in between my legs.

All around us, the witches were cleaning up from the battle. Creely had assembled a team to repot plants. Grandma was back there, barking orders at the witches who were recovering unbroken spell jars. Others gathered pottery shards into large bins. They didn't waste a thing.

Rachmort stood a short distance away, talking on his cell phone. No doubt he had a lot to explain to headquarters.

I couldn't believe everyone had survived the battle. It was a first, and it was a huge victory.

Dimitri slipped an arm around me. "What are you thinking?"

I gazed up at him with love. "That we're a great team." He'd always been there when I needed him most. And he'd given me the freedom to be the best version of myself. "That even when you're not with me, you're there."

His love helped me believe in what could be. I could be confident without selling my soul. He'd made me stronger. I didn't need demon powers to feel good .

"I'm glad," he said, leaning down to me. He kissed me and as his lips moved over mine, I thanked the heavens for my husband, this drop-dead sexy man who would move heaven and Earth to be with me. Who loved me more than I could ever imagine.

Nearby, Carpenter groaned.

I broke away to find the necromancer staring at the sky. "What is with you people?"

Dimitri grazed his hands over my back, found my waist, and tugged me playfully against him. "I hope you find out someday," he said to the necromancer.

"Don't hold your breath," I said, rubbing up against him. It would take a special kind of woman to handle Carpenter.

Pirate, the little devil, wormed in between our legs. "What's next?" he demanded.

I looked down to find him waging his tail, his expression eager.

Dimitri shrugged. "I'm starving. Want to grab an In-N-Out Burger?"

I tried to wrap my mind around it. "That's so…normal." We'd just survived a demon attack. We needed to clean up and do other things. I wasn't sure what, but there had to be something more responsible that needed my attention.

But I hadn't eaten since that lunch with my dad and we were already into the next day. "What time is it, anyway?"

"Nearing six," Dimitri said. He glanced out at the witches. "When we realized you were gone last night, we started work. We haven't stopped since."

They'd risked their lives and their home for me. "I suppose we do owe them takeout," I said.

Although we'd have to take Shiloh's convertible in order to fit it all.

I shared a smile with Dimitri. He could be supernatural and enjoy the natural world as well. And maybe I could too.

†††

At about three in the morning—the devil's hour in case anyone is keeping track—we sneaked down to our little beach on the edge of paradise.

We'd helped the witches get everything back together, and persuaded the necromancers to stay on a few days as their guests. We'd said good-bye to Shiloh and her husband, who had retreated to the Four Seasons to "rest." And we'd left Pirate and Flappy to get some sleep.

Dimitri and I should have been falling over sideways. Instead, we got a second wind. We had one more thing left to do.

I grasped his hand tightly as we hurried down the wooden boardwalk toward the beach. I pulled ahead, eager to make it down to the darkened seaside. He tugged me back into a scorching kiss.

Nice try.

"Come on!" The sea grass reached out and tickled my back as I broke away and ran the last ten feet. He caught me around the middle and a screech of delight burst from my lungs.

"Keep a lid on it." He laughed, doing absolutely nothing to dissuade me as he spun me around. I couldn't stop laughing. He leaned me tight against his chest and planted a kiss on the top of my head. "They're going to hear."

Yeah, like Sarayh would mind. We glanced up toward the row of town houses on the rise and thankfully—surprisingly—no lights had popped on.

I turned around to face him. "Are you honestly complaining?" I asked, running my hands over his shoulders.

He gave a husky chuckle. "Hell no."

I let out a small cry as he picked me up suddenly before lowering me down to the sand. I nuzzled his neck and drew a line of openmouthed kisses up his throat and to his ear. He gasped lightly as I nipped the soft spot right behind his earlobe.

"We already have a reputation for sex on the beach," I murmured. "We might as well earn it."

He drew back, his eyes shining with love. "Anything for you."

Slowly, we removed each other's clothes and used them to make a bed in the sand. His strong, naked body stretched over mine and it startled me to realize how lucky I was.

I may never relate to my father as a person, but now I understood what it was like to go down that dark path, and how hard it was to come back from it.

I cupped Dimitri's face in my hands and gave him a long, slow kiss.

This man, his love, had made all the difference for me.

My father had never loved anybody enough to open that door. He didn't accept anyone close enough who could purify his soul.

I'd offered and he'd rejected that.

My dad had skipped town as soon as the Earl died. He'd offered no apologies. No good-byes to me or to his congregation.

At least the souls of his followers were free.

His church would grow out of fashion now that it lost its source of eternal youth. It would be another fad that came and went in Beverly Hills. I had to be satisfied with that and realize I couldn't change anyone, least of all my father.

I simply had to be grateful for the people in my life who did love me: the witches, Pirate, and most of all, Dimitri.

I kissed my husband slow and deep. I spread my legs, opening myself up to him in the most primitive way possible. I moaned as he settled his body between them.

He'd shown me happiness. He'd shown me love. He'd shown me what it meant to have a life.

And I couldn't be luckier to spend the rest of my life with him.

ABOUT THE AUTHOR

Angie Fox is the *New York Times* bestselling author of several books about vampires, werewolves and things that go bump in the night. She claims that researching her stories can be just as much fun as writing them. In the name of fact-finding, Angie has ridden with Harley biker gangs, explored the tunnels underneath Hoover Dam and found an interesting recipe for Mamma Coalpot's Southern Skunk Surprise (she's still trying to get her courage up to try it).

Angie earned a Journalism degree from the University of Missouri. She worked in television news and then in advertising before beginning her career as an author. Visit Angie at **www.angiefox.com**

Made in the USA
San Bernardino, CA
24 September 2014